GH01018512

Alyssa
Awakens

Alyssa Awakens

SAGE MALLORY

THE *Alyssa* SERIES

Published by Cardinal Wellingham

ISBN: 979-8-9909085-0-5

For my very own Baby

1

SUNDAY NIGHT, VALENTINE'S DAY

OH GOD. ARE they at it again? Alyssa thought as she glared at the hotel room wall. The noises of rough sex, screaming, slapping, and dirty talk coming through it had started about midnight and had continued for the last three hours. Despite other guests yelling "shut up" and "be respectful," the two fucking next door had not broken stride. Alyssa didn't usually think of sex as "fucking," but there was no other way to describe the sounds. There was no making love next door, just two animals fucking as hard as they could.

"Fuck me hard! Make me yours! Slap that ass! I'm gonna come again!" The woman next door loved what the man was doing to her. She had screamed her approval all night. Initially, Alyssa thought they were showing off for the rest of the guests. As the woman begged for more cock, moaned, and growled through the wall, Alyssa determined they were genuinely having a powerful fuck session. She resented that it was keeping her awake, but at least it sounded legitimate. She had heard of screamers before, but losing sleep to one was new. Alyssa wondered how long it would go and what the couple looked like.

Alyssa didn't need to sleep now, her morning flight canceled because of the ice storm. She had nowhere to go, so she planned to sleep in. Houston was shut down, and her flight had been pushed back two days. Nonetheless, she wanted to sleep.

The spanking and choking next door was not like any sex Alyssa had ever had, but the way the woman loved it made Alyssa's pussy throb. She had been pressing her legs together to soothe the ache for the last hour, making sleep impossible. If Robert were with her, she could have some sex of her own and settle down for the night. He had stayed home with their son, Clay, while she delivered their daughter, Susan, to college. Getting Susan back for the spring semester was done, but getting home would take a little longer. With the wailing next door, and no Robert to take the edge off, it was going to be a long couple of nights.

Alyssa thought about the last time she and Robert had sex. *It was fine. I came.* Robert knew just how to get her going after twenty-three years together, and he was efficient with it. *I almost always come, but not like my neighbor.* The effort spent on foreplay had diminished over the years. That was how it had been on Friday before she and Susan left for Texas. Quick yet satisfying enough. The memory fluttered Alyssa's stomach. She squeezed her thighs tighter.

Resigned to being awake, Alyssa paid attention to the noise next door. She moved the pillow off her head and cupped her left breast through her thin nightshirt. The beds were obviously arrayed so the headboard of Alyssa's bed and that of her neighbors shared a wall. Though the headboards were screwed to the wall (*just like my neighbor*), she could hear the mattress rhythmically bumping near her head. When the woman gasped, "Spank me again," a loud slap followed a low-pitched groan. Alyssa teased herself, rubbing the underside of her breast but not yet touching her nipple. She rewarded its tingle of anticipation with a quick flick of her thumb.

"Mmmm," she moaned as the woman next door demanded another spank, followed by another low-pitched groan. Alyssa pinched her nipple gently, making it hard. She used her other hand to pinch her right nipple.

"You love that cock, don't you, slut?" The question refocused Alyssa's attention on the couple next door. She had never been spoken to like that in her life, but when she heard, "Oh god, yes. Give me your cock," desire surged through her nipples and down to her pussy. She pulled both nipples and sat up to remove her shirt. *Might as well go all in.*

Alyssa turned across the bed so her ear was close to the wall. She kept one pillow under her head but threw the others down. She wanted to hear, and she wanted to climax. Alyssa held and massaged both breasts, shifting from a gentle rub to slow circles around her areolae, then pinching and flicking her nipples. She loved having her breasts played with. Their sensitivity could put her right on the edge of orgasm, priming her for a quick climax when hands or tongue moved between her legs. When "oh, fuck me" stretched out through the wall, Alyssa pulled her nipples up and away from her chest, then held them there a few seconds, the pain of the pinch and the pressure of the stretch sparking between her nipples and radiating the pleasure lower. She reached down and cupped her vagina, just holding it and feeling its heat and the moisture absorbed by her panties.

The couple next door rustled around on the bed, clearly

changing positions. Alyssa reached into her panties, cupping and rubbing her sex with her whole hand, building some tension. The woman next door surprised Alyssa with, "Slap my tits." The softer slap didn't resound like the spanks before, but the woman wailed, "Oh god," into the wall. Alyssa couldn't believe how that would be a good part of sex, but she stripped off her panties to provide a little more room to work.

She circled her clit a few times and slid her finger along her slit, pulling the moisture to her clit for lubrication. Her right leg was up on the headboard and her left leg splayed lewdly down the bed. She slipped her finger into herself, then followed it with a second. She alternated pulling her nipples with her other hand. The flutter in her belly began to grow quickly.

"Fuck me hard and choke me, you bastard" set Alyssa off. She pulled her nipple and plunged her fingers in and out of her slit as quickly as she could, pushing on her G-spot each time she withdrew. Her palm slammed her clit with every instroke.

The woman next door let out a throaty noise that could only be described as a release. The man bellowed, and Alyssa imagined him coming deep in the woman he was choking. Alyssa tensed her legs, arched her back, and came harder than she had in months. Her pussy clenched her fingers.

Eventually, Alyssa released her nipple but continued to hold her breast. She kept her fingers inside herself until all the aftershocks from her orgasm subsided, maybe a few minutes. She dragged her hand up her belly and lazily rubbed her juices on her nipples while waiting for the noise to restart next door. Some soft snoring sounded instead, and she closed her eyes.

2
MONDAY

ALYSSA AWOKE LATE the next morning to the sound of renewed sex next door. Her neighbors were spanking and grunting, but it didn't arouse Alyssa; it just made her get up and get dressed. She picked up her panties and put them back on. She had only packed enough clothes to get through today, and she was going to be in Houston until Wednesday.

The snow and ice had stopped falling, leaving an inch of ice and four inches of snow behind. The coldest weather in more than a century was expected to last all week. Houston's lack of winter weather equipment meant there would be little plowing of roads or runways. Just the same, Alyssa counted on her Wednesday flight out.

The power was on, and the staff had told the guests that the restaurant would open in late afternoon to serve dinner. She headed toward the lobby Starbucks for coffee and a light breakfast. The cold air hit her when she stepped out of the elevator. Alyssa's nipples hardened, but her bra hid that fact from the other guests. Alyssa thought for a moment about last night's guilty pleasure. *Not as much fun when they're hard from the cold.*

She noticed the entrance and the check-in line, which explained the temperature. There must have been forty groups wanting to check in, and every time they brought in luggage or children, the twenty-degree air came in with them.

The desk clerk who had helped Alyssa check in on Saturday stopped as she crossed the lobby. "It started last night. As people lost power, they headed here. We are going to be full soon if this keeps up. I'm glad we extended your stay last night after your flight got canceled, Mrs. Davis."

Alyssa refreshed her memory by reading the young blonde's name tag. "Good morning, Beth. Yes, I'm glad you took care of it right then. To be honest, I'm surprised these people could even get here, with the roads covered."

"Yes, ma'am. Some people drove hours from places that are normally twenty minutes away. There are wrecks, and the blackouts have affected the signal lights. The city is using the hotel and convention center as a command center, so people know we have power."

"That explains all the police cars here last night. I worried there was a problem."

"Oh no, ma'am. The city reserved a couple hundred rooms to house essential staff and their families during the storm. They told us the power is off through most of downtown, and to be ready for more guests because restaurants and other hotels won't have power. If you want breakfast, our Starbucks may be the only option."

The Starbucks line stretched at least fifty people long. *Jeez, Starbucks isn't good enough to stand in that line, but these tennis shoes are useless for walking in the snow, and I'm not getting an Uber with the roads like this. Ha! I wouldn't trust a Houstonian to drive in this weather anyway.* When she reached the register an hour later, she snagged the last piece of banana bread and a venti Pike Place. She was downright cold. She had the barista nuke the bread, stuck it in her purse, and snuggled the coffee in both hands as she headed upstairs to get warm.

Even after eating the warm bread and drinking half the coffee, Alyssa hadn't warmed up. She would double up getting clean and getting warm with a shower. Besides, the restaurant would open at five, and a shower could replace daytime TV while she waited. When the shower was steamy, she stripped off her clothes and hung them on the towel racks to let the wrinkles fall out while she bathed.

Alyssa had washed her hair and conditioned it before she warmed up. She scrubbed her face and moved to her body, taking a little extra time on her crotch after last night's play. She must have been rougher than she'd thought—she was a little tender. As she rinsed, a loud thud came from the wall. Then another. The sound of the shower covered any other noise, but it was clear the neighbors were fucking in the shower, right up against their shared wall. Alyssa had only wanted to get warm from the water, but her own warmth kindled above her pussy and crept outward. She hefted her breasts so the shower sprayed directly on her nipples. It felt so sinful. Every drop hardening her nipples, making them ache to be touched, the next drop meeting that need but intensifying the ache nonetheless. Her fingers tickled as they traced down her belly, the contact firming and lessening along with her quickened breathing. She reached her pussy, cupping it with her hand and stroking her middle finger along her lips. *It's warmer than the shower. And slicker.*

Alyssa closed her eyes to let the thudding from the wall fill her head. She pictured her neighbors only a few inches away. The man, muscular but faceless, the woman clinging to him with arms and legs as he slammed his cock into her, buckling the fiberglass insert with her back. Alyssa imagined herself in the woman's place. Strong fingers pressing into her ass cheeks, her weight bearing down on them, but nothing like the pressure of the cock against her pussy, her own weight driving it deep inside her. Its power resisting her muscles as they grasped it as much as her arms and legs gripped his body.

Her heartbeat throbbed in her pussy. Two fingers chased her orgasm at double the tempo of her neighbors. Alyssa pressed her clit as she imagined the man's pubic bone would on every single thrust. The shower on her nipples felt like a man's stubble as he kissed and bit her breasts. The thuds from the wall accelerated, and so did her hands. She was close to orgasming when the thuds stopped. "Oh god, not now," she said aloud, and she turned off the water to hear any other noises. She wanted to finish with the extra stimulation. She worked both hands but stopped in the quiet.

Alyssa ran into the bedroom still wet, hoping to hear the neighbors. The room was quiet. She pulled on her nipples, trying to revive the diminishing orgasm before it disappeared completely. She lay back on the bed and rubbed her clit, holding her breath to force her body to respond, but the orgasm only whimpered instead of the roar she sought but couldn't catch. *Sometimes I get that from Robert, but I want more.* Alyssa put both hands to work on her breasts, rubbing, pinching, and pulling, but her arousal stayed at a low simmer. When her fingers reached to stroke her slit and circle her clit, that familiar warm buzz returned to her belly and started to spread. She stroked her labia and used her juices to lubricate the full-on strumming of her clit she had progressed to. As the orgasm built, she plunged two fingers into her slit and jerked them in and out. Her belly spasmed, her legs tensed, and the strong orgasm she needed radiated from her sex across her body. "Ah, fuck," she cried out, allowing herself the first loud orgasm in years. *Don't wake the kids.* She sagged into the bed, satisfied and sweaty. After a while, she put on the hotel robe and dried her hair. She kept the volume low as she surfed the TV channels, listening for any noise next door.

About 3:00, boredom and horniness got to her, and Alyssa called Robert. She smiled and twirled a lock of her hair in her right hand while it rang. "Hey, Babe. How are you two holding up?"

"Probably better than you are. We are the only spot in the country where the weather is good. We have been hanging out, just cooking and doing little chores. You are the one stuck in the snow. Are you okay?"

"The hotel is taking care of us, and it's probably full now. We have power, but most of the city is dark. The restaurants nearby are closed, not that I have any clothes for walking in this weather. The restaurant opens later. They are only opening for dinner."

Alyssa smiled when Robert gave a long "hmmm." He always did that when he tried to solve problems without being too pushy. He was taking care of her from a thousand miles away.

"Get two meals. If they are only opening for one meal, take your second meal to go, so you have food for tomorrow. Things could get dicey if the food runs out. You only have to make it until your flight on Wednesday. Food for tomorrow gets that done, even if it is a little light."

"Do you think the flights will go out? It isn't supposed to warm up, and the news said that Houston doesn't have much snow equipment. What if I can't get to the airport?"

"The airport won't operate if the workers can't get there, so if the airport is open, the roads will be passable. Don't worry. You will be okay."

"You're right." Alyssa paused and thought about being in the hotel another two nights. "I could use some sleep anyway. I didn't get any last night."

"Why not?"

"You won't believe it. The couple next door were talking loudly around midnight. They jiggled the door between our adjoining rooms, which scared me."

"Did you call the front desk?"

"Don't jump ahead, Babe. Then they started having nookie. It was loud, and she was screaming and begging him to spank her, which he did. Loudly. He called her slut and whore and even pig, which makes me wonder how big she is. She even demanded that he choke her and give it to her hard. I didn't know people talked like that during sex." Alyssa traced around her tingling nipple with a fingertip through the robe.

Robert laughed. "Talking dirty. It's not just for pornos anymore."

"Funny for you; not so much for me. They kept at it until after four o'clock. Some of the other guests yelled at them to keep it down, but they didn't stop. I guess nobody got upset enough to call the front desk."

"Wow. That sounds like a fantasy story, where they are both beautiful, sexy, and well endowed. The real-life versions may look like a couple of seventy-five-year-old fat people missing some teeth."

Alyssa didn't drive the image of two beautiful people fucking like animals from her mind. Could she get Robert to fuck her like an animal when she got home? Would he talk dirty? Might be fun. Firmer pressure from her finger was met by a sensitive and hardening nipple.

Robert's chuckle brought her thoughts back to the call. "What did you do?"

I fingered myself until I almost exploded. She and Robert hadn't masturbated in front of each other since before they were married. "I lay there with a pillow over my head until they quit. I slept in a little this morning." *Can I talk him into phone sex? We've never done that, but I'm bored and horny. He's working from home, but maybe he would take a break with me for a minute, especially if Clay isn't home yet.* "You know, Babe, listening actually got me a little excited. What would you have done to me if you had been here? Tell me every detail, and I'll tell you what I would have done to you. I'm a lonely wife right now."

She knew the answer from his quiet voice. "Baby, are you trying to get me to talk dirty with you right now? You know I'm still working today."

"I know. I'm bored and thought we could play a little. It's okay. You work." She shifted to everyday mundane topics for a few minutes. Her smile faded as her hand moved from her breast to the arm of the chair, leaving her tingling nipple to soften.

Robert's responses shortened like they did when he responded to emails, like he thought nobody noticed his inattention. He took a breath and departed the previous topic. "Why don't you go hang out in the lobby? You could people watch. I know you hate not having people around. You can get dinner when they open."

"I will. At least I won't be in the room."

"Okay. Enjoy it. You and your fellow stranded travelers can swap stories at the bar. Love you, Baby."

"Love you, too, Babe. We can talk again later." Alyssa hung

up. Her nipples tingled after reminiscing about last night's entertainment. Her simmering horniness would only lead to masturbating again if she stayed in the room, so she got dressed in yesterday's clothes and headed downstairs.

❧

The lobby was packed with people. It had warmed up, and Alyssa found a seat near the restaurant. The bar was open. Alyssa ordered a merlot. She tasted a little more alcohol than the brand she drank at home, but it was good and she sipped away. Scanning the crowd while she waited, Alyssa noted three different types of people also waiting. The police officers, even those out of uniform, looked like a crew-cut convention. The families had turned the kids loose to burn off energy while Mom and Dad drank some of their exhaustion away. The stranded travelers seemed to be in singles and couples, ranging in age from early thirties to late seventies. With the crowd, not everyone had a seat. Some people stood, while others found spots to sit against the walls or columns. The din kept conversations private, but people were smiling, enjoying the warmth, and waiting for the restaurant to open.

While Alyssa drank her second glass of merlot, the little girl sitting next to her had a full meltdown. Mom and Dad finished their drinks and took her to the elevator. A thirtysomething couple came from behind Alyssa and took the seats. "Do you mind if we sit here?" asked the tall redheaded woman.

"No. Please feel free. You saw the family that just left, I'm sure. That little girl needs a nap before dinner."

"Yes, her parents looked like they would take one, too…or do something to take the edge off."

Alyssa sputtered a laugh through her wine. She would not

have imagined making such a statement to a stranger in a hotel lobby, but two strong glasses of wine and the last twenty-four hours of stimulation made the comment amusing. "Probably a nap. With kids that age, you get sleep when you can. Taking the, ahem, edge off becomes less frequent for a few years."

"We wouldn't know. No kids. I'm Kate. This is my husband, Paul."

The muscular blond man with glasses and perfect white teeth leaned over Kate to shake Alyssa's hand. "Nice to meet you. Thanks for letting us sit down. We've been waiting for, oh, three drinks?"

"Alyssa. Glad to meet you. I notice you beat the old lady with the walker to the seats. Lucky for you."

"Ha! She should have been quicker, and it has been four drinks," laughed Kate. Alyssa noticed her perfect teeth as well. Alyssa was a pushover for great teeth. Kate's bright-green eyes squinted when she smiled. "Here is to outpacing old ladies." Kate raised her glass of white wine to Alyssa and finished the last swallow. Alyssa took the last sip of her merlot as well.

"You ladies need a refill. White wine for you, dear. What is yours, Alyssa?" Paul stood, took their glasses, and smiled at the two women.

Alyssa leaned her head back to look him in the eye. "Merlot, please. Whatever they are pouring from the well is good so far. Thank you."

Paul walked toward the bar.

"Wow. How tall is he?"

"Six-five. It's great because I can wear heels with him."

"Are you tall also? I didn't notice before you sat down."

"I'm five-eleven. Even with four-inch heels, I look up to him. There are other benefits as well. You know what they say about big feet." Kate laughed again, and Alyssa felt her face flush. She also felt that tingle in her nipples.

"I know what they say—" Alyssa paused to glance around for eavesdroppers. "—though I never dated a guy that tall, so I can only imagine." She shocked herself at continuing the conversation.

"It's true, and it's great. Oh, sorry. That is probably too personal from someone you just met. I've been drinking since we got here." It was Kate's turn to blush.

"Don't worry about it. I've been drinking, too, and it is so loud that nobody would be able to hear us. Besides, I like getting personal."

Kate looked shocked.

Alyssa's jaw dropped. "Oh, wait. That didn't come out right. I mean that you confirmed what they say…"

Kate laughed loudly. "You should see your face! Don't panic. I know what you meant. It was funny to hear though. It is good to meet someone who likes to—" She cleared her throat. "—get personal." They both cackled.

That is a big bulge. Paul returned from the bar. *Stop it. You are married, and so is he. You are just sitting with him and talking with his wife while you wait for dinner.* She chased the little itch between her legs as he handed her the wine by shifting in her seat. As they continued to talk, Alyssa crossed and uncrossed her legs in search of relief, but Kate's revelation about sex with Paul and the beauty of her companions worked against her. Her panties kept getting wetter.

Thirty minutes and a glass of wine later, the restaurant opened its doors. Kate stood. "Why don't you join us, Alyssa? They will want us to sit as many to a table as possible."

"Great. If you two don't mind, I'd love the company."

They snagged a three-top along the wall and sent Paul to the bar.

Paul returned with the wine. "It's burgers or pizza tonight. They are trying to manage the volume in the kitchen, and it isn't built for this many people without more staff. We can order at the bar. The few servers they have will be running food and busing dishes. What would you two like?"

"I'll have one of each," Alyssa piped up, remembering Robert's advice. "Pizza will be lunch tomorrow."

"That's a good idea. Paul, let's get two burgers and two pizzas also."

Paul went to order, while Kate drained half her wine.

"This wine is good."

Paul returned to the table after placing the order. The three chatted and drank wine and laughed and drank more wine for the two hours it took the limited staff to bring their food.

"Three burgers and three pizzas. Oh, hello, Mrs. Davis."

"Hello, Beth. You are a busy person today."

"Yes. Most of our staff can't get here, so tonight we work the restaurant. Mike, our general manager, is cooking." Her eyes flicked to Paul and Kate.

Both Kate and Paul looked the young blonde up and down while she placed the food. Alyssa eyed her, too, and noticed how her blouse hugged her breasts even though the buttons below the neck had come undone during her shift. She looked beautiful, if somewhat harried. Alyssa had not noticed yesterday or this morning, but tonight Beth's good looks made her nipples itch. *Really? I'm getting horny over a woman? I've never even thought about a woman before, but she is beautiful.* Kate winked at Alyssa when she looked away from the younger woman's chest.

"Thank you for getting your own drinks, we just don't have enough people…"

"Don't apologize," Alyssa interrupted. "You guys are doing all you can. We can get our drinks. Thank you for everything."

Beth smiled and sighed. "Not everyone is so understanding. Have a great night."

All three of them watched her tight ass walk away. Paul picked up the empty wine glasses.

Kate caught Alyssa staring at Paul's crotch as he walked by her. "You have been thinking about what I said earlier, haven't you?"

"What part do you mean? We have been talking for almost four hours."

"About the truth of men with big feet. I saw you looking."

Alyssa blushed and looked down at her food. "I'm sorry for looking at your husband that way, only enough to see if it looks big in his pants. I have been thinking about it, and I shouldn't have. Are you upset?"

"Oh no. It is natural to look, even if I hadn't planted the thought in your head. Let me assure you, it is big—long, straight, and thick. It takes me to the moon." Kate paused and looked toward the bar where Paul stood waiting. "Would you like to see?"

"What? Oh my, no. I could never mess with your marriage that way, or mine either. I appreciate the offer, but I think we're both a little drunk." Alyssa knew some people who had had affairs, and most got divorced over them. She and Robert usually lost at least one friend in the process. Experiencing what Kate offered might be fun, but she would never actually do it. So why had her pussy simmered for the last four hours?

"I am more than a little drunk. If you would like to see, you won't mess with our marriage. We define monogamy a little differently."

Alyssa shifted in her seat, still seeking the relief that had eluded her all evening. "Oh. Um, I, uh…" Alyssa interwove her fingers, then squeezed them together at the knuckles. The pain of bone on bone focused her thoughts. Kate implied that they weren't monogamous. Alyssa imagined offering to show Kate

Robert's dick. It was a good dick; nothing to be ashamed of, but a wife should keep it to herself. Just like Robert would never show Alyssa's breasts to anyone. That kind of sharing had never even merited a conversation between them. She squeezed her fingers together again, shifting so the warm metal on her left hand focused her thoughts.

"It's okay. Most people stammer when we say our marriage is open. At least, the few we tell. We only tell those who need to know." Kate made eye contact as Alyssa processed. Kate's lips parted, and the tip of her tongue slid between her teeth.

Alyssa's nipples pushed against her bra and ached to be touched. *Did Kate just invite me for sex? That's more than just showing off the goods.* She shook her head, shocked at the thought of bringing someone to bed with her and Robert. That act would destroy the very foundation of their marriage. They had married each other, and only each other.

But what if we liked it? Her pussy shot a jolt of energy up through her belly to her boobs. Warm tingles started at the tops of her breasts, moved up her chest and neck and onto her ears. *I wonder what it would be like to kiss that mouth? Wait…enticed by a second woman in one dinner?* "I would never judge you two. You are such great company. How your marriage works isn't my business."

"You didn't know and therefore couldn't judge. I think you understand that I'm telling you I'm interested. I think Paul is too. No, I'm sure Paul is interested." Kate held Alyssa's gaze a few seconds, again with her sexy tongue between her perfect white teeth.

Alyssa stared back, lightly biting her lower lip. *She is beautiful. Paul is gorgeous and has a big cock. I've been horny since last night, and Robert is a thousand miles away. Oh god, Robert… I would never do that to Robert…to me.* She remembered Robert breaking into tears when he learned that his brother had died.

Her stomach tightened. *This would be worse. The pain of our marriage dying would be bad enough. The pain of knowing I murdered it would break him.* Alyssa spun her wedding rings with her thumb while that last thought lingered. After a pause, Alyssa looked down at her food, then back up. "I knew what you meant. I'm flattered that you beautiful young people would be interested in an old mom like me. I am quite intrigued. I am also quite married, and I couldn't jeopardize my family. I hope you understand."

"I understand. We fought for a monogamous relationship, before we changed. I don't want to make you uncomfortable, so I won't mention it again." She leaned over the corner of the table to Alyssa's ear. "Remember that we are interested, if you change your mind." And she gave her neck a light flick of her tongue.

Alyssa's hand jerked to her crotch under the table, and her eyes closed. There was no way Kate could have known that Alyssa's neck got her so turned on, but she'd hit the right button. Warmth flew from Alyssa's neck across her body in tight, targeted ropes. Her nipples fully hardened, and her pussy dampened. Kate leaned back, and Alyssa reopened her eyes, only to see Paul returning to the table, smiling with his perfect teeth and his bulging trousers hinting at what was beneath. Alyssa gave her mound a firm squeeze before removing her hand.

"It is a good thing you arrived, honey. We couldn't wait much longer to eat. Alyssa was just telling me about her family and how important her marriage is." Paul and Kate locked eyes, and Alyssa noticed a flash of something—disappointment?—cross Paul's face.

He smiled at Alyssa. "Ours is as well. It is the absolute foundation of everything we do. A solid marriage is the difference between joy and misery. I'm glad all of us have good ones." He took Kate's hand. "I can't imagine a marriage more fulfilling than ours."

The three of them ate and sat drinking for a long time. They enjoyed one another's company, and the topics stayed away from sex.

Kate, who was drinking faster than Alyssa and Paul, laid her head on the table. "That's our signal to go. I can manage her, but would you mind carrying our pizzas to the room for me? I can't carry her and them."

"Glad to. Even as big as you are, she looks like a handful. Wait here while I pay." Alyssa walked to the bar to pay the tab.

Beth was there, leaning back against the speed rail, drinking water. "Finishing up, Mrs. Davis?"

"Yes. When someone puts her head on the table, it is time to stop. It was probably time to stop a couple of drinks ago. You still have a full house. How are you holding up?"

"I'm enjoying the lull while the next round of food cooks. Mike wants to feed everyone. We will probably be here a couple more hours, then I'll collapse into bed. Here is your tab."

"This seems a little low. Dinner is here, but you only included some of the drinks. I drank more than this."

"Oh, Mr. Stevens paid cash most of the time when he picked up a new round, and you guys have been so patient with the delays that I didn't charge you a couple of times. Some people have not been as understanding." Her soft eye contact with Alyssa lingered.

Alyssa gazed right back at the young woman. "Beth, thank you. You didn't need to do that. You won't get in trouble, will you?"

"No. I can take care of understanding guests. It's my way of saying thank you."

"Well, thank you." She filled in a generous tip. *I wonder if she tells everyone this for the tips? No, she is just filling in.* "I hope you get some rest tonight. See you tomorrow."

Alyssa picked up the pizzas at the table. "You paid for my

drinks. You didn't have to. Thank you though. Between you and Beth, I feel absolutely taken care of tonight."

Paul smiled at Alyssa. *Those perfect teeth again.* "I was glad to. You have been such good company, it was the least I could do."

Kate turned her face up from the table to Alyssa. "I'll take care of you, too," she slurred.

Alyssa's face warmed as she looked at Paul. "I bet you would, sweetie. Instead, let's get you to your room."

Paul helped Kate stand. He held her hand over his shoulders and wrapped his own around her waist. When they stepped into the elevator, Alyssa scanned her key card and pushed eighteen. "Which floor?"

"Twelve."

She pushed the button, and the doors closed. Kate looked at Alyssa and then at Paul. "Is she coming with us?"

"Yes, honey. Alyssa is bringing our pizzas to the room while I carry you. You are pretty drunk."

"I want Alyssa to carry me. I bet her tits feel soft, and her neck tastes great. I really want to eat her."

"I know, but we are just going to get you to bed."

Kate had nodded off again.

Alyssa's entire torso fluttered. Her arousal had diminished during dinner but hadn't abated, and now it returned full force. Kate's dirty talk hardened her nipples, and Alyssa rubbed the pizza boxes against them. It didn't help. It only made her pussy itch and weep. The doors opened, and they headed down the hall.

"Here we are, 12035. I must apologize, but my hands are full. Would you mind getting the key card out of my pocket, please?"

Alyssa couldn't believe it, but she immediately reached into Paul's left front pocket. It was deep and empty, and his large cock was right behind it. Alyssa grasped it. It was semihard yet filled her hand. The corners of Paul's mouth turned up so slightly when she looked up at him that Alyssa wondered for an instant if she had seen it at all. She held and rubbed a little longer before reaching over to the right pocket and pulling out the key. She put the pizzas on the coffee stand inside the door, then held it open while Paul brought in Kate. His chest brushed against her breasts as he came by, and then Kate's breasts followed. Alyssa was on fire. *You are married. Don't make a mistake.* She closed the door and pulled down the bedcovers where Paul could lay Kate down.

"Could you help me with her a moment, please? Like you said earlier, she's quite a handful, and she won't want to sleep in her clothes. I can hold her up if you can undress her."

Oh god. I can't take more. But Paul was just asking for help with his wife. This wasn't sexual, even if Alyssa might find Kate attractive. "Of course. Her dress is too pretty to risk tearing a seam or a zipper." Alyssa licked her lips subconsciously.

Paul raised Kate to a sitting position, and Alyssa unzipped the back of her dress. Alyssa then slipped the dress off Kate's shoulders and down her arms so Kate was naked from the waist up. Paul moved behind Kate. With his hands under her arms, he lifted her hips off the bed. Alyssa pulled the dress down her hips and legs. Paul laid Kate down while Alyssa removed her heels. She raised Kate's feet and finished taking the dress off.

Alyssa reached to cover Kate but took a long look at the beautiful woman before finishing. Her legs were long, even for her height, firm and defined without being overly muscular. They extended from painted toenails up to a set of narrow hips clad only in a pair of black lace bikini panties. Her belly was flat with some definition and a long torso. Kate indeed had great boobs. The large breasts with light-pink areolas and small nipples sagged only slightly to the side as she lay on her back. As she stared, Alyssa rubbed her own breast through her shirt. Her pulse throbbed in the erect nipple when she pressed harder.

"She is the most beautiful woman I've ever known."

Alyssa started when Paul spoke. He had slipped behind her during her reverie. He put his hands around her onto her belly, then kissed her neck.

God, not my neck. But yes, my neck. Alyssa closed her eyes, moaned, and moved her hands to cover his. She leaned back to feel his body against hers and pressed into his crotch, savoring the growing hardness in the cleft of her ass. She pulled his hands to cup her breasts while he kept kissing and nibbling her neck. Her breathing quickened, increasing and reducing the pressure as she panted.

You are married. The reappearance of Robert's weeping face wrenched her gut. Alyssa opened her eyes, pulled Paul's hands off her breasts, and stepped between the two queen beds. She looked at him a moment while her breathing slowed. "I can't do this. I really want to, but I couldn't live with myself after. I love my husband and can't betray him. I'm sorry if I led you on."

"It's okay. Kate let me know you didn't want to play. I thought you had changed your mind when you fished for my room key." He smiled again. *Those perfect teeth.* "If you change your mind, you are the hottest woman in the hotel, and we'd love to entertain you." He stepped back and gestured toward the door. Alyssa hesitated, then walked by him, turning back at the door.

"Thank you for understanding. You two are the hottest people in the hotel, and I'm flattered. Perhaps we can still have dinner tomorrow, but I'll understand if you are looking for someone to…entertain." She opened the door and walked out before her resolve failed.

⦊

She was glad the elevator was still on the floor, and she rode it to eighteen. She stripped off her clothes in the quiet room. Her body was burning. She needed to come. She sat in the lounge chair and draped her legs over the arms, fully opening her slick pussy. She slipped a finger inside, then reached for her phone. She called Robert. "Hey, Babe. Got a minute?"

"What's up, Baby? I'm playing Madden with Clay. His buddies aren't online tonight."

Shit. I can't have phone sex with him playing video games. "Oh. Nothing urgent. You play with Clay, and we can talk tomorrow. I know it is getting late. Love you."

"You sure?"

"Yeah, go ahead. We can talk tomorrow. Love you, Baby." *God. And the neighbors aren't providing any stimulation either.*

"Okay. Love you, Babe. Sleep well."

Alyssa hung up and put a second finger inside. She pressed on her G-spot, but she wasn't getting the relief she needed. The big orgasm she wanted had a requirement: engage all of yourself, not just your fingers. *I've never watched porn much, but I need something.* She turned on the TV, but scrolling through the menu revealed that the old days of pay-per-view hotel porn were long gone.

She opened her phone to search. "Big dick porn" sites filled her screen. Playing a video, she put the phone in the chair so she could use both hands on herself. Alyssa watched a small woman take every inch of a cock that should reach higher than her navel. *There's a reason I don't watch much porn, but I'll try.* Alyssa humped against her hand and pulled her nipple. The phone fell to the floor, and it fell again when Alyssa got moving a second time.

Leaving the phone on the floor, Alyssa closed her eyes, imagining the stretching and fullness that caused the moans and dirty talk emanating from the fallen phone, imagining it like she had the night before. Her pussy clenched at the emptiness above her fingers, wanting something to resist it, something to stretch it apart.

She groaned and slammed her hand on the arm of the chair. Her pussy ached to be filled by more than the fingers she was using. Her nipples tingled more than her pinches and pulls could satisfy. She tensed her entire body, unable to get the relief she needed, and thwarted at every turn. Sleep and sanity would elude her until she set this climax loose. *Fuck it. I'm desperate. I'll keep the secret.* She slipped on her shirt and skirt, grabbed her hotel key, and went to the elevator. She knocked softly on room 12035.

✎

Alyssa shuffled from foot to foot after she knocked. *Please don't let them be asleep.* "Are you sure?" sounded like a yell in the silent hotel. Alyssa looked up the hallway, then down it. She faced the peephole.

She nodded.

Her stomach dropped like on the first hill of a roller coaster. *I'm along for the ride now.*

Paul opened the door. He was naked, and his hard cock stood out from his flat belly. Alyssa paused to look at his body. Large arms and shoulders led to wide pecs and flat abs with a little blond hair across them. His cock looked as long as Alyssa's forearm and was thick. His pubes were shaved, as were his large balls. His long, muscular legs had what looked like surgical scars on both knees. She finished looking and rushed to him. He closed the door behind her with one hand while kissing her mouth.

Paul broke their kiss a moment later. "What about your husband?"

Alyssa gritted her teeth. "I have decided I want to fuck you. Don't mess it up by mentioning my husband."

She pulled his mouth to hers and shoved her tongue inside. He returned her kiss. He cupped her ass cheeks with both hands and pulled her against him. The hard cock pressed into her belly. She rubbed his ass. It was firm, almost as hard as his cock, and warm. Paul pulled the hem of her skirt up over her hips. He grabbed her naked ass firmly. He pulled her cheeks up, then apart. Alyssa flashed back to dinner when the decadent sound of her wet lips parting fit perfectly between two slow breaths from the bed where Kate lay, still asleep. *I'll take you up on that offer now, Kate. Thank you for sharing him with me.*

While they continued to kiss, he moved his hands to her breasts. He lifted and rubbed the whole breast while flicking her nipple with his thumb. His touch made her shiver even through her shirt, but Alyssa wanted to move faster. She grabbed the hem of her shirt, pulled it over her head without unbuttoning it, and threw it on the floor. Paul removed his hands only long enough to get the shirt off, and he returned to fondling her tits.

He moved his kissing from her mouth to her neck below her earlobe. "Oh, that's it. Kiss me there." Alyssa's pussy leaked down her thigh. She didn't remember ever being so wet. Paul nibbled down her neck and chest to her breasts. He sucked as much of her breast into his mouth as would fit, then pulled back to sucking just the nipple while pinching the other nipple with one hand. Alyssa's knees buckled at the sensation coming right on the heels of her neck being kissed. She caught herself on his shoulders before she fell. Alyssa moaned. "Please, do that again. I need that again." Her pussy throbbed as he repeated that treatment a couple of times on each side.

Paul kept up his assault on her sensitive tits. He used his off hand to drag slowly up her thigh from just above her knee to her pussy. He cupped it and squeezed but didn't brush her clit or put a finger in. She ground her sex against his hand, enjoying more friction for a moment. He dropped his hand to the other thigh and repeated the process. Alyssa shuddered as his hand teased up her thigh. Rapid breaths were a bellows, stoking the orgasm burning inside her belly, not yet ready to erupt. Paul sucked her tit into his mouth, squeezed the other nipple, and this time, when his hand reached her pussy, he pinched her clit. He bit down on her nipple. The three sensations came together in her belly as an explosion. Her body went rigid, and she screamed. Her legs shook, and she sagged forward onto Paul as her scream descended to a low, tired moan. He laid her on the bed beside Kate.

Paul kissed his way down her body, kissing circles over each breast, then kissing the seams of the muscles in her belly. The warm, wet sensations flowed from her body to increase her pussy's need to be filled, the ache that brought her to this room in the first place. Her vaginal muscles grasped at the nothing inside them when Paul stopped to remove the skirt still bunched around her waist, then flexed again as the last few warm kisses fluttered through her lower belly to her cunt. He put her thighs on his shoulders and licked up from her perineum almost to her clit, stopping just short of it.

"Stop. I'm still too sensitive," Alyssa managed to say through her orgasm-induced haze.

"You are going to like this," Paul said before the wide tongue lapped upward on the outside of both outer lips at once. He continued to lick and nibble her outer labia before moving to her inner ones, grasping them in his lips and pulling them out. Alyssa opened her quivering legs wide so a thick finger could spread her wetness over her lips. The pressure flowed from the finger pressing her lips to ripple the walls of her vagina. He licked up from her perineum again, but as he reached her clit, he pushed his finger inside her and pressed the front wall of her pussy. He licked her clit and started flicking it with his tongue while working his finger in and out over her G-spot.

Alyssa jerked her head up to look at Paul while she held her breath. *This will be a big one.* He repeated the lick and, this time, inserted two fingers. Alyssa thrust her hips forward, wanting more pressure, more finger, more tongue, then clamped her thighs onto Paul's head. The climax tensed her lower body until she expelled her breath, gasped, and felt the tension diffuse outward until it reached her neck. She had rarely come twice in one session, and never this quickly. Paul continued his ministrations as Alyssa's throaty moan subsided and her thighs allowed him to breathe again.

"Are you ready for my big, hard cock now? You said you wanted to fuck. Let's fuck." Paul climbed on top of Alyssa, whose legs had flopped wide open. He crawled along her until the tip of his cock touched her opening. He held it there for a moment, then grasped it and slid it along her, wetting the tip and tapping on her inflamed clit at the top of each stroke. Alyssa whimpered.

"You can't tire out now. I was jacking off when you showed up, thinking about shoving my dick inside you. I'm going to make that fantasy real." He looked down, still tapping lightly on her clit.

Alyssa was indeed ready. She was almost destroyed by the orgasms she had experienced, but she had to have that cock inside her. She looked at Paul. "Yes. Put it in me."

"What did you ask? Do you want me to fuck you?"

"Yes. Please."

"Say it. Ask me to fuck you."

"Oh god, yes. Fuck me. Fuck me with that giant cock of yours. I need it. I need it now." Alyssa was nearly sobbing.

Paul put the head of his cock on her opening and pushed. She was not used to such a big cock, and her pussy was still tight from her orgasm, so he stopped just after he got the head inside. He held it there while she moaned.

He's going to split me apart. Oh, but what a way to go. "Yesss. Give me more."

Paul pushed forward another inch and then pulled back again. He repeated that a few times, going a little deeper each time. Her cunt was milking him, her muscles spasming as they stretched to accommodate his size. She whimpered with each advance, not comprehending why her lips felt so pinched as his cock stretched them to their limit, but reveling in it nonetheless. She held his back and pulled when she was ready for more. After a few minutes of this slow progress, Alyssa groaned when his cock hit her cervix, then slid against the top of her vagina beside it. Her muscles, stretched to their limit, strained to grip him as hot tendrils rippled outward from deep in her belly to lash inside her nipples, her neck, her clit. *Oh god. No man has touched me this way. I need more of this.* She flexed her ass, pressing herself further onto him.

He stayed still to allow her to adjust. Almost two inches remained outside her. When Alyssa pressed forward, he pulled all the way back, stopping with just the head inside. The emptiness popped Alyssa's eyes open so she was making eye contact with the large man pressing her into the bed. "No. Put it back in. Fuck me now!"

Paul grinned. He slammed his dick in until it hit beside her cervix, and Alyssa wailed as the pleasure again whipped out from that spot, that spot his cock pressed every time he filled her, that spot that connected to every other pleasure center in her body, that spot that tensed her body in another orgasm quicker than the last one. Paul sped up, filling her again and again, hitting that spot each time.

Alyssa unclenched and pulled him in by his sides. She wanted him to keep hitting her back wall, even though she knew she would be sore tomorrow. She kept pulling him in until his balls finally slapped her asshole. She had taken it all. She was so full. She could feel her belly distend with each stroke. He was giving her a hard pounding the likes of which she had never experienced. Her body alternated between orgasm and almost orgasm quickly. Alyssa moved her hands to her nipples, rubbing around and over them, her fingertips acting like lightning rods to the pleasure tendrils coming from her belly. She felt her juices running down the crack of her ass and soaking the bedspread below her. Her body had never produced so much cum.

The pinching sensation in her lips returned. Her vaginal muscles ached as they stretched further. The big head ramming beside her cervix spread wider. Alyssa opened her legs further, wanting even more of him inside before he finished.

"Where do you want me to come?"

Through the bouncing of Paul's powerful fucking and her own ragged between-orgasm breathing, Alyssa managed, "Come on my tits… Oh god… Come on my tits… It's so dirty." He gave her a few more hard strokes, pulled out, and aimed his cock at her. The first shot of cum landed on her face, from her hairline to her chin, the heat connecting to the pleasure radiating from her empty pussy. The next seven or eight did the same where they landed from her throat to her belly, with two good ones electrifying her nipples. Paul jacked the last few drops onto her gaping pussy, uniting her entire body into one final warm spasm. Alyssa wiped a drop of cum from her eye and sagged back, completely spent. Paul sat back on his haunches, his cock still in his hand between her legs. Sweat dripped from his chin onto Alyssa's thigh.

"That was really hot."

Alyssa and Paul both snapped their heads toward Kate.

"What? Even this drunk, I couldn't sleep through that roller coaster of a fuck. I had to hang on to the covers to keep from bouncing to the floor." She reached over and gently stroked

Alyssa's hair. "Are you okay, sweetie? I know you just got a great fuck, but are you okay? You said you didn't want to play."

Alyssa closed her eyes. She felt a couple tears slide down her temples into her hair. *Am I okay? What I just did I vowed never to do. I love Robert. But I really liked it. I have never had that much pleasure. I have never felt so satisfied, well fucked, and full. Never. I'm alone here and stranded. Drunk. Bored. Horny. I just had a once-in-a-lifetime experience. And my pussy will be sore tomorrow. Am I okay? …Yes, I think so.* Alyssa opened her eyes to see Kate up close. "I am okay. I had intended to go back to my room, frustrated and faithful, but I couldn't take it. I'm glad I came here tonight."

"Oh, I am so glad." Kate wiped a drop of cum off Alyssa's face and sucked it off her finger. Alyssa thought it was the sexiest thing she had ever seen, and her nipples came back to life. "Um, would you mind if I licked up Paul's cum? I love eating it, especially off someone as sexy as you."

Alyssa didn't respond, so Kate tenderly kissed her head near the hairline on the first glob of cum. Her lips felt warm and soft. *Different from a man. No stubble, more patient.* Kate shifted and repeated the gentle kiss on the bridge of Alyssa's nose, and again just beside her mouth. Alyssa's eyes closed, and she let the red-head nibble her face, each kiss warming her chest like drinking hot coffee on a cold day. Kate paused after a kiss on Alyssa's chin before kissing Alyssa on the mouth.

Alyssa surprised herself by kissing Kate back. *She is a good kisser. I'm just enjoying the kiss, like everything else I've enjoyed tonight. Do I like women too?* Her abs tightened and her neck tensed at the thought. A long exhale through her nose calmed Alyssa's mind. *I'm about to find out.* Their tongues flicked each other's lips a while.

Kate broke the kiss before it escalated. She kissed away the cum on Alyssa's neck and chest, just as she had on her face. She moved to the older woman's breasts, kissing all over them instead of simply eating the cum, each kiss building the comfortable warmth around her heart. Kate's patience and thoroughness made Alyssa feel concurrently comfortable and teased like she had never experienced. She was coated with saliva before Kate sucked the first bit of cum from her right nipple.

Alyssa's sensitive nipples worked against Kate's slow pace. The spark that flew from Alyssa's nipple, through her belly, to her cunt popped her eyes open. She let out a low groan and put her hands in Kate's hair. When Kate shifted to suck the other nipple, Alyssa held her head there.

Kate kept sucking and licking Alyssa's nipple as it hardened and grew to a nub more than half an inch long. She gave it a light nip with her teeth, sucked it with her lips, then pulled gently back and off her breast, descending with a trail of kisses and cleaning the cum off Alyssa's belly. There was less cum here, but Kate made her way down to Alyssa's navel, flicked it with her tongue, then moved to that sensitive spot between her abs and obliques. She sucked and licked there until Alyssa curled her hips to the side, seeking respite from the sensation.

Kate followed the last of the cum trail to Alyssa's pussy. It still tingled from Paul's magnificent fucking, and Alyssa raised her thighs as Kate nibbled toward it, fearing a jarring assault on her vulnerable clit. When small, soft nibbles landed on her tired outer lips, Alyssa's legs relaxed, collapsing toward the bed in an open invitation for Kate to have her way. Kate roamed over the lips, along and across, building more of the warmth in Alyssa's chest and a renewed tingle along her opening. Kate dropped her own pussy onto Alyssa's shin and rubbed her slit on the bone as she licked the inner labia upward with a broad stroke of her tongue. Kate stopped just short of Alyssa's clit and dropped back down.

Alyssa's full attention focused on Kate. She again snaked her fingers into the red curls between her thighs, not holding Kate in place, but encouraging her to dig in. She flexed her leg up into Kate's pussy, and she felt the wetness accumulating on her shin. Kate's licking was more tender than any man Alyssa had ever been with, and Kate spent more time around Alyssa's pussy than on top of it.

The tingle building just inside Alyssa started to want Kate to finally touch her clit. "Oh yes. That is so good. Don't stop this time. Lick my clit. Please."

Kate hummed into Alyssa's pussy on the next stroke and feathered her clit. Alyssa pulled the red curls toward her pelvis, enhancing the light sensation with something harder.

The mattress sagged underneath her shoulder, and Alyssa turned to see Paul's rejuvenated cock just before it tapped her lips. "Suck this while she eats you, honey. It's ready."

Alyssa looked into his eyes and opened her mouth. She licked the big head and could taste her own pussy. She had given blow jobs before but never after it had been inside her. She didn't so much enjoy the tangy saltiness as the depravity of tasting herself on a cock made her mouth ache to be filled. She had never felt that when giving head, but she opened her mouth to satisfy it. She guided the shaft into her mouth as far as she could, maintaining contact between her tongue and the veiny underside. She didn't suck cock often, but she knew how. *Now I show him what I can do.* She sucked hard and pushed back when he hit the back of her throat. She fluttered her tongue on the underside of his cockhead while twisting her hand before pulling the big dick back to her throat.

Kate's three fingers shoving all the way in her cunt broke her rhythm. "Argh, god. Oh shit." The surprise of it almost matched having Paul's cock for pure sensation, and her orgasm began.

Her belly rolled, and she pulled her nipple. She squeezed Paul's cock, though its girth and hardness prevented her fingers from touching her thumb. When she let go to pull the other nipple, Paul moved to the end of the bed behind Kate, cock in hand.

Kate's mouth bumped into Alyssa's throbbing pussy again and again as Paul fucked her. Even with the motion, Kate kept her fingers working Alyssa's G-spot, her tongue flicking her clit, and most importantly, her eyes focused directly on Alyssa's. The erotic connection with those eyes fluttered her belly even more than the rhythmic pounding she felt as Paul fucked his wife.

Alyssa's juices became a steady stream down her ass, and her body shifted from orgasm to almost orgasm just as quickly as it had when Paul had fucked her minutes ago. This time, though, Alyssa stayed focused on Kate's eyes. She knew when Kate would come even before she stopped fingering and licking.

Kate's eyes went wide and rolled back. Her neck strained and flushed a bright pink. Her hands pushed Alyssa's thighs farther apart. Her wail announced her satisfaction to everyone on the floor. After the seconds that seemed to last minutes, her body collapsed forward onto Alyssa. At that moment, Paul echoed his wife's wail and came deep inside her. He climbed up the bed and lay beside Alyssa. Alyssa nodded off, completely spent.

3

TUESDAY

Alyssa awoke in the dark, an unfamiliar snore coming from the man holding her breast. The instant of terror woke her enough to forestall a scream when she remembered she was with Paul. She counted to ten, her method of settling down after a nightmare. Kate's heavy breathing from the other bed told Alyssa she must have decided not to sleep between Alyssa's legs. Her pulse back to normal, Alyssa replayed the night's events in her head. With the beginnings of a hangover replacing last night's drunkenness, regret and guilt crept into her mind. She moved Paul's arm and got out of the bed. Enough light came from the illuminated bathroom mirror that she found her skirt and shirt on the floor. She slipped them on, felt the key card in her skirt pocket, and tiptoed out the door barefoot.

Her room was quiet. Alyssa turned on the bathroom light, opened a bottle of water, and closed the bathroom door. The light escaping under the door allowed her to navigate to the window and open the curtains before sitting in the armchair. She stared out at the few lights in the dark city. She spun her wedding rings with her thumb.

Alyssa, what have you done? You've never cheated on Robert, nor has he cheated on you. You don't keep secrets from each other, and you are a lousy liar. She had no hope of keeping this secret. *Your marriage is solid, but is it strong enough to withstand this?* The reasons sounded more like excuses. *A little drunk, horny from the neighbors' fucking, lonely, bored? After two nights? Robert would be right to throw you out. If that isn't bad enough, will Susan and Clay even speak to you if you ruin the family?* Tears ran down her cheeks, her earlier assessment of "okay" shattered by a perspective that didn't involve the afterglow of too many orgasms.

As the sky lightened, Alyssa stopped crying and took a drink. She was cried out, and the self-pity and guilt had run out of her with the tears. She thought about her marriage. *I don't want to lose my marriage. I love Robert and Robert only, more than I ever thought I could love anyone. I still love him the same way this morning that I did yesterday. I won't lie to him about last night, but I'll tell him in person, when we can talk face-to-face. I'll work it out with him, like we have worked out our problems before. I'll do what is necessary to save our marriage, then there is nothing to tell the kids.*

What about last night? Alyssa stared out the window for several minutes as the morning strengthened. *I'm ashamed and worried that I broke my wedding vows. That said, I really enjoyed the sex. Not just the sex, but the forbidden aspect of sex outside my marriage.* She smiled, remembering great sex with a great cock. *My pussy is wonderfully sore, and I loved making it sore. I liked having a different experience: different caresses, different kisses, different foreplay, a different dick size, different fucking technique, even different cum.* It was like being a kid at Christmas—a surprise every minute.

And, god, having Kate lick and kiss and eat Paul's cum off me was so erotic. She was different, too, so tender. Until she rammed three fingers into me. God, she made me come so hard. I can't believe I came that hard without a cock or a vibrator. I never thought about being with a woman, but Kate made me feel so good. When it was happening, the dirtiness of cheating and the iniquity of being with a woman had me halfway to coming before she touched any of my good parts. She was so beautiful looking up at me while she ate me. I could have come from the gleam in her eyes. She trailed her fingers over her belly, using the pleasant flutter their touch caused to loosen the huge knot of nausea her worries had created.

How do I feel about all that? What do I do about it? After only another moment's hesitation, Alyssa's thoughts crystalized. *I'll talk to Robert when I get home. I told myself last night I would keep the secret, but I won't do that to us. He deserves, our marriage deserves, honesty. I may have cheated, but I won't lie. We will go to the back porch, and I'll tell him what happened and beg his forgiveness. I'll explain how much I love him and how important our marriage and our family are to me. I'll do whatever he demands to repair the damage, and I'll never cheat again. He can even monitor my phone if he needs to rebuild his faith in me.*

Alyssa bit the inside of her lip, the pain a reminder that she had to get through today and tonight before solving her problem tomorrow. *If Paul and Kate want to play, and if I want to, I will. I don't want to hurt my marriage further, but I won't feel guilty for enjoying a once-in-a-lifetime experience. I won't seek it out, but if the opportunity comes along, I'm open to taking it. God, I want that opportunity.*

Alyssa closed her eyes, surprised at her own clarity. Before, impactful decisions caused days of consternation, that uneasy knot growing bigger each day. Of course, the last big decision was deciding to get pregnant with Clay, and nineteen years had matured her. The knot in her stomach released, confirming her mind was made up for the better. She relaxed in a crash, not even having the energy to move to the bed. She stretched her feet out on the ottoman and allowed herself to sleep.

Alyssa's neck woke her a few hours later. Sleeping in the chair had sounded like a good idea, but she had to raise her head with her hand because her neck had been stretched over for too long. The remnants of a hangover hammered behind her eyes, and she was glad that the sky outside her window remained overcast. As she worked to sit up, her thighs and pussy ached. A slight smile arose with her memories as she settled to a more comfortable position. When she pulled the bottle of water from the window-sill, pungent underarm crinkled her nose and broke her trance. She finished the water and went to the shower.

While the water warmed up, she hung her blouse and skirt on the towel racks to steam out the wrinkles. She caught her reflection in the mirror and turned to ponder herself. Her dark-brown hair was a mess, but there was no gray thanks to good genes and a good hairdresser. The small creases around her eyes and beside her mouth showed less than her friends', she knew, but she noticed them. The taut skin of her neck and chest showed just a few freckles more than when she was in college. Having kids had left her with larger breasts, and they sagged a little. She hefted them with her hands as if offering them to her reflection. The larger nipples still sat in the center of wide, firm orbs that jiggled when she pulled her hands away. Her belly was flat, though the small bulge above her C-section scar had never diminished after Clay. Her cleanly shaved mons jutted just enough that it bulged in a swimsuit. The lips themselves were tight, which made her pussy look small between her legs. *You can't even tell how hard it got pounded last night.* Her legs were long for her height. They were firm, and the tops of her thighs had a young woman's gap between them. *The benefit of those aerobic tapes. Not as cut as they used to be, but still really good. Robert loves them.* She turned to look over her shoulder at her back and ass. The knots of muscle on her shoulder blades flexed as she twisted. Her hips were broader than they used to be, but her ass was firm with good globes of muscle. *Remember this the next time you want to skip exercising.* Alyssa smiled seductively at her reflection. *Paul called me the hottest woman in the hotel. Not a chance, but not bad for a forty-four-year-old mother of two. Nuh-uh, motherhood and age aside, I'm still sexy.*

The mirror fogged, so she stepped in the shower. The warm water eased the crick in her neck. She scrubbed the dried cum and juices off her body. She considered staying in longer to relax, but hunger pangs refocused her. Alyssa got out, dried her hair, and looked for clothes so she could go eat. Having only packed for a three-day trip, she needed to rewear the jeans and long-sleeved T-shirt she had worn Saturday driving down. They weren't too dirty—she had been in the car all day. She pulled Saturday's panties and bra out of her dirty-clothes bag. They smelled a little worse than the jeans and T-shirt, so she hung them in the bathroom to air out. She would go commando for now. *So this is how Robert feels,* she thought as she slid her jeans up over her naked body. She liked the sneaky roguishness of it. She donned the T-shirt and noted the two stiff points on her chest in the mirror. *I'm not that much of a rogue. I'll wear my cardigan to cover my nipples.*

᪻

There was no line at Starbucks when she reached the lobby, but she found there was no food either. She got a cup of coffee and walked toward the restaurant. The handwritten sign by the entrance indicated they would open at five o'clock. Alyssa closed her eyes. Her hunger wouldn't wait four hours for the restaurant to open and another couple hours for the food. She heard a noise. Beth was coming out from behind the front desk and over to her.

"Hey, Mrs. Davis. It's good to see you this afternoon. We will open in a little while. I hope you like burgers and pizza. That is the menu again tonight. By the way, you tipped way too much last night."

Right! I left a pizza in Paul and Kate's room. Maybe I can get it before I starve. "Good afternoon, Beth. It's good to see you, too, and you earned every penny of that tip. You ran hard all night. For tonight, burgers and pizza sounds great to me." She looked at the pretty blonde a second and said, "Are you okay? If you don't mind me saying, you look tired. How late were you here?"

"We finished about three. I didn't have to be up when Starbucks opened, but yesterday was a long day. Being short-staffed means we are all doing everything. Nobody expected to be full, and not everyone is as kind as you are." The girl's eyes showed a rim of tears, and her chin quivered.

Alyssa hugged Beth while she regained her composure. She rubbed Beth's back with one hand and felt a couple of tears soak into the shoulder of her T-shirt. Beth hugged her back tightly and held on. Without her bra, Alyssa's nipples hardened against Beth's chest. After a long minute, Beth sniffled and released her grip.

"The hard thing is I miss my daughter. I dropped her with my mom before I came in on Sunday. I'm still here and it's Tuesday."

Alyssa felt her eyebrows raise. "You don't look old enough to have a daughter. I bet she is beautiful, like her mom."

"Oh, thank you. I think she is. She keeps me going some-times and wears me out all the rest. It's a good thing she's with Mom. I wouldn't even see her, as busy as we have been." Beth looked at Alyssa a moment. "I bet your daughter is gorgeous too.

She is if she is like her mom." That last bit was under her breath, but Alyssa heard it. Beth and Alyssa both blushed.

"Beth, I remember being a young mom away from my babies for the first time. You will get through it, and your daughter will be just fine staying with Grandma. That said, if you need to talk, I am here with both ears open and precious little matronly advice. It's only fair, after you have taken such good care of me." Alyssa grasped both of Beth's shoulders and held her gaze. "Promise you will take me up on that if you need to."

"I will. Thank you for understanding me. I'll find you if I need to talk." Beth hugged Alyssa once more and walked into the restaurant. Alyssa watched her go before turning for the elevator.

Alyssa's empty stomach filled with butterflies as she walked down the twelfth floor hallway. *Are Paul and Kate upset that I left in the middle of the night? Did they find another playmate this morning? Will they even open the door so I can get my shoes and pizza? Am I walking right into an afternoon of sex?* Her free-swinging tits and sensitive nipples wanted her to. They loved rubbing against the inside of the T-shirt as she walked. Her pussy moistened as she walked down the hall, nodding its approval. Her brain dissented. *One drunken night can be forgiven. Going back the next day, intentional and sober, will be judged more harshly. You decided to tell him about last night; will you tell him about this? Your intentionality? If you walk in there and fuck, there are no extenuating circumstances.* Alyssa had stopped walking. *Fuck it. I need my shoes and my pizza, so I'm going in. If they want to play, I'll play. This remains a once-in-a-lifetime experience, and I intend to participate. Then I'll tell Robert when I get home, just like I promised myself.* She knocked on 12035.

Kate opened the door far enough to stick her head out. "Alyssa! I'm glad you are here. Thought you might come by. We have your pizza. Come in." She opened the door wider but stayed behind it. The shower was running. Kate gave her a full hug and kissed her cheek. "Are you okay? We weren't surprised you were gone this morning. You weren't in the lobby when we went down for coffee, and we have been thinking about you."

Alyssa should not have been surprised by Kate's nudity. It was her hotel room, and they had fucked last night. There were no pretenses of modesty. Nevertheless, Alyssa gawked at the red-haired beauty standing in front of her. She was as flawless in the daylight streaming through the window as she had been in last night's soft lighting. Alyssa looked her up and down.

"That's the nicest thing anyone has not said to me," laughed Kate. She held her arms out in a "take it all in" pose.

Alyssa regained her composure and smiled. "I'm okay. I woke up beside Paul in the middle of the night. I wanted to think, so I went to my room. I stared out the window until after dawn, then crashed. That's why I wasn't at Starbucks."

"You forgot your sandals. They are on the desk by your pizza. Would you like to eat and talk?" Kate picked up a robe from the bed and slipped it on.

"That sounds good." She sat in the desk chair and ate a piece of the cold pizza before saying more.

Kate handed her a bottle of water.

"This is what I needed. Some food and a talk."

"I'm glad to provide both, and I'm glad you're here. So what did you think about this morning?"

"My marriage and my family remain the most important things in my life. I love my husband. I'll tell him that I broke my vows. I hope to repair the damage." Alyssa put her pizza down and released a long breath as she watched the corners of Kate's mouth turn up enough to look attentive and friendly without smirking.

"As far as last night, I really, really enjoyed it. Both the dinner and the sex, though dinner doesn't cause any moral dilemmas. I decided to not feel guilty about feeling such pleasure. It's been a long time since I had sex with anyone other than Robert, and last night was wonderful. Paul is an amazing lover, and you…well, you are the first woman I've ever been with. If I had known how good a woman can be, I would have tried it earlier."

Kate's neck flushed as she opened her mouth to speak, stopped, and grinned instead.

Alyssa returned Kate's wide smile. "I also decided that last night was just that, a wonderful, pleasurable experience. I don't love you or Paul, and you two don't love me. Our sex hasn't made me love Robert less. You didn't steal me away from him last night. I consider last night's sex an adult vacation, something to be enjoyed, but not something to build a life around. Does any of that sound sane?"

Kate's face became serious. The shower stopped running, and she glanced at the bathroom door. "It does. You must be one smart lady. It took Paul and me three years to come to the same conclusion."

"I don't understand."

"Paul and I both started having affairs by the second year of our marriage. He was traveling all the time selling decking systems, and I was home teaching aerobics. We were young and horny. His clients wanted him to entertain them at titty bars, and I spent evenings getting sweaty with fit people in tight clothes. We both gave in to the temptations." She stared into space as if savoring a memory. "Sometimes we caught each other and fought like cats and dogs. We didn't realize it then, but the make-up sex was stellar, and we never talked about getting divorced. A divorce would have been easy then; there was nothing to split. We didn't though." Kate took a bite of pizza.

"That went on for three years. We would cheat, get caught, fight, make up, repeat. Three goddamn years of nasty fights and amazing sex, with a lot of horrible loneliness in between. I still don't know how we stayed together. The last time, Paul came home early from a trip and caught me in bed with a woman from my class. She was eating me and fucking me with a vibrator, and my howls obscured the sound of his arrival. When he walked in the bedroom and dropped his luggage, everything stopped." Kate closed her eyes and shook her head.

"What happened then?"

"His face went red, and he took two big strides toward the bed. He stopped and let his eyes refocus from the laser beams that bored into me. He noticed Marjorie, a lovely blonde who was, as you can imagine, terrified. He released the tension from his neck and shoulders. His face softened. He stood still just long enough that she and I were no longer afraid of him. He looked at my friend and said, 'It sounded like you were doing a great job of fucking my wife. Do you mind if I join you?' She hesitated and looked at me with questioning eyes. She could tell this was a surprise to me too. I nodded at her. She looked at Paul for another minute before nodding. Paul undressed slowly and gently kissed both of us when he got into bed. We spent the rest of the afternoon pleasing one another. It was wonderful. Marjorie left to make supper for her boyfriend, and Paul and I talked. We didn't fight, just talked. We enjoyed the afternoon, but while the various bedmates had been great, we only loved each other. For the first time, we verbalized that the affairs and other partners had only been sex to combat the loneliness, and that we needed professional counseling. That was four years ago. We have been very happy since. Sounds like you are quicker on the uptake than we were."

Paul chimed in from the bathroom door, where he had been waiting. "That was the single scariest and most wonderful day of my life. I started to throw both women out of the house just as naked as I found them and let them bear the consequences. I realized that Kate's friend thought I might do that and worse. It was Kate's look of absolute woe that stopped me. She knew she had ruined our marriage, and that it would end in that bed. She dropped her eyes and slumped her body forward, resigning herself to that fate. That was the worst I ever made her feel, and it broke my heart. My reaction had yanked her from the heights of pleasure to the depths of despair, and I loved her too much to hurt her that way. Instead, I wanted to show how much I loved her, and how much I missed being with her when I was away. So I asked to help please her. Thank god Marjorie was up for it, or we might be divorced today. It was the hardest and best thing I ever did. It literally was a last-second save of our marriage."

"And since then, you two have had a…um, what's the term? Open marriage?"

"We don't use that term, but as I understand it, yes. We can both have sex with whomever we want, together or separate. The one rule is that we tell each other about it." Kate looked at Paul before grinning and saying, "Telling the stories really gets us hot. The sex is always better after somebody gets some strange."

"And you don't get jealous? Not even a little?"

Paul weighed in. "I like to think of it like I am reclaiming Kate after she has sex with someone else. She comes home, tells me, and our lovemaking reminds her why she keeps coming home."

"I think about it the same way. I let Paul know it is fine to play around, but what he has at home will thrill him better than anyone else."

"You guys decided this that day?"

"Oh no," Kate laughed. "Months of therapy helped us figure that out. Cooperatively editing your wedding vows takes work. Well, it took us a lot of work, at two hundred and fifty dollars per hour. It took a long time to differentiate sex and love, and to accept that we not only enjoyed sex with others but wanted to continue doing it."

"We learned from our experience and talking with other open couples that an open marriage is as hard as a monogamous one." Paul paused a moment. "The stresses of everyday life remain, which pressures any marriage. People fall out of love, or one partner isn't as good with the open arrangement as the other. Any of the reasons that marriages end still exist. An understanding about sex with others just eliminates one legal reason for divorce."

Kate looked Alyssa right in the eyes. "You seem to understand that love and sex are different things. This morning, did you ponder how to include other partners in your marriage? Is that why you are asking these questions?"

"No, I don't see changing our marriage at this stage. My resolution separating love and sex is for this trip. I expect to go back to normal when I get home."

Alyssa didn't realize what she had said, but Paul did. "So this trip is open for you? You came to our room for more than just your things and an interview on open marriage?"

Alyssa's nipples hardened, creating visible lumps in the thin T-shirt. *Did I? Kate looked so good naked, and Paul is still just wearing a towel.* She smiled. "Perhaps. I decided that if you invited me and I wanted to, I would."

"Consider yourself invited," Kate said at the same time as Paul said, "Then get over here."

"Ooh yes." Alyssa moved to the bed to kiss Paul. Kate slid behind her and nibbled her neck. Alyssa lay back. The other two followed, the three of them kissing and groping together. Paul's large hand felt hot and heavy as he slid it under her shirt to rub her belly. Kate's smaller fingers feathered across her breasts through the T-shirt. Both left Alyssa panting as she alternated kissing them. The three weren't in a hurry, but there was no reason to delay with seduction.

Paul and Kate cooperated to raise Alyssa and remove her T-shirt. "Ooh. Only a bad girl goes to a man's hotel room without a bra," Kate laughed. "I think you came here to seduce my husband." She and Paul each sucked a nipple into their mouths, and Alyssa moaned her appreciation. She untied Kate's robe and reached inside. Her first light touches slid uninterrupted around and over Kate's breast, the skin smooth and perfect—soft like satin laid over the firm tissue beneath. A small divot where the ribs met the breast broke the smoothness; the rough texture inside teased her fingertip. *Almost perfect.* Kate shuffled the robe off without removing her mouth from Alyssa's breast.

Paul unsnapped Alyssa's jeans, and she raised her hips to let him remove them. "No panties either. You *are* a bad girl. I think you came here to seduce my wife," he said, smiling at both women.

"I didn't intend to seduce, but I did intend to eagerly surrender." Alyssa opened Paul's towel. His huge dick was already hard. She lay back. Paul's skin felt just as soft and satiny over the hard tissue inside his cock as Kate's breast had felt, but veins and ridges interrupted the smoothness as she held and stroked it. She slid her other hand down to cup Kate's mound, also smooth with a hint of stubble scratching her palm. Alyssa jacked Paul's cock in time with caressing Kate's lips, enjoying the silky roughness in each hand.

She didn't realize how horny she had been until Kate slid her finger between Alyssa's lips and dragged the moisture up to her clit. Alyssa gasped when Kate rubbed it. Paul sucked on one tit and fondled the other. Every time he flicked her nipple with either his thumb or his tongue, Alyssa jumped at the shocks that simmered low in her belly. Alyssa pushed Kate's head away to break their kiss.

"I want to lick your pussy. I want to pleasure you like you did me last night. I don't know what I am doing, so please guide me. Paul, can I focus on Kate for a while before returning to your magnificent cock?" Alyssa rolled toward Kate without waiting for an answer.

On top of Kate, Alyssa gave one long kiss, then raised her head. Kate's perfect teeth peeked from behind her open lips. *Mm, those teeth.* Alyssa lowered again, kissing the neck muscle below Kate's ear, then pulled back again. She kissed the divot between her collarbones, her lips feeling Kate's pulse throb. Alyssa kissed across Kate's upper chest, smiling at the white skin turning pink and feeling her own nipples tingle with anticipation.

Alyssa mimicked what Kate had done to her the night before: nibbling around the whole of each breast, spiraling in toward her engorged nipple. Alyssa would remember the scent of lavender every time she tasted a woman's nipple for the rest of her life. She licked it a few times, then sucked hard, Kate's soft moans letting her know she was getting it right. She repeated the process on the other breast, to the same confirmation.

Alyssa raised her head when Kate touched her breast. "No, no. This is about me making you feel good. Please, just lie back and let me make you come. Tell me what you like so I can do more of it."

"Keep licking my nipples."

Alyssa sucked as much of Kate's boob as her mouth would hold and slowly pulled her head back until only the nipple remained between her lips.

"Oh. That's good," from Kate encouraged Alyssa to do it

again and again. Alyssa did, and her own pussy lips pulsed with her heartbeat.

Kate began to writhe under Alyssa's nipple play, so Alyssa took her cue to descend farther down the redhead's body. She licked Kate's navel and abdomen while dragging her fingertips along the gaps between her ribs. Kate jumped when Alyssa trailed her fingers along the outside edge of her ab muscles. *Remember where that is.* She moved her mouth to the corresponding spot on the other side, teasing both sides at once. Kate curled her hips upward and moaned deep in her throat. She pulled Alyssa's hand off her stomach and just held it as her body slowly unfurled.

When Kate's hips returned to the bed, Alyssa moved between her knees. She ran her fingers up from the bottoms of Kate's feet, across her ankles, and up her calves, lingering at the backs of her knees. She shifted her fingers to the insides of Kate's thighs and feathered her fingertips up almost to her pussy. When she stopped and moved back to Kate's feet, Kate's head pushed back into the bed and her back arched. Alyssa wanted to please Kate until she pushed her away again. Her power over Kate's pleasure filled her chest with pride. Alyssa repeated the excruciating process again, and a third time. Kate's pussy lips swelled and darkened. Alyssa's tingled from her opening up through the inside of her vagina, anticipating Kate's release perhaps more than Kate did.

After the fourth trip of her fingers up Kate's legs, Kate's inner lips parted, revealing a glistening wetness. Alyssa replaced her fingers at the tops of Kate's thighs with her mouth, kissing and licking them over and over, still avoiding her pussy. Alyssa kept tracing up and down Kate's calves. Alyssa looked up to see Kate rubbing her breasts and pulling her nipples with both hands. Alyssa's belly fluttered; she was unsure exactly how to proceed, worried that she would ruin Kate's building pleasure.

Time for my first pussy. She licked the length of Kate's slit with a flat tongue. Kate moaned loudly and put one hand on top of Alyssa's head. Alyssa repeated the lick and finished by flicking Kate's clit a couple of times. Kate grabbed Alyssa's hair. "Oh fuck. Do that again. I'm going to come." Alyssa didn't do it again. She wanted Kate to hover on the edge of orgasm for a while, the way she herself had last night. Alyssa rubbed Kate's calves and kissed her thighs. The butterflies in her belly flew to her breasts, tickling behind her nipples, Kate's reaction physically pleasing Alyssa's own body. When Kate's hand relaxed in her hair, Alyssa dove back into her pussy. She licked the slit and pulled the inner lips with her mouth. She stayed clear of Kate's clit, knowing that Kate's clit tingled and sought release as much as her own did.

Kate's hand firmed up in Alyssa's hair, pulling yet pressing her into her sex. Kate's thighs squeezed Alyssa's head, and Alyssa felt Kate groan her approval through the thighs preventing her from hearing it. Alyssa stretched her tongue to flick Kate's clit and pushed two fingers into her opening. She pressed on the front wall, feeling around until she found the spongy G-spot. *Hers feels different from mine.* She rubbed it with a come-hither motion. Kate squealed and arched her back. *But it gets the same reaction.* Alyssa's pussy squeezed in on itself, seeking something to squeeze against.

Alyssa's nose was buried in Kate's skin, and Kate's thighs held her there as Alyssa refocused from the throbbing in her pussy to her need to exhale. She kept licking and fingering until Kate relaxed her thighs. Alyssa sucked a big breath through her nose and kept stimulating Kate until Kate's hand reversed its pressure and pulled her away from her crotch. *Mission accomplished.*

Alyssa looked into Kate's eyes as she crawled up her body. "Did I do that right?"

Kate embraced Alyssa and kissed her. "Did you do it right?

49

Oh fuck, you did it right. I'm a mess. You have really never been with a woman?"

"Never. I was so nervous." She kissed Kate softly. "Are you sure I did it right? I want to repay you for making me feel so wonderful."

"Oh, you did that and then some. Now it's your turn." She looked at Paul sitting against the headboard, rubbing his cock just enough to keep it hard. "I'm fucked out right now. Honey, can you please pay this lady the pleasure I owe her?"

Alyssa licked her lips and looked at Paul. "Oh no. You can repay your own debt to me later. Right now, I need to thank Paul for letting me have you first." She crawled over Kate toward Paul. Kate licked Alyssa's nipples as they dragged over her mouth, but Alyssa kept moving. Her eyes locked with his, and she slithered past his feet and over his leg. Her hand replaced his at the base of his cock. Her fingers could not wrap all the way around it. Alyssa's wet and needy pussy ached as she spread her legs to straddle Paul's knees. The hard bone split her lips, laying her open to grind her clit, powerful shocks making her thighs tremble when she sat down on his shin.

Now balanced, she used her other hand to cup his balls one at a time. Her eyes never left his, even when he peeked at her body. She released his scrotum and started jacking his cock with both hands. She had felt how large it was last night, but now she could see that it was longer than both hands could hold. *Jesus, I had that in me.* The corner of his mouth turned up as if he was reading her thoughts. Alyssa felt her neck flush.

She looked down at the large purple head, then leaned forward to suck it into her mouth. Her mouth stretched wide to take it in, but she succeeded. The pinch she felt in her lips echoed the pinch in her pussy lips last night, with the same pleasure in her lower belly. She moved her top hand back to his balls and descended until the tip tickled the back of her throat. Her gagging sent saliva dripping down the shaft to her hand. She pulled back until the tip was between her lips and descended until gagging again. Her mouth was fuller than it had ever been. She could barely flutter her tongue under his shaft, and she stretched to ensure she didn't bite. She used the saliva to lubricate her hand and began to pump and twist the part of Paul's cock outside her mouth. Soft moans reached Alyssa's ears, growing the building warmth in her chest. Alyssa pulled off and wiggled her jaw to relieve her burning muscles. *I won't be able to do this long. I almost never suck Robert, and Paul is so much bigger.*

"Are you okay?"

Alyssa held the hard cock in her hand, smiled, and resumed.

Alyssa worked Paul's cock with alternating tenderness—slowly jacking him while fluttering her tongue on his frenulum and licking the large head—and aggression, jacking it hard and squeezing his balls while taking his cock to the back of her throat. With every gag came a load of saliva. It ran down her hands and his balls, creating a wet spot beneath him.

Paul reached underneath Alyssa to fondle her breasts. He continued for a minute or so, then grabbed her nipples when she pulled back on his cock. The gasp of breath only fanned the fire he started in her nipples, spreading it inside her from her neck to her thighs. He pulled her up, stretching them, the pain of the sting creating throbs of pleasure in her cunt.

She fanned the pleasure in her clit with another grind against his shin, and Alyssa released his head from her mouth. "Are you ready for more? You want these tits now?"

"Why don't I suck them while you ride me?"

Her empty pussy clenched at the question. She kissed Paul on the mouth as she walked her knees forward until her belly bumped his. She positioned his cock between her pussy lips. She didn't let it enter her, she just rode her pussy along the underside, spreading more lubrication and grinding her clit. Its girth let it rub her clit like his shin did, but it also ground her swollen lips between its silky hardness and her pubic bone, just a warm-up to the sensations coming in a minute.

Paul gripped her ass cheeks and lifted. Alyssa's belly lurched at the surprise of being raised, but the strong fingers lifting her and the strong will taking what he wanted from her turned the uneasiness to hunger. A wave of heat flowed from her clit, down across her lips. She would swear later she felt the wetness flow from her. "That feels good, but it's time to fuck."

She reached down and placed his cock at her entrance. She rubbed the head a couple more times along her inner lips, then he lowered her. She paused when the head stretched her open. *Oh god, so big. It is going to tear me apart. I can't wait.* "Let me go slow. You're huge."

Paul smiled and strengthened his grip on her ass, still supporting her while she took more of her weight onto her legs. "Take your time. Your pussy feels exquisite." He leaned his head to kiss her neck, then kissed the other side. She trembled atop his cock.

Alyssa rose until his cock was just touching her pussy, and descended again, farther this time, until she felt more pain. Her pussy responded with another rush of juices, and her head rolled back. *Do that again. The pain is so good. I'm going to come soon.* She retreated and descended again, farther down.

Paul sucked her right nipple into his mouth. He swirled his tongue around it and then curled his tongue into a tunnel that completely enveloped the bud. Alyssa moaned and bounced on his cock, taking more than half of it this time. When she came down, he repeated the nipple play on her left breast, and her pussy gripped his cock, rippling along the part that was inside and squeezing the nothing beyond where he had yet reached. Her back arched, and she gushed fluid down over his balls in an orgasm. He held her up when her head fell forward onto his shoulder.

Alyssa raised her head and repeated her slow attack on Paul's cock. She was tighter after her orgasm, and the little aftershocks every time she took more of him kept her pussy leaking. She felt him hit the top of her vagina and looked down. She was more than an inch from taking all of him. *Motherfuck, this is good. I'm so full and feeling everything. Now it's time to really fuck.*

She rose and plunged down until the massive cock stopped her, her weight driving the big head against the top of her tunnel. Alyssa increased her pace to establish a good rhythm. She brushed her sweaty hair out of her face and looked at Paul. His teeth were gritted and his face a twisted grimace that told her how good he felt. She took all her weight on her own legs and pulled his hands to her tits while she did the work. He cupped and squeezed her breasts, raising and lowering them in time with her thrusts. He pinched her nipples hard a couple of times, sending jolts of pleasure through Alyssa's belly to her pussy.

Paul gave a hard pinch, then released her nipples. "Let them swing free. Show me how hard you are fucking me." His hands moved to her hips. She established a resonance that kept her breasts bouncing as she fucked him. "Oh yeah. Look at those gorgeous tits bounce. You are working so hard. Keep going. I'm getting close."

"Me too. Pinch my nipples when you come. We'll come together." Alyssa's thighs burned with the exertion, and she put her hands on his shoulders to help her finish the race to orgasm. She pulled up until the head of Paul's cock was just at her opening and dropped down, legs limp, slamming his cock against her cervix and the tender spot around it. Rising until she was empty made her pussy ache to be refilled. Repenetrating with a drop, taking all of him at once stretched her wide from opening to cervix, the lack of transition exploding pressure and pleasure from inside out. Her belly tightened, and the soles of her feet cramped from curling her toes. Her arms straightened across Paul's muscular shoulders. She pounded down twice more, then felt Paul's cock, unbelievably, swell even larger inside her. The head flared against her walls, and she knew he was coming before he moved his hands to pinch her nipples and pull them hard.

"Oh god, yes. Come inside me." Paul filled her full as she ground her hips down to take him so deep. He was coming directly on her cervix; the heat and tapping feeling warmed her belly and made her come. She gripped him tightly as they orgasmed and wailed in each other's ears. *His cum feels like a hot douche. So much cum. Oh fuck, that is good.* Paul held her to him as she collapsed with her eyes closed.

Alyssa awoke to the feeling of Paul's cock slipping out of her followed by a rush of fluid. Still astride him, she kissed his neck. "How long have I been asleep?"

"Long enough for me to go soft. Maybe three minutes. You should have slept longer, as hard as you worked. You were fantastic. Let's lay you over. My feet are numb." He kissed her head and laid her beside him.

Alyssa stared into his eyes as the afterglow diffused through her limp body, slowly melting into the bed.

He turned to Kate. "Do you think all of us can fit in the shower? We should clean up before dinner."

"Ooh. It will be tight, but starting early gives us time for any delays that come from such close quarters." She kissed Alyssa's eyes, then nose, then mouth. "That was amazing. You were on fire. I have never seen a woman fuck on Paul's cock the way you did. You were slamming down on him like you couldn't get enough. I bet you are sore in the morning."

Alyssa roused under Kate's kisses. "It felt so good. I got so horny with you that I couldn't get enough of Paul. I can't believe I took all of him." She paused. "I really liked being with you. It was so different kissing you, teasing you, eating you. Are you sure you enjoyed it?"

"Oh god, honey. You ate me like a pro. If you learned that from your husband, I want to meet him. Oh. Wait. I'm sorry. I shouldn't have said that. I'm sorry. I'm sorry. I don't want to mess with your marriage. I'm sorry. Please forget I said that." Kate's eyes widened as she backtracked.

"It's okay." Alyssa stroked Kate's cheek. "I know what you meant. I tried to mimic his technique from years ago. We don't often spend much time on foreplay. He's good at it when he wants to be. He would take the compliment you intended. So will I." *If things go well, I can tell him about driving her wild. It might inspire him to do me more often.*

"Why don't we get a shower?" asked Paul during the pause. "Let's see if we can all fit."

The three of them squeezed into the shower. They took turns washing one another's hair. Alyssa found both washing Paul's hair and having Kate wash hers more sensuous than erotic, but her entire body responded when they squirted body wash and lathered one another up. Paul paid special attention to Alyssa's breasts and nipples, while Kate gently soaped her sex, her soft massage welcome after the hard ride Alyssa had just taken. Alyssa stroked Paul's cock with two foamy hands and feigned surprise as he hardened.

With a sputter, the water stopped flowing. No one said anything for a moment, and Alyssa turned the handle off and on again a couple of times. Nothing came out. The horny mood dissipated. The three stepped out of the shower and toweled off, and the women dried their hair. They dressed and went to the lobby.

Mike, the general manager, stood on the front desk and spoke with the throng of guests who had assembled to ask questions. Beth and four other staff members stood behind him in front of an open door into the back. "Folks, the water is off because the line that feeds the hotel has burst. We do not know when it will be repaired. Ordinarily, this would close the hotel and you would have to relocate. Let me be clear. We will remain open. Most hotels across the city are full. Our generator is running, so we will have heat and power. We are trying now to determine how to feed you without any water. We will let you know as soon as we can.

"As far as the water in your room goes, we will give each of you some bottled water. Use it for drinking and brushing your teeth. When the water eventually comes back on, it will be contaminated, so please do not drink it or bathe with it. For toilets, ours are pressurized, so do not try to open the tanks. I repeat, do not open the tanks. You can get hurt and damage the toilets. We are filling barrels with water on each floor. Use your trash cans to get some of that water to pour in your toilets after you use them. This will flush away the waste. Of course, the water for flushing is not potable. Do not drink it, and please use sanitizer on your hands after using that water to flush.

"We will do everything we can to make you as comfortable as possible. This is a challenge, and we will work through it. We ask that you remain patient with us as we do so. We will let you know through the PA system on the floor when things change. Thank you all for your understanding."

"Oh boy." Paul shook his head. "The staff is under the gun now." The three of them lingered while the crowd picked up its water. Most guests were polite, and some asked questions, but a few were angry and yelling. Mike and Beth responded with grace and manners. After almost an hour, the crowd disbursed. Alyssa, Kate, and Paul headed across the lobby. Beth's haggard look brightened, but Mike looked braced for another confrontation.

"You folks handled that with aplomb," Alyssa said when they reached the desk. Mike's shoulders relaxed, and Beth smiled. The others offered their thanks and scattered. "You are in a tough spot. Regardless of how well you get through this, some people will be angry."

Mike burst out laughing. "That's every day in this business. Thank you for saying that, but we are used to it. This just causes issues we don't normally address. Are you folks holding up?"

"We are fine," Paul said while putting his arm around Kate. "We drive out tomorrow, so if we can just eat tonight, everything will be perfect."

"I'm flying out tomorrow also," Alyssa chimed in, "so the same goes for me."

"We are glad that everything is working out. Let's get you some water, and then Beth and I must start dinner. Without water, I'm not sure what options we have, but we will put something together. Thank you again for staying with us." Mike turned to Beth. "Beth, can you please give them some bottles and join me?"

Beth handed them several bottles of water.

Alyssa turned to Paul and Kate. "I'm going to take these to my room and give Robert a call. See you at dinner?"

"Sure," Kate replied. "See you down here in an hour."

Alyssa turned back to Beth. "Are you all right? This just got harder, and you seem to be Mike's right hand. You must be running ragged."

The young woman looked at Alyssa and nodded but couldn't bring herself to speak. Alyssa stepped around the desk and embraced Beth. "It's going to be all right. Mike seems to have things in hand. I'm here if you need a friend."

As if on cue, Alyssa's phone buzzed. She opened the text from the airline. "Shit. Shit, shit, shit. They just pushed my flight back to Friday." She hung her head a moment, then looked up. "Beth, can we extend my stay to Friday, please? It looks like you're stuck with me a little longer."

They extended the stay. Beth gave Alyssa some toilet paper and Kleenex from the back room. "You will need these. Thank you for being so kind. I really appreciate it. See you at dinner!"

∽

Back in her room, Alyssa called Robert. "Hey, Babe. I have some bad news. They pushed my flight to Friday. It seems the airport doesn't have water."

"Doesn't have water?"

"Frozen pipes. We lost our water this afternoon also."

"People are going to become desperate. First, you need to extend your stay."

"Already done. I'm good through Friday."

"Good. What food and water do you have? The restaurant may not be able to cook."

"I have some bottles of water and a can of peanuts I bought when Susan and I got her supplies Sunday morning."

"That isn't much, but it should get you to Friday. You'll be hungry if there is nothing else. As for the toilets, use the ones in the lobby until they are gross. It is better than having a toilet full of crap in your room. I'm sorry you are stuck there, Baby."

"They are providing barrels of water to flush with. They told us it is not potable, so I don't know where they are getting it."

"What about your clothes? You didn't pack for this. You can't wash them in the sink. You could hang them out in your room. Maybe they won't smell as bad when you wear them."

Alyssa smiled. "That's a good idea. They are hanging everywhere now. Even what I was wearing."

"You're naked?"

Alyssa used a breathy tone while twirling a lock of hair in her fingers. "Yes. Does that excite you?"

"Are you warm enough?" Alyssa heard background noise. "Oh hey, Clay. Say hello to Mom."

Alyssa heard a faint hi from the phone. "Love you, Clay." *So much for getting Robert excited.*

"Have you heard from Susan? I talked with her last night. The university has power and water, so she is fine. She is bummed that you guys rushed there so she could go to class, just before they canceled all week."

Alyssa realized she had not spoken with Susan since dropping her off on Sunday. She closed her eyes. *What have you been focused on, you horny girl? Too busy cheating on your husband to check on your daughter?* "No. I thought I would call her before dinner. I'm glad to hear she is okay." They talked a while longer about nothing important, just reconnecting the way they did every day. Alyssa's stress about being stuck in the hotel diminished while her anxiety about talking with him about Paul and Kate increased. *Can our routine life take the shock of what I did?* "Babe, it sounds like they are making an announcement," she lied. "I'm going to go. I don't know if we will talk later. Dinner took forever last night. Love you. Give Clay a hug for me." She hung up and wept beside the window.

Susan lifted Alyssa's spirits. *She is warm, and she has hot food, running water, and her friends.* Susan offered to bring Alyssa to the dorm, since her roommate wasn't there, but Alyssa told her to stay put. Between the ice on the roads and the nonfunctioning streetlights, Alyssa didn't want Susan driving. When Susan hung up to visit her neighbors, Alyssa wondered what Susan would think about her mother's behavior. She was growing up and had made significant social strides from the shy, studious girl she had been in high school. That said, Alyssa was pretty sure Susan wouldn't understand her cheating on Robert. Alyssa started down that mental path, then stopped herself. *Don't. I need to dress and eat before thinking any more about this. I'm down because of what is happening here. I need to eat and be around people so I can think.*

⁂

Paul and Kate had secured a table. A glass of merlot sat at Alyssa's place. "Oh, thank you. I need this." She took a big gulp of wine and sagged into her chair. "What's for dinner? I didn't look at the sign."

"Burgers and chips for everyone. I guess it is what's available without making too much mess." Kate grinned. "Besides, it beats those awful protein bars that Paul has. Those are bad by themselves, and worse with wine."

"Delightful. I'll need a second one to go, for lunch tomorrow."

Kate's head jerked to look at Alyssa. "What? You have a flight—"

"That got canceled this afternoon when the airport lost its water. Houston isn't built for a stretch this long and cold. Pipes are bursting all over town, according to the news. The airline texted just after you went upstairs." Alyssa took another long drink.

"Oh my. I'm so sorry." Kate squeezed Alyssa's hand. She cast a questioning look at Paul, and he nodded. "Look, we leave tomorrow for Las Cruces. We plan to stop in San Antonio, thinking what usually takes two hours may take eight or nine if they can't clear the roads. You can come with us, and maybe that airport will be open."

Alyssa squeezed Kate's hand and looked her in the eye. "Thank you, but I'll stay. I have a flight on Friday. If getting to San Antonio takes all day, I'd be on a Thursday flight, at best. My best bet is the airport here. You two have a long trip, and if the roads are clear, you can go a lot farther than San Antonio before you have to stop. Thank you, but you guys go tomorrow. I'll be fine." She looked at Paul.

"If that is what you want," he replied. "If you change your mind, the offer stands. Are you sure? You don't have water here."

Alyssa smiled. "I'm sure. Your offer brightened my evening. Thank you. Are you hungry? We should order," she said as she rose.

Alyssa crossed to Beth at the bar. "Hey, Beth. Another long night after a long day?"

"Yes, Mrs. Davis. With a short staff, everyone is stretched thin. We will make it. Mike is doing what he can to keep our spirits up." She forced a smile. "Three burgers and more wine?"

"Four burgers. I need some lunch for tomorrow. And yes, more wine."

"We aren't supposed to let anyone have more than one burger tonight, Mrs. Davis. If you will eat your three, I can bring another one out when you leave. Nobody should notice."

Alyssa looked around the dining room. The tables remained as full as they had been last night, but many of the patrons wore looks of stress and displeasure. The background noise was a low rumble, where it had sounded like a cocktail party last night. "Oh, thank you, Beth. Don't feel like you need to make an exception for me. I don't want to get you in trouble."

"I won't get in trouble. Mike mentioned how nice you and your friends were this afternoon while we cooked. I'm sure he won't mind."

"Well, thank you. If that changes, please don't get into

trouble on my account." Alyssa took the wine back to the table. After a couple of hours and several more glasses, Alyssa leaned into the center of the table. "I'll tell Beth I'm ready for my burger to go. I like sitting here talking and drinking, but what I'd really like is a farewell session in your bed. That is, if you will have me."

"Wow. That was unexpected." Paul smiled. "Not that you want to, but that you have struggled with cheating and now you are asking us for it."

"It's been a long week, and I'll be bored tomorrow. I've done what I have done. The repercussions will be tough when I get home. For good or bad, I might as well enjoy tonight. Does my idea sound good to you two?"

"I haven't heard a better idea all day." Kate leaned like she was whispering to Alyssa, but instead just rubbed her thigh and licked her neck. Alyssa's nipples hardened as she looked over Kate's head to make eye contact with Beth. Beth's eyes bugged for a moment, but when Alyssa mouthed, "We're ready," Beth nodded and went to fetch the burger. She returned a moment later.

"Oh no! Huh-uh! Ain't no way!" The woman standing a few tables away and pointing at Alyssa brought the entire restaurant to a standstill. "They already ate, and she told us everybody only gets one! That little thing there don't look like she could eat two, anyway." Her red dress held her like a two-pound casing for a three-pound sausage, and her eyebrows met in a deep *V* between her eyes. As she strode toward the table, other guests backed up.

Alyssa stared at the menacing woman. "What? What are you saying?"

"You are getting an extra burger. I'm hungry, too, and you don't need one."

Beth stepped toward the woman. "You don't understand. She didn't eat. She is getting it to go, and she'll eat later."

The roundhouse slap knocked Beth onto the table. The

woman picked up a glass from another table and threw it at Alyssa. It missed Alyssa but hit a lady behind her in the head. The next glass shattered against the wall. The lady picked up a steak knife from the same table and lunged at Alyssa, losing her balance and planting the knife into the tabletop, just missing Beth's face. The woman rose without the knife but with a cut on her hand, slinging blood as she flailed.

Paul grabbed the woman in a bear hug before she could strike again. She began shrieking just as two off-duty cops arrived from across the dining room. The three of them wrestled the woman into submission. After a momentary struggle, she lay on the floor, handcuffed and screaming.

Alyssa knelt to check on Beth. The red handprint on her cheek looked to be the worst of it, though her wide eyes focused on the bloody knife standing in the table. Her nose was running with tears but not blood. Her lips weren't swollen, and there was no blood in her mouth. Once Alyssa moved Beth into a chair, she hugged her and let her weep. After a long minute, Beth relaxed. Her eyes showed defeat as the events of the past few days overcame her cheerful personality. As Alyssa pulled back, she smelled the wine that had soaked her shirt when Beth fell. She felt the cold and wet that adrenaline had negated. *No time for that.* She brushed Beth's hair out of her face and caressed her head as Beth's tears flowed.

Mike had come from the kitchen and was talking with the cops when he saw Beth sitting. He knelt beside her, and they spoke quietly. Alyssa looked at Kate, who had her head buried in Paul's chest. Alyssa looked across the emptying dining room. Mike had told the servers to close out the checks and let everyone leave without paying. A few people cast angry glances at her, but most glared at the angry woman, handcuffed and being tended to by the officers. Two additional cops had joined the crew in the restaurant to provide first aid to the woman hit by the wine glass. The cops walked the angry woman toward the door. One of the original cops came to their table. "Folks, we saw what happened. You aren't in any trouble, but the other lady is. We request that you come with us so we can get your statements."

"I… I don't want to press charges," Beth said from her chair. "She was just stressed."

"Perhaps so, ma'am, but please consider these three things. First, you may change your mind after you process the initial emotions. You can always drop the charges later. Second, the lady needs to cool down, and our holding area across the street is a great place for her to do that. Third, people are under a lot of stress here, and they need to see that we won't tolerate this kind of behavior. If this lady gets let go, things could get out of hand."

"Oh. I see. Um, I guess I can give you my statement. Where will we go?"

"We have a satellite processing facility in the convention center. With the homeless being brought there to get warm, we have officers there to handle this quickly." He looked at Alyssa, Paul, and Kate. "I'll need you three to join us as well, please."

"I'll come with you, Beth," Mike said as he stepped toward her.

Beth looked at the door of the restaurant. "Mike, those upset-looking guests want to speak with you. There is a lot of cleanup to do in here. I'm just going to give a statement. I'll be fine."

"Mike, I won't leave her," Alyssa assured him. "I'll stay with her until she's done and will bring her back to her room."

"We will be there, too," echoed Paul. "She is in good hands."

Mike looked uneasy. "Are you sure, Beth? I can talk with guests and clean up the mess later. I'll support you with whatever you need."

"Thank you, Mike, but I've got it. If I need you, I have your cell." She didn't look as self-assured as she wanted to, but Mike relented. The four of them followed the cop through the elevated walkway to the convention center.

4
WEDNESDAY MORNING

THE QUICK STATEMENT session ended up being a few hours of waiting. A fight in the homeless housing had the station busy processing the combatants. Alyssa, Beth, Paul, and Kate sat in a bright but chilly hallway on a bench. Kate and Alyssa leaned against Paul, and Beth leaned against Alyssa. They didn't talk much, just tried to stay warm. Each of them went back to give their statement.

Beth walked out around 2:00 a.m. into Alyssa's waiting arms. "That was awful. I saw that lady in there, and she yelled at me. The cop said, 'And all it got you was a night in jail,' and she sat down. I'm tired. Can we go?"

"Let's go, sweetie." Alyssa kept her arm around Beth's waist as they crossed the street and walked to the elevator. When they got to the fourth floor, Alyssa stepped out with Beth and turned to Kate and Paul. "I'm going to get her settled, then I'm going to bed. Are you heading out early tomorrow?"

"Not now. We will probably leave after ten." Paul held the door open. "We are headed to bed. I hope we see you in the morning."

"Me too. I'll drop by when I get up. Thanks for helping so much tonight, guys." Alyssa touched Paul's hand, then turned to walk Beth to her room.

Alyssa and Beth sat on Beth's bed beside each other. Beth looked at Alyssa and began to cry. She crushed into Alyssa's arms and buried her face in Alyssa's neck. Alyssa held her while she sobbed. "It's been a lousy day," she mumbled into Alyssa's neck.

"I know. I know." Alyssa just rubbed her back and moved one hand to stroke her hair.

"I don't know why that woman did that. She was mad…but why hit me? Then she almost stabbed me. I'm just trying to take care of everyone. And I miss my little girl." She started crying again but for only a few seconds. "Thank you for staying with me tonight. I'm sorry to cause trouble."

Alyssa kissed the top of Beth's head. "It's no trouble. I like you, Beth, and you have been taking care of me, remember?" Alyssa hugged her tighter. "We moms have to stick together to get through this."

"Yes, but…thank you anyway. Nobody else would understand like you do." Beth pulled back and smiled at Alyssa. "I am so glad we met." She looked down. "Oh! Your shirt. You have wine all over you. Let's get you cleaned up." Beth walked across the room before Alyssa could respond. She pulled a pack of baby wipes from the diaper bag on the desk. "With no water, these will have to do. Give me your shirt. I'll see if the seltzer water in the minibar can get that wine out."

Alyssa stood up. "Beth, it is late. I don't need to get cleaned up, and you need to rest."

"Nonsense. It will only take a minute, and then bed does sound good. You can't go out of here smelling and looking like a drunk. Please let me help you get clean. It's the least I can do after you have been so nice." Beth held out her hand to the older woman with a pleading look in her eyes.

Alyssa paused a moment. *Whoa. Just strip right here? Not normally, but I won't hurt her feelings. She wants to repay my kindness.* "You are too kind. Thank you." She reluctantly began to remove her cardigan. Its dark-purple color would hide the stain but not the smell. She hesitated again before grasping the hem of her T-shirt and pulling it slowly over her head.

Beth stood still, watching Alyssa remove her clothes. Alyssa moved even slower, still unsure about disrobing in front of the younger woman. Her skin tingled with goose bumps as each inch of skin met the air.

"Wow," Beth uttered under her breath as Alyssa's bra-clad breasts came into view. "Now the bra," she whispered as Alyssa dropped the T-shirt on the bed.

Is she getting turned on? Does she want me? Does she think I want her? Alyssa fumbled with the front clasp of her bra. She held it in place and looked at Beth. Beth was staring intently at Alyssa's breasts with her mouth open. Alyssa's body responded with a churning in her belly before she could think through the situation. *She is beautiful. Besides, do I want to reject her after the day she has had?* Alyssa pulled the cups from her breasts and shrugged the straps off her shoulders, letting the bra fall to the floor behind her. *No. I don't.*

"You are beautiful." Beth slowly raised her eyes to Alyssa's, then returned them to her hardening nipples. She licked her lips with the tip of her tongue. She placed her hands on Alyssa's waist before leaning in for a barely there kiss on her lips. Alyssa opened her mouth as Beth pressed the kiss harder and flicked her tongue on Alyssa's lips. They began urgently kissing, tongues wrestling as each slid her hands across the other's body.

Alyssa moved from squeezing Beth's firm ass to unbuttoning her blouse and pushing it and Beth's jacket off with both hands. She quickly dispensed with Beth's bra. Their breasts mashed together as both women embraced. Beth's warmth chased the goosebumps from Alyssa's skin and built in her chest. Alyssa unzipped Beth's skirt. Beth wiggled her hips as Alyssa pushed it down and dropped it to the floor.

Beth opened Alyssa's jeans and slid her hand down to cup her mound, the small fingers barely covering both lips when she squeezed it. Alyssa missed the pressure when Beth hooked the jeans and panties with her thumbs and pulled them downward. Alyssa squirmed until the jeans were at her knees, then lay on the bed to allow Beth to finish removing them. Her chills returned, ignited by the cool sheets, running up her sides to her belly before reaching her nipples, the tingle hardening them.

Beth climbed up Alyssa's body, dragging her hard nipples along her legs, hips, and belly. Sparks snaked from the firm points, tracing pins and needles over her skin until they met in her pussy lips. They throbbed and crackled as each new spark arrived. When their breasts touched again, Beth attacked Alyssa's mouth with sloppy kisses. The two women cupped breasts and pinched nipples, squeezed buttocks, and raked sides and bellies with firm fingers. Every point where Beth's skin touched Alyssa's, more warm sparks tingled outward, all finding their way to increase the heat building inside Alyssa's vagina.

Alyssa reached inside Beth's panties and inserted a finger in her wet pussy, then added another. Beth humped her hips against Alyssa, and Alyssa pressed hard inside her, enjoying Beth's enthusiastic response.

Beth stood to remove her panties. When she returned to kiss Alyssa, she spun her hips around and raised a knee over Alyssa's head, lowering herself into a sixty-nine. Momentarily stunned,

Alyssa stared at the young, clean-shaven cunt. The outer lips were swollen, the inner ones visibly wet and agape from Alyssa's fingering. *That is a beautiful pussy.* Beth nibbled Alyssa's clit with her lips, shocking Alyssa out of her trance. She grabbed Beth's ass with both hands and pulled that beautiful pussy to her mouth.

Alyssa couldn't tease Beth as she had Kate earlier, but she didn't want to. Beth had shifted from timid and beaten to aggressive and powerful by their second kiss. This woman wanted to come and to make Alyssa come. Alyssa drove her tongue inside, fucking Beth with it before licking downward where she flicked the clit, then nipped it with her teeth.

Beth pulled off Alyssa's pussy and wailed before diving back in. When her clit stretched as Beth sucked it, a lightning storm of sensation drilled into her, making the earlier shocks accumulated in her pussy react and squirm like a knot of hot snakes sliding over and around each other. Her ass clenched. Her breath caught in her throat. She flexed her hips, seeking even more pleasure from the mouth on her clit. The two women raced to make each other climax. Beth shoved two fingers in Alyssa's pussy and rubbed her G-spot. She lashed Alyssa's clit with her tongue.

Alyssa inserted three fingers, fucking Beth with them, feeling the compression when Beth's pussy squeezed while Alyssa bit and sucked on her clit. When Beth's thighs tightened, she curled all three of her fingers to tap on Beth's G-spot. *It's ridged, like mine. I wonder if it feels as good when I do this.* Alyssa pressed hard. Beth's head jerked back. Her body tensed. Splashes of fluid squirted from her pussy over Alyssa's face and into her hair as her thighs clamped against Alyssa's ears. For an instant, Alyssa started to smile at the pleasure she gave, but then Beth's fingers flexed, and that pushed Alyssa into her own orgasm. Her back arched, and she yelled into Beth's pussy.

After catching her breath, Beth spun to lie beside Alyssa. She laid her face beside Alyssa's and pulled the covers over them. She held Alyssa's breast while Alyssa held Beth's buttock. They kissed before closing their eyes to sleep.

✍

Light leaking between the curtains woke Alyssa. She listened to Beth breathe, still nestled against her side. The clock showed 8:26. *I should say goodbye to Paul and Kate.* She got out of bed and donned her dirty clothes. *These won't get washed, they'll get burned.* She took a spare key from the small folder on the desk, then went to 12035.

Kate beamed when she opened the door. "Alyssa! Come in! We hoped you would come by." The door closed, and Kate kissed her deeply. "You taste like morning breath and pussy but not my pussy. You are wearing last night's clothes. I thought you were tired." She winked.

"Beth needed a shoulder to cry on, and then she wanted to clean my shirt. The rest just kind of happened after that. She was a wreck, and I didn't want to reject her."

"That was good of you." Kate smiled. "And good for you, too, I bet."

"Let's say I'm glad I didn't reject her."

Paul called through the open bathroom door, "How do you feel about last night? Are you okay?"

"I haven't thought about it much, but I think I'm okay. The lady was scary, but you kept her from hurting anyone, and the cops will keep her locked up. Did you notice the tension in the dining room beforehand?

"Yes. No water, limited food... Tensions are high. I won't be here to tackle the next nutcase. Are you sure you want to stay?"

Alyssa smiled. "I'm sure. I'll make it home Friday." She

sighed. "Frankly, that is what I dread." The comment hung there for a moment. "But that isn't why I came. I came to wish you a fond farewell. Are you ready to go?"

Kate giggled. "Paul always gets up in 'go mode' when he travels. We weren't leaving before ten though. We were hoping to see you before we left." She licked her lips. "So how fond a farewell did you want to wish us?"

"I dreamed about eating you while Paul fucks me. Would that be a good 'one for the road'?"

"You naughty girl," gasped Kate. "That would delay our departure a bit. What do you think, hon?"

"I think we can spare the time if Alyssa really needs to say goodbye this way."

They hugged each other and kissed. They undressed in a circle: Alyssa undressed Kate, who undressed Paul, who undressed Alyssa.

A bit of fondling and sucking later, Alyssa lay on her back at the end of the bed. "Sit on my face, you beautiful redhead."

Kate swung her leg to straddle Alyssa's face. Alyssa licked from the bottom of her slit almost to her clit, and back again. She grabbed Kate's ass cheeks, driving her tongue deep between Kate's lips, teasing but neglecting her clit.

"Oh, that's good, but lick my clit!"

Alyssa spread her legs wider when strong hands touched inside them. The firm tongue licked her outer lips and then the inner ones. The stretch when Paul sucked first one, then the other into his mouth felt cool and warm as the air and his tongue touched inside her for the first time. Alyssa squealed and humped her hips upward against the rapid shocks of his tongue flicking across her clit. His two thick fingers rotated inside her, slowly stretching her while the shocks in her clit continued. Alyssa's pussy wanted to be filled when his fingers moved, spreading her ass cheeks as his tongue tickled her anus. Alyssa tightened from neck to toes and moaned. Paul licked it a bit more before continuing up to her clit, flicking it, then repeating the process.

Oh fuck. Nobody's ever licked my ass before. It's so dirty and so good. I never knew. Alyssa stretched her legs wider and tilted her hips up so Paul could have better access. He licked and rubbed it with his thumb before inserting three fingers into her cunt and spreading them. Alyssa stopped eating Kate to get used to the stretching. She resumed when she was ready for Paul's cock.

Paul slapped her clit with his cock before lining it up at her opening. She savored the rubbing of his head on her lips before he pushed into her. She was ready for him, but that meant he could get only halfway in. When Alyssa groaned, Kate pressed down on her mouth.

Paul withdrew until the tip of his cock just parted Alyssa's lips, then inched forward. Alyssa writhed, but Kate's hips kept her from pushing toward Paul. Instead, Alyssa shuddered when Kate pinched, then pulled her nipple. Alyssa moaned with pleasure, and Kate's hips circled on Alyssa's face.

Paul tapped the end of Alyssa's channel, then stilled. Her rolling hips stretched her around his huge member, but her pussy clasped at him, tightening around him even as she tried to loosen herself. He thrust into her at a steady pace, and Alyssa relaxed. His increased pace and short strokes kept her feeling full even as the impact of his thrusts bounced her body. The cock inside her swelled further, stretching her vagina, prying it apart, little pinches and rings of pressure accumulating in a swirl of pain and pleasure.

He pulled out and said, "Kate, lie down in front of her face. Alyssa, roll over and keep eating her. I want to fuck you from behind until I come."

The women moved, and Alyssa dove into Kate's smooth

snatch. She mimicked what Paul had done to her, sucking the inner lips, nibbling the clit, using her fingers to stretch Kate open. She lowered her head to lick Kate's anus before returning to her clit. *Not disgusting like I imagined.* Then her attention whipped to Paul shoving fully into her. Stretched to her limits, Alyssa wailed into Kate's pussy. Her back arched as she came.

Paul didn't let her rest. He fucked her faster and harder, her body relaying Paul's assault on her pussy to Kate's. The two women grunted in time with his thrusts. Kate held Alyssa's head, forcing Alyssa's mouth to her clit while she groaned and shuddered. Paul rubbed his wet thumb around Alyssa's anus before inserting past the first knuckle.

Alyssa's entire body tensed. Her ass clenched Paul's thumb as her pussy did his cock. Her hands spread Kate's thighs apart and back as her teeth bit Kate's clit. Kate's legs fought Alyssa's hands as Paul erupted into Alyssa. His giant orgasm filled Alyssa so full that cum leaked around his cock and dripped down Alyssa's lips. He lay beside the two women, who had collapsed where they were.

The three stirred a few minutes later. "That's what I call one for the road," said Kate. "I'm glad Paul is driving. I may just stare out the window, googly-eyed, for a while."

They laughed. "Me too." Alyssa paused. "Guys, thank you. Not just for the great sex, but for being my friends and letting me experience your lifestyle. You have given me much to think about, and I won't forget you."

"Please stay in touch," Paul responded. "You have our numbers. Maybe we can see each other again—with or without the sex."

"Absolutely," Kate echoed. "After you talk with Robert, we are here to listen. There aren't too many people who will understand what you have been through...here and in your marriage."

"Thank you both for that. I probably will need to talk. But

you need to go or you will never reach San Antonio." She slid on her jeans.

Paul picked up her panties from beside the bed. "You forgot these."

Alyssa looked at him with the hint of a smile. "You took those panties off me. Please keep them as a souvenir."

Paul held the panties to his nose and sniffed loudly. "Mmmm. Alyssaaaaa."

"You pervert," cackled Kate. "You act like they are some kind of trophy you will jack off to."

"Okay. You keep them," he smirked, tossing them at his wife.

Kate caught them with one hand and sniffed them loudly. "Mmmm. Alyssaaaaa. I'll jill off with these every night."

When they were dressed, they hugged and kissed goodbye.

Alyssa returned to Beth's room. The light was still dim, so she stripped and slipped into bed next to Beth.

"Mmm. Hi. Where did you go?"

"I said goodbye to Paul and Kate."

"Said goodbye? Or a little more? I saw Kate rub your thigh last night before everything went to hell."

"Well, a little more. We had an adventurous time together. I wanted to see them off properly."

"And you wanted to come back to me after?" She looked at Alyssa with hurt eyes.

"Of course I wanted to come back to you. I like you very much. No, I care for you, and I want to be here for you. I was the reason things went bad last night. And...our sex last night was amazing."

"You care for me?" Beth touched Alyssa's rings. "You're married."

Alyssa's stomach clenched like the floor had fallen away. She took a deep breath while it recovered. "I am married, but you knew that. You have called me Mrs. Davis since checking me in. I love my husband and can't wait to see him when I finally get home, but I am…learning about myself in these unusual circumstances. But when they end, so does my"—she cocked her head—"education."

"And part of that is caring about me?"

"I actually care. I like you. You are a special girl." She lifted the covers and gazed at all of Beth. "You are beautiful, from head to toe. Your kindness makes everyone around you feel better. I can tell you are a great mom. All that and more makes me care for you."

Beth kissed Alyssa and held her tight. She released her grip and kissed her way to Alyssa's breasts. She licked around them in ever-shrinking figure eights, working her way in before sucking the nipples. When Alyssa's nipples were fully erect, Beth kissed down Alyssa's belly to her mound. She licked and kissed over it, moving from thigh to thigh before lining up at her slit and licking from bottom to top. She repeated the motion before pushing in to lick between the inner lips and sucking her juices. She took a breath and looked up. "God, I love eating cum out of a pussy." She dove back in, licking and sucking.

Alyssa was in heaven. Her pussy, ravaged by Paul's huge cock, was dripping its own juice again under Beth's therapeutic kisses. Alyssa raced to her third orgasm of the morning. When Beth inserted a finger to scoop out more cum, Alyssa exploded. She cried out. The veins and tendons in her neck strained against her skin. Her pussy gushed juice into Beth's mouth, flushing more of Paul's cum with it. Beth lapped it up as fast as she could, but most flowed down her chin to the sheets.

When Alyssa breathed again, she pulled Beth up and rolled on top of her. She began a tortuous descent down the young mother's body. She nibbled her ears and neck before licking her chest down to the tops of her large breasts. They sagged to the side, so Alyssa lingered, kissing the valley between them before moving to first one orb, then the other. She left her mouth short of the nipples, preferring to watch them harden and distend without her stimulation. A few kisses later, and proud of her patience, she sucked a long nipple into her mouth while rolling the other with her fingers. When Beth's hips began writhing, she kissed her way down the young woman's belly, paying special attention to the faint, tell-tale stretch marks from pregnancy. She reached Beth's shaved pussy but instead dropped her head to Beth's splayed knees and kissed the insides of them alternately. She kissed and nipped up the inside of her sensitive thigh, again stopping short of Beth's visibly wet pussy, then repeating the trip up from the other knee. On her third trip up, Alyssa blew hot breath on Beth's clit. Beth shoved her pussy up into Alyssa's mouth, and Alyssa attacked it with her tongue. She licked it inside and out, from the perineum to the clit, with no pattern, just energy. Beth wailed, flexed, and came.

Alyssa slowed just enough to let the younger woman catch her breath but not enough to come off the orgasm. She put two fingers inside and licked her sensitive clit as rapidly as she could. Beth flexed, and though Alyssa couldn't tell if Beth had a second orgasm or just continued the first, pussy juice flowed over her fingers and down her wrist. Alyssa sucked a big drop of it from the pad of her thumb, then spread her fingers wide inside Beth and circled her clit with her lips. Light suction caused Beth to arch her back and cry out. Alyssa removed her fingers from Beth's spasming cunt and dragged her tits up the younger woman's body until they rubbed nipple to nipple. She rested her weight on her elbows and held Beth's head in both hands. Beth opened her eyes, and they kissed.

"Oh. That was so good. I haven't had a woman as good as you in a long time. Do you have women lovers?"

"No. I've never been unfaithful to my husband. Well, until Monday night. I had never been with a woman until then either. I feel bad about it, but I also feel good. I am realizing some things about marriage and life that I hadn't before." Her eyes wandered to the wall and back. "What about you? You said you love to eat cum out of a pussy. You seem quite experienced for so young a woman."

"I didn't end up with a kid at twenty without some experience. I was a wild teenager. Discovered boys, discovered drugs, discovered how to get drugs from boys, discovered that boys like girls who like girls. Then I discovered that I like both boys and girls. I was quite the partier."

"All to get drugs?"

"Not all. I liked the attention. I got arrested a couple of times but didn't learn. When I got pregnant at nineteen, Mom moved us from LA to Houston. She didn't want me to have an addicted, deformed baby. It was hard. She didn't work for a few months. I kicked the drugs because she stayed with me every minute and didn't let me out to find any. She slept in my bed with me, searched my room, and took me with her when she left to get groceries and supplies. I hated her for it. When I felt Carly moving inside me, I understood what she had done for me. When Carly came out perfect and happy, I understood why. We have been close ever since. Carly and I are in our own place, but I still see Mom almost every day. She gave up her entire life for me and Carly."

"That is what moms do." Alyssa squeezed Beth's hand.

"I steer clear of trouble now. I work, go home, see Mom,

and take care of Carly. It isn't exciting, but I'm making a good life for us. Jeez, that's probably a lot more than you wanted to know." Beth took a deep breath. "I don't have much time for sex, to answer your question. I'm glad you came back this morning." She gave Alyssa a peck.

"That is some story. You come across so kind. Your toughness gets covered up. I'm glad I came back also." She hugged Beth and kissed her forehead. "We should get dressed. You probably need to get to work, and I need to check in with my family."

"You are right, though I hate to get out of bed." Beth held tight to Alyssa, then the two got up. Beth walked across the room and picked up the baby wipes. Without turning around, she asked, "Alyssa?"

"What is it, Beth?"

"You know you won't get a shower."

"I know. It's deodorant and cleanish clothes for now."

"Um, you could…"

"Just say it, sweetie."

Beth turned to face the older woman. "Can I wash you?" She looked again into Alyssa's eyes and held a soft gaze. Neither looked away, and Beth stepped forward, pulling a wipe from the pack. She touched the wipe to Alyssa's forehead and slowly rubbed it across and down both cheeks. She lightly wiped her eyelids, down her nose, and across her mouth and chin. She repeated the process. "Let's get that girl cum off you."

Alyssa stood still and let Beth work down her neck and chest before slowing to clean Alyssa's breasts, particularly the underside where she had been sweaty. Her nipples stiffened and her areolae wrinkled under Beth's gentle hand. Alyssa sighed when Beth moved along her sides, under and along her arms, and then to her belly. The cool of the moisture intensified as it evaporated. Alyssa shivered.

"You don't have any stretch marks. You are so beautiful." Beth got a fresh wipe, knelt, and placed a kiss on Alyssa's clit before wiping down her body and cleaning her pussy. Alyssa moaned. Beth rubbed harder to remove the dried cum from inside Alyssa's thighs, then moved to her knees and shins, finishing with her feet.

Alyssa put one hand on Beth's shoulder while Beth raised and cleaned her feet, even between her toes, then kissed each foot before placing it back on the ground. When she had wiped Alyssa down from head to toe, she grabbed Alyssa's hips and spun her around to clean up from the bottom, again taking her time between Alyssa's ass cheeks, causing Alyssa to bend forward. When Beth leaned in to lick her anus, Alyssa growled.

"Has nobody ever done that to you?"

"Not before this morning. Paul licked and put a finger inside."

"Did you like it?"

"It's so shockingly dirty that it sends a wonderful surge through my belly. It turns me on."

Beth leaned in for another lick.

"Ooh… Stop it. You are supposed to be getting me clean, not wet."

Beth wiped Alyssa's back and shoulders, then palmed both butt cheeks.

"Mmm, yes." Beth slid her hands around Alyssa's waist, then cupped her breasts while hugging her from behind. Alyssa's head rolled back when Beth rolled her nipples. Beth kissed her shoulder blade.

"Okay. Let me do you."

"Yes, please." Beth handed Alyssa the wipes.

Alyssa copied how Beth had wiped her face, paying attention to her pussy juice around Beth's mouth. When she finished, she kissed Beth's clean lips. She wiped down Beth's neck, lingering at the soft spots behind the jaw and between the collarbones. She used a wipe in each hand, slowly working her way down the chest before circling Beth's breasts, hefting them slightly, finally pinching and rolling to clean her turgid nipples. She finished each breast with a kiss below the areola.

"Oh god. Don't do that again or we will never leave. How did you know that feels so good?"

"Robert taught me that. He hits all the right spots when we have time for foreplay. Too bad we usually need to hurry."

Alyssa wiped Beth's abdomen, probing her navel and rubbing the sensitive joint between abs and obliques more than was needed to get clean. She traced up her sides and under her arms before caressing down her arms, then back up to Beth's shoulders, only to return to her waist and repeat the tortuous movement.

Beth squirmed. "Oh, stop. No, don't stop. No, do stop. I need to get downstairs. It's cold and it feels so good at the same time. Look at my goose bumps. Please stop." She kissed Alyssa's mouth and let her tongue slip inside.

"Okay," giggled Alyssa. She knelt to work Beth's legs from toes upward, reaching around to caress the backs of her knees before wiping her thighs. She saw Beth's pussy leak a drop down her thigh and licked it off before continuing to wipe the strong legs. When she reached Beth's soaking slit, she rubbed only a couple of times before Beth grabbed her head with both hands and flexed her legs, her entire core rigid. Alyssa's thumb flicked Beth's nub, and Beth came. Beth finished spasming, and Alyssa whispered a kiss on her clit. Beth's hands grasped Alyssa's hair, keeping her in place before releasing her. Alyssa wiped the fresh juice off the insides of Beth's thighs, then stood.

Alyssa used Beth's hips to turn her around and began a less provocative cleaning of Beth's well-defined and muscular back. *I remember what carrying a baby did for my back. One of the benefits of motherhood.* She knelt and wiped up Beth's legs before reaching her taut cheeks. Using both hands, she caressed them more than necessary for cleaning, then she spread them to clean Beth's crack, rubbing the puckered opening. *Twice in one morning. Should I?* She rubbed it again, ensuring it was clean. She licked Beth's anus. *Musky like Kate's, but with alcohol.* She licked several more times before pulling back.

"Ooh. I want some more of that later. I love your tongue." Beth met Alyssa's mouth for a French kiss. "I need to get ready." She went into the bathroom, taking a bottle of water with her. Alyssa gathered her clothes while listening to Beth brush her hair and teeth.

Alyssa slid her dirty jeans and shirt on, dropping the wine-stained bra in the trash. She watched as Beth put on fresh underwear from her bag, a fresh blouse and skirt, then yesterday's blazer. Beth slid into her heels and held her hand out to Alyssa, who took it and stood.

"See you at Starbucks? They may not have much by now. It's nearly eleven."

"Yes. I'll get fresh clothes and check in with Robert, then I'll be down. I'll have a slow day."

"Okay. Keep the room key if you want to come back tonight. I would love the company. That is, if you want to. I mean, no pressure, but I loved sleeping next to you. Oh, I know you are married and probably don't want to get involved. Ugh. I sound like you're my girlfriend. Please, just forget I said anything."

Alyssa let the flustered girl ramble before putting two fingers to Beth's lips. "Shh. You are fine. I'll keep the key. I liked sleeping next to you last night also. I need to think, but I expect I'll be back." She planted a kiss beside Beth's smiling mouth. "Now let's get you to work."

5

WEDNESDAY AFTERNOON

Back in her room, Alyssa stripped off the dirty clothes. She threw the shirt in the trash and stuffed the jeans into the dirty-clothes bag. *Ugh. I've worn these for three days. They smell like it too. Good thing the heat works.* She flopped into the chair, not caring she was naked beside the open window. Spinning her wedding rings, Alyssa mentally wandered across the previous three days: being stuck in the hotel, having her flights canceled, limited food and water, the crazy woman in the dining room. *Somebody doesn't like me. So much for warm, sunny Houston. So much for a drive down and a quick flight back.* She scanned the room. Clothes hung everywhere so she could rewear them. Bottles on the desk represented her only drinkable water. The bed was unmade; no lights were on. The daylight filtered through clouds, creating a dusky mood. She reached to turn on the lamp behind the chair. *By the toilet are two trash cans so I can flush. Oh, to be home.*

Her mind transitioned to the memory of that first sleepless night in the hotel. She replayed the sounds that had awakened her. Unconsciously, she traced a finger under her breast. *I'm hornier than I've been since college, and those two kicked it off. Do I thank them or curse them?* She replayed her sexual adventures since then: masturbating Sunday night and Monday to the sounds of the neighbors, Monday night and Tuesday with Paul and Kate, last night and today with Beth, and again with Paul and Kate. She moved the hand not tracing her breast to her pussy, cupping and then rubbing it in a gentle massage. She had taken a pounding and wanted to rub out the soreness. *And if I come from it, so much the better.*

Without stopping her ministrations, Alyssa shifted from pleasurable memories to the bigger questions her behavior had created. *Do I know what I am doing? With Paul and Kate gone, I won't sleep with another man, but what am I doing with Beth? I've never been attracted to women, but I'm attracted to her, just like I was to Kate. Am I becoming a lesbian? Clearly no. I really loved fucking Paul. So not a lesbian. Maybe bisexual though. They showed me how different and wonderful women can be.* Her belly fluttered inside. *I am desperate to get home and, how did they say it, have Robert reclaim me.*

Behind her eyes, Alyssa envisioned walking through the airport. As she stepped through the secure exit, Robert, still in a suit from work, guided her to the glass elevator to the parking deck. When they had risen but not yet cleared the lobby ceiling, he hit the stop button. "What are you doing?" she asked.

Robert kissed her as he raised the silver satin of her dress to her waist. With two strong hands, he yanked the wispy lace panties apart, dropping the tatters to the floor. He lowered his pants, revealing an erection larger than Alyssa remembered. "You can't go home until you belong to me and everyone knows it."

The cold glass chilled her back as he lifted her against it, sliding inside her while she wrapped her legs around him. Her ass chilled with his first thrust, but the cool was defeated by the hot cock that filled her completely, warmed her, touched the end of her vagina. That warmth flowed through her to heat the very glass of the elevator.

The elevator echoed with her gasps, one every time he filled her. She levered her back against the glass, thrusting her pelvis forward to take more of him, letting her weight and leverage stretch herself over the tip of his cock. She felt him swell and drive into her even harder than he had been. They locked eyes.

"I belong to you," she said as his cum splashed inside her.

When Robert lowered her feet to the floor, Alyssa looked down. The lobby was full of people watching her, not saying a word.

Back in Houston, every inch of Alyssa's skin burned to be touched. She obliged it with feathery touches all over her body, chasing the tingles to where they converged between her legs.

I want and love Robert. I can't wait to be home with him. Is that enough now? Do I want others going forward? Maybe. Can our marriage survive that? It has to survive what I have done before we think about the future. Will Robert even forgive me for this week? Maybe if we talk after I fuck him silly. That's what I want, and soon. His cock curves just right to hit my G-spot on every stroke when we do it missionary. Alyssa's massage evolved to firm fingering, again without her direction. Her juices dripped down to the chair.

I'll have to repay him for this week. He's not vindictive, but he is brutally fair. Alyssa loved that despite abandoning religion, Robert held firm views on right and wrong. His resoluteness gave him strength to be good at whatever he did. It made him a good husband and a great father. *He has no idea how standing up for what he believes affects me. I fall in love all over again. He hasn't noticed that he always gets laid after he does that, even when he stands up to me. He'll definitely stand up to me when I tell him I cheated. If we have make-up sex after, it will be spectacular.*

Alyssa worked her crotch with both hands now, shoving two fingers in and out of her pussy with one and tapping her clit in time with each thrust with the other. She had hooked her legs over the arms of the chair, and pinched her clit to hasten the orgasm growing under her hands. Her legs tightened, but the arms of the chair kept them apart, allowing her to drive her pleasure higher. Her body curled forward as her belly and chest inflamed. The veins in her neck strained against the skin, and her mouth opened in a silent scream. When she could, she sucked in a breath and collapsed into the chair, spent.

Lieutenant John Frazier of the Houston Police Department stood in his hotel room, staring across the white, dark city. Babysitting the homeless on the far side of the street and the politicians on this side was not fitting work for a detective. He needed to be on the street where there was always action for a man willing to use his badge. His orders said stay here, protect the city officials. He felt like a caged lion, looking from a distance at the jungle he ruled. In here, he followed orders. In here, he waited for the snow to melt.

A light coming on two floors down in the perpendicular wing drew his eye. A woman sat in the chair by the window. He retrieved the binoculars from his off-site gear bag. Several feet back, in the shadows of the dark room, the 12X magnification brought the naked woman right to his window. He gazed over her slowly, then recognized her face. "That's the woman from last night's dustup," he mumbled to no one. "She's fucking hot." He put down the binoculars to free his short, thick cock. He stroked it as he watched Alyssa.

Though he had tried to stop thinking out loud, the bad habit returned in times of stress. "She's rubbing her tits. I'd rub them for her." He yanked his cock faster. "Oh fuck, yeah. Rub that pussy, honey. Make me come." His cock swelled, and he shot his load on the floor. "It's not the first cum that's been on this floor."

Frazier took some photos with his phone through the binoculars while Alyssa's masturbation intensified. "Not great, but viewable." His cock hardened again, and he dropped the phone again in favor of some self-satisfaction. "Holy shit. She's slamming it with both hands. Oh fuck." His balls tightened again. "Oh yeah, baby. Come for me." Just as Alyssa came all over her chair, Lieutenant Frazier shot a second load onto the carpet. "I got to get me some of that." A plan flickered behind his eyes, and he logged into his police laptop.

≪

When she got chilly, Alyssa crawled into the bed and dialed Robert. "Hey, Babe. I miss you."

"Hey, Baby. I miss you too. How are you holding up?"

"I'm ready to be home. I'm bored and dirty. Most of all, I miss you, Babe. I'll need a hug when I get back." Alyssa paused, then lowered her voice. "You know, I'm lying here in nothing but a sheet. What are you wearing?"

"Ooh. Um, that's a little unexpected. I like the idea, but I have a conference call at one thirty. Can I envision you naked later?"

"I knew it was a long shot that you could be naughty this time of day. I want more priority when I get home though." *Can I be more important than a fucking conference call one time? I need some attention from you, damn it. Being here is lonely when I'm so damn horny.*

"We can arrange that. Can you make it until Friday?"

"I will, but this isn't fun. I had great conversations Monday,

87

but now everybody is tense. A lady even attacked a hotel worker last night at dinner. That's why I didn't call. I was with the police until late."

"The police? You need to be careful. You said they are staying in the hotel?"

"Yes, they were there, but it was unsettling. The lady was one scary customer."

"Just stay away from anybody volatile. If you have a bad feeling, trust it and get away."

"I will. That may keep me in my room until Friday though."

Robert chuckled. "If you must. I have to get on that call. Be careful. Love you, Baby."

"Love you too."

Alyssa hung up, and her stomach rumbled. *Please, Starbucks, feed me.* She dressed and went to the lobby. She got a coffee and sat on a sofa near the bottom of the escalator.

"Nothing to eat today?" Mike, the general manager, said to her as he walked across the lobby.

"Starbucks sold out before I got here, so it's coffee for lunch. The barista said that the power and water outages have shut down the supply houses, and apparently that is true for all of Texas. This is some cold snap. It even snowed in Mexico. So… Starbucks is out of food."

"Let's see about that. It seems we should find you something after that unpleasant experience last night." He walked behind the Starbucks counter and returned with a pack of cookies. "They keep a few of these back there for emergencies. It isn't a hot lunch, but it's more than coffee."

"Thank you, Mike. You are so kind."

"No. I'm providing a special guest some special treatment. It's one of the perks of my job."

"Oh, I'm not a special guest. I'm just an old lady trying to get home."

"Au contraire. You are a special guest. In your five days here, you have tipped the staff well, been kind and reasonable, and been understanding with our inconveniences, and Beth speaks higher of you than any guest we've ever had. Plus, please forgive me for being forward, you are quite striking, and your smile absolutely lights up the room. All those things in one person? You are indeed special. Don't let anyone tell you otherwise. The rest of the staff have noticed as well."

Alyssa blushed. "I've just been reasonable, polite, and kind. You speak as if you never see that."

Mike shook his head. "We don't see it as often as we would like. That is why everyone notices someone special like you."

"If that is special, then I'm glad I'm special. I must say, you and your staff have been outstanding during this. Keeping everyone fed and calm, coming up with a way to flush the toilets, it really means a lot. The smell after a day of no flushing would drive me to sleep outside in the cold." She made eye contact with Mike, and her stomach fluttered. "So if you folks keep giving me reasons to smile, I'll keep smiling."

Mike maintained the eye contact. His smile shifted from pleasant to hungry. "We will do everything we can to keep you smiling, then. If you run out of reasons to smile, please let me know, and I'll get right on it."

Alyssa looked him up and down. He was tall and thinner than she typically liked, but his angular face was handsome, and his hands had long fingers. Alyssa's nipples began to tingle. "I think I'll keep smiling, but I'll remember that." *God, Alyssa. Again? What are you, a huntress?*

"Excellent. Call the front desk and ask for me. I'm staying here, so I'm always available." He held her gaze a moment longer before returning to the back. She watched him go. *Thin, but a nice ass. He made me horny. Or was he around when I got horny? Either way, now I'm horny. Shit. I've been horny since Sunday. Do I really want to fuck yet another person?* She slid a hand to her crotch. *If this itch continues, I might.*

Alyssa ate the cookies and drank coffee. She watched the staff, mainly Mike and Beth. They were indeed good at what they did, and the rest of the staff followed their lead. She noticed the subtle physical contact between them. *Is something there? I'll ask Beth. I wouldn't want to intrude. Shit! Maybe I should think about my family instead of my needy vagina.*

Alyssa called her daughter. Susan jabbered. Classes were canceled, but the school's generator and wells meant they had power and water, and some of her friends had arrived, unleashing a weeklong funfest. Alyssa didn't want to pull her away, so she discarded the idea of Susan coming to visit. They talked a while before Alyssa let Susan return to the fun. Clay couldn't talk; school didn't let out until after three, then he had rowing. She knew not to call Robert because of his meetings. *So much for family calming my hormones. My nipples haven't settled down, they've hardened, and now I feel moist.* She played on her phone until it was time for dinner.

⁓

Alyssa sat at the bar for dinner. She took her time and had some drinks. A couple of obese middle-aged men sat beside her a while and smiled. *Whoa, they never had braces, maybe not even a toothbrush.* They chatted about the situation in the hotel and traveling out when the airport opened. Neither one looked higher than her tits the entire time. The conversation offset the repulsive vibes Alyssa felt in the pit of her stomach. The one closest to her put his hand on her knee as they finished their drinks. "You must be lonely, here by yourself. Want to continue this elsewhere?"

"Way to ruin a pleasant conversation. Beat it." *I'm horny but not that desperate.* She turned to face the other direction. Beth winked at her from down the bar. Alyssa held up her drink, and Beth arrived with a refill. She heard the men leave the bar.

"Do I look that easy?" Alyssa asked her friend.

Beth laughed. "You were just separated from the herd. They have ogled and propositioned any lone woman since Monday. They haven't gotten lucky, but they haven't learned either." She noted the empty seats around Alyssa and leaned in. "You caught Mike's eye. He asked me about you. He said you had an interesting conversation. Are you looking for another diversion?"

"No. No, I'm not. Well, maybe. I don't know. Watching you two work together kept me horny all afternoon. Are you and he an item?"

"More like coworkers with benefits. We relieve tension together sometimes. It's convenient when you work in a hotel. He's married, but they have an arrangement, I guess like your other friends."

"Oh my. I didn't mean to keep you apart. You said you didn't have much time for relationships."

"We don't have a relationship. We fuck from time to time. It keeps my edge off, and he dallies after his wife plays with someone else. Doing it at work makes it hot."

"When you asked, were you thinking of inviting him to join us?"

"Um, no. I wouldn't do a threesome with Mike."

"I thought you liked threesomes?"

"I wouldn't with Mike." She looked around again for

eavesdroppers. "You see, Mike has a special skill. God, I can't believe I'm saying this. See, his dick is long, but it's skinny. Really skinny, like less than an inch across. He has learned to use it. It's the perfect cock for anal, and he loves pleasing women that way. That's too much risk of cross contamination to do a threesome with him."

"That is a lot to share. Thanks for letting me know."

"I didn't mean to shock you. You liked it when I licked you there, and I thought you might want him for that. Sorry if I upset you."

Alyssa's nipples hardened and her vagina tightened as she remembered how electric the rimming had felt. "You did shock me. This was not the conversation I expected." She looked around before leaning closer, grinning. "And I did like it when you licked me there."

Beth smiled. "The feeling is mutual." A bell rang in the back. "I have to go. Enjoy another drink." She smiled. "When you're hungry, let me know which option you want tonight, burger or burger, and I'll make sure you get it." Beth winked and left.

Did that conversation just happen? I must seem like some horny, desperate housewife. Well, I am a horny housewife. Not desperate yet? I've had sex with three people in three days. After twenty-three years with one man, I fucked a man and two women. Why am I even considering Mike? Because he's not bad looking and specializes in anal. I could try it, just this once. I gave myself a guilt pass this week, but Robert won't understand a week of debauchery. If I like anal, maybe Robert will too?

She lingered over a sip of her drink. *No, Alyssa. You're rationalizing what you want. You have been thinking about it since he brought you cookies. Anal makes it dirtier, and the dirtiness makes you wetter. You've decided to let Mike fuck your ass, and now you are determining how to tell Robert.*

She threw back the rest of her drink. *I'll experiment with*

Mike. If I like it, I'll tell Robert I want his big cock back there. If I don't, it will be just one more thing to apologize for. Jesus. I have to get home soon, or I'll fuck this entire hotel.

Alyssa motioned for another drink, and Beth delivered it. "Are you ready to eat?"

"Yes. Go ahead and bring the food when my turn comes." She ensured that the seats beside her were empty and leaned forward to talk. "I'll have the Mike special tonight, if it's still available."

Beth's face dropped. "I'll bring your food and let him know."

"Wait, Beth. Is something wrong?"

"I hoped to see you tonight. I liked waking up next to you this morning. I'd like to do that again, but you will be with Mike."

"Oh, I see. I planned to experiment with Mike, not an all-night thing. I want to wake up next to you too. Doesn't he go back to his family when we are done?"

Beth smiled. "Really? You want to be with me? That sounds good." Her grin turned wicked. "You know I said I wouldn't do a threesome with Mike? That's true, but I will offer this. If you will have him cum on you rather than in you, I'll lick it off, if you want me to." She looked around for eavesdroppers. "I won't go all the way to eating it out of your ass. I'll lick and tease, but nothing that comes out of there goes in my mouth."

"Okay, so that's a lot to process, and so incredibly hot. I may not sleep tonight."

"Don't feel like you have to, but you turn me on so much that I'll do that. Let me go place your order."

Over the next two hours, Alyssa drank some more wine, ate, and daydreamed of losing her anal virginity. She stayed wet, and nervous. She couldn't talk to Beth about what to expect after the bar filled with other diners. As the dining room emptied, Alyssa signaled for the check. *I just need some liquid courage, not enough to pass out.*

"Done for the night?" asked Beth.

"Done drinking. I still have some things I want to do in my room." She winked at the beautiful bartender.

"I'll let the kitchen know you're done and bring your check."

"Thank you. You give such great service."

Alyssa put another large tip on the check and headed to her room.

✧

Despite the number of drinks she'd had, Alyssa's body crackled with energy. Her nipples hardened, her pussy was wet, and her ass tingled, a first. She stripped and rubbed her breasts just enough to heighten the sensations before putting on the hotel robe. *If I sit down, I'll masturbate, and I want to be this horny when he arrives.* She paced, enjoying the robe sliding across her breasts and ass, especially when the braided edge rubbed her inner thigh.

This is so dirty. Exciting. Wearing only a robe, waiting for a man to have anal sex with me... No, to fuck my ass. She had set it up like ordering off a menu. Who knew people lived like this? She was so naive. *What else will I learn? I like this branching out.* She hoped he would get there soon. *I'm about to come just thinking about this.* What about her marriage? *Fuck. I'll deal with that later. Tonight I'm going to feel good. No. Tonight I'm going to be slutty.*

The anticipated knock on the door broke her stride. Mike stood in the corridor with wet hair and a small tool bag. "Hi, Mike. Thank you for coming to fix this," she said to anyone who may have been in the hall. She locked the door behind him. "I didn't expect you to be finished cooking yet." She sniffed. "And how did you take a shower?"

"Mrs. Davis, I left the restaurant as soon as Beth prepared your check. One of the other chefs made it in, so he can finish cooking. When Beth told me you wanted to meet, I wanted to lose the grease smell, so my wife washed my hair in the sink with a bottle of water. I am a little disappointed."

"Disappointed? Then why are you here?"

"Only disappointed that I didn't get to seduce you longer. Beth made this businesslike, don't you think? A woman as captivating as you should be pursued." He kissed the back of her hand.

"Thank you for the kind words. Beth did make it business-like, but she is your saleswoman. Perhaps she earned a bonus." She smirked. "Of course, if you would rather delay, you can supply secret Starbucks cookies until I depart. I don't think that will meet my needs though." She grasped his hand before he could release hers and pulled him closer.

"Your needs? What might those be?" His empty hand grazed the side of her boob as he reached to rub her back.

"Like I said, Beth is a good salesperson. She understood that I need something new. I want to try anal, and she says you are the best at it. So tell me, can you fulfill my need?" Alyssa snaked her free hand to tug what she felt in his pants.

Mike dropped his hand to squeeze Alyssa's ass cheek through the robe. "I can do that. You can decide if I am the best." He kissed her. She opened her mouth to receive his tongue. Their hands released and moved to the others' bodies, rubbing and fondling. Mike opened the loose robe, and Alyssa shrugged it off her shoulders. Mike stepped back. "You are indeed exquisite. I am going to take my time pleasing you."

Alyssa closed the distance between them, making quick work of his shirt and pants. He had worn loafers, no socks, and no underwear. "Pretty sure of yourself, were you?"

"My wife's idea. She thought you would appreciate the easy access."

"She was right." She stroked his cock. It was exactly as Beth described, except it had a wide head, much wider than matched a cock that narrow. *I bet I can deep-throat that.* "Let me pleasure you first. Can you come more than once?"

"Yes. Quick recovery is one reason I make women so happy. You will see."

"I intend to. There is something I want to try first." She knelt and engulfed the head of his cock. She flicked the underside and sucked so her cheeks pressed on it as she bobbed her head. She used one hand to gather her spit and slather it on his shaft and the other to cup and squeeze his balls. The first time the head touched the back of her throat, she gagged. The second time, she swallowed as it arrived and took most of it down before pulling back. Her throat closed on the narrow shaft, keeping full contact on his length with no discomfort. Mike groaned. She repeated the action several times, each time taking more and pausing a little longer.

"Fuck, how do you do that? That feels incredible. Keep going!"

Three more passes put her nose on his abdomen and his long cock encased in her throat. She moaned from the feeling, and his cock hardened. Mike had kept his hands at his sides, content to let her please him. Now that she was fully engaged, she felt his hands guide her head along his shaft. She let him control the speed, rewarding her hungry pussy by dropping the hand that had been jacking his shaft and inserting two fingers. She maneuvered to thumb her clit while thrusting in time with swallowing the long cock. The pleasure rose through her body and escaped as a moan around his shaft.

"I'm about to come."

Alyssa looked up and smiled around his cock. She intensified her efforts with her throat and her hand. She felt his balls tighten before he shot the first glob straight into her stomach, triggering her orgasm. She pulled back, wanting the rest of his cum in her mouth. She swallowed once more and collected another mouthful. When he finished spurting, she pulled off and drooled the cum from her mouth onto her chest. *God, so dirty.* She rubbed some into her nipple with one hand while finishing her spasming pussy with the other.

"Oh fuck, that was good. Your throat is astounding. And you look so sexy with my cum on your tits. I was right. You are truly special."

Alyssa looked up and leaned back, showing her body. "That was round one. How can I get you ready for round two?"

He wagged his long, soft dick. "Why don't I rub this between your beautiful tits?" He offered his hand to help her stand, then picked her up and laid her on the bed. He put one knee over, bringing his still-dripping cock across her chest.

Alyssa rubbed the head of his cock in the valley between her breasts, spreading the cum with it. When her valley was coated, she brought the head to her mouth and sucked and licked until it began to swell. She let Mike's cock pop out of her mouth, moving her hands to press her breasts around it. She maneuvered them up and down her chest. She felt his cock harden between them, and Mike thrust his hips in time with her motions. He pinched and pulled her nipples as Alyssa kept bobbing her orbs along his cock. She watched the head disappear and reappear from her cleavage. When it showed a drop of precum, she stopped moving. "I really want you in my ass now. What's next?"

Mike pinched her nipples hard one last time and reached for the tool bag on the nightstand. He pulled out a bottle of clear lubricant and a hand towel and knee-walked down Alyssa's body. He kissed her mouth, then her breasts before climbing off and pushing her knees back and apart. This rolled her hips upward and spread both her holes for him. He licked both before raising his head to reply. Alyssa moaned and gasped a ragged breath. Her pussy leaked down the crack of her ass.

"That tastes good. Usually, ladies like me to fuck their pussies doggystyle for a while. It lubricates me and loosens their pelvic muscles. I open your ass with a couple of fingers and lubricant while I do that. Then I lubricate my dick some more, roll you on your back, and enter slowly. After that, I do what you tell me. If you can speak, that is."

Alyssa groaned, "Oh fuck, yes. Fuck me now." She clambered to all fours and presented her rear. She watched over her shoulder, proud that Mike admired the view before shoving his cock halfway in her open pussy. Alyssa shuddered and pushed back, not giving him a chance to withdraw. She stopped when his balls tapped her clit. They thrust together several times, and Alyssa understood. *That's different. My lips are barely spread, but the head is like a ball rolling around in there. I...* "So good. Oh shit."

Mike's two fingers rubbed over her rosebud before stretching her open. Slick with lube, they went all the way in, and the thin tissues between her pussy and her ass squeezed between his cockhead and his fingertips as he fucked her. "Jesus, that's good. Keep doing that." She pushed back harder and faster in search of another orgasm before Mike grabbed her hips with both hands and rolled her on her back.

"Oh no. Keep going. I was about to come."

"You are ready, then. Hold your knees back with your hands and let me please you." He squirted lubricant in his hand and jacked his cock. He used that same hand to wipe her open asshole and spread the remaining lubricant inside. He looked into her wide eyes, lined up his cock, and pressed into her.

The pressure made Alyssa's entire body tense. Heat spread up her neck and face while she held her breath. She pulled back on her knees to thrust her hips upward, pushing to get the entire wide head past the stretched ring of muscle. When it popped in, she groaned. Every part of her pelvis tingled, feeling full and excited. Her ass clenched at Mike's cock as he worked forward an inch at a time. Alyssa's head rolled back when she inhaled again and unclenched her abs, and Mike put two fingers in her pussy and his thumb on her clit while shoving the rest of his cock into her ass. Alyssa came with a wail.

Rather than let her absorb the orgasm, he assaulted her sparking nerves. Removing his thumb from her clit, he rolled his hand and pressed down with the fingertips, squeezing her tissues between his cock and fingers. He sped up and lengthened his thrusts, pulling back until the head pressed against the inside of her ring before slamming in his full length over and over, accelerating. His free hand alternated between rolling one of her nipples and tapping on her clit in time with his thrusts.

Alyssa's mind could not process the sensual assault. All her erogenous zones flamed and screamed for more. Mike's cock gave an internal massage, only fast and hard. Her pussy leaked and probably squirted juices, based on how it clutched and spasmed around his fingers. Her breasts felt the pull of being bounced by the hard fucking. She lost count of her orgasms, or maybe they became one long one. The stream of sound coming from her switched from unintelligible speech, to moans, to high-pitched squeals. Her head flopped from side to side.

Neither of them could stand this stimulation long. Mike asked as he huffed, "Where do you want the cum?"

Alyssa somehow remembered Beth's depraved offer. She fought to form the words. "On... Unh... Unh... On... Pussy." Mike popped the head of his cock out of Alyssa's ass. The sudden stretch followed by snapping closed set off Alyssa's largest orgasm, and she curled upward and screamed. Mike shot cum across her pussy. The spurts covered most of her lips, then dripped down. The last few drips fell between Alyssa's ass cheeks.

Alyssa collapsed when her body released its clench. Her legs fell to the side, leaving her gaping. Her head lolled to one side, her eyes closed, and her mouth opened. Her breathing slowed, and she lazily rubbed her breast with one hand and smeared Mike's cum across her pussy and down her thighs with the other.

Mike lay down beside her, stroking her heaving belly while she painted herself. When Alyssa turned to him, he asked, "Did I meet your needs?"

"Yes. That was amazing."

"It was that. You were amazing."

Alyssa closed her eyes and breathed a moment before responding. "Thank you. I'll give your sales staff a testimonial. How did you learn that?"

"My wife taught me. You notice I have a thin shaft. She enjoyed sex but wanted something different. Neither of us had tried anal, and she thought it would spice things up without hurting too much. She loved it the first time, and we kept experimenting. We browsed the internet for ideas, but mainly I fucked and she talked, moaned, or grunted, and I listened. You received our favorite technique."

"Tell her thank you for me. I'm all worn out and smiling. That makes you the best hotel manager ever."

"Glad to be of service, Mrs. Davis."

"After that many orgasms, call me Alyssa," she laughed.

Mike got up. "I hope we can do this again. Right now, I'm going to give your appreciation to the boss. She loves taking the other woman off me and reclaiming me. She's waiting."

"I mean it, tell her thank you. No, give her a big kiss for me."

Alyssa sat, then flopped back down. "I'd walk you out, but you took my energy. Thank you, Mike. This was wonderful."

"Yes, ma'am. I'll see you tomorrow." He grabbed his tool bag and left.

⋘

Alyssa recovered her strength. She ate a couple of handfuls of peanuts and chugged a bottle of water. Mike's cum sliding between her cheeks restored her unbridled libido. *So decadent. I want more.* She tied her robe, leaving it open to below her navel, picked up the two room keys, and headed to the elevator.

The elevator door opened, revealing two young men. They stared at her with knowing grins. *I'm showing cum in my cleavage and otherwise look freshly fucked. To hell with it.* She swiped Beth's room key, hit four, and turned to face them. *I'm sure I smell freshly fucked too. They have all the details when they jack off remembering this dirty girl.* The elevator stopped on eight, but the men shrugged and kept leering at her. When the doors opened on four, Alyssa said, "Sweet dreams, gentlemen," and walked down the hall laughing.

Alyssa opened the door to darkness. *I made a mistake. She's already asleep.* She locked the door behind her, then waited. When the glow of the alarm clock and the moonlight coming between the drapes was enough to see, she stepped to the foot of the bed. Beth's head peeked above the covers. Her breath was even. Alyssa smiled, and her libido geared down to low. *She is beautiful. I won't wake her. I need some sleep too.* She dropped the robe where she stood and spooned behind Beth, draping her arm across her waist. Alyssa kissed the back of Beth's head and closed her eyes.

6
THURSDAY MORNING

Alyssa awoke with Beth spooned behind her, Beth's fingers grazing the underside of Alyssa's breast. Beth's breath filtered through her hair to tickle the back of her neck. Goose bumps covered her body, and her nipples tingled.

"You awake?" Beth whispered.

"Yes," Alyssa whispered back, not wanting to break the quiet mood.

"I felt you wake up. Just a subtle tension. I'm glad you're here."

"Me too. I liked sliding in bed beside you."

"Sorry I was asleep. I couldn't keep my eyes open."

"Don't be. You looked so beautiful lying there. I snuggled behind you and put my arm around your belly. My heart glowed just holding you."

Beth laid her head atop Alyssa's and hugged her. "Me too." She pecked Alyssa's cheek.

They lay there not moving for what felt like twenty minutes but could have been only three. Alyssa finally broke the mood. "Beth, I love lying here, but I have to pee. I'll come right back."

"I did that earlier."

When Alyssa returned to the room, Beth held up a hand to stop her. "I want to look at you." Alyssa stood relaxed while Beth drank her in. "You have no idea how beautiful you are, do you? You have bed hair and dried cum everywhere, and you are absolutely beautiful. Anyone waking up beside you is the luckiest person in the world."

That should be only Robert. Don't think about that now, Alyssa. Alyssa smiled at Beth, taking in the compliment without comment. She slid into the bed and kissed Beth. As they kissed, they traced light touches on each other's backs. With their lower hands, they did the same to each other's breasts and stomachs.

Their kissing intensified. Tongues dueled. Lips nibbled necks and pulled at earlobes. The light finger touches became caresses, then progressed to rubbing, squeezing, pinching, pulling. Alyssa climbed onto Beth, but Beth put both hands on Alyssa's hips and rolled her over, pinning the older woman. Beth kissed her hard before working her mouth down to her breasts. Alyssa pushed Beth's head toward her needy snatch. Beth jerked Alyssa's wrists above her head. "If you wanted me to clean you quickly, you should have let me do it when it was wet. This dried cum tastes more like you, and I'm going to enjoy this. So lie back and let me clean you." She kissed Alyssa without breaking eye contact. Alyssa nodded and kept her hands above her head.

Beth licked Alyssa's breasts clean over the next few minutes. The warm moisture and gentle firmness of her tongue was only interrupted by the scraping of hard teeth. The combination kept Alyssa moaning and yelping as her body ached for more. Beth bit one of Alyssa's nipples and pulled. The shock tripped Alyssa's first small orgasm. "Oh, so good. Keep going."

Beth gave a mischievous grin, then let the nipple slip from her teeth. She licked her way down Alyssa's belly to her mound and cleaned as she had her breasts. Beth worked her way around from above Alyssa's clit to the insides of her thighs. She followed the trail of cum to the back of Alyssa's thigh, then continued to the instep of her right foot. Beth licked and cleaned back up Alyssa's leg, lingering at her knee and the inside of her thigh beside her pussy. Alyssa's breathing came in shallow gasps as she awaited Beth's first lick of her pussy, but instead Beth moved to follow the trail of cum down Alyssa's left leg.

Alyssa moaned. "Oh god. Don't tease me like that."

Beth grinned at her and kept licking her thigh. The cum trail stopped on her thigh, but Beth continued licking down to suck Alyssa's toes. She ran her tongue between them as she sucked.

"Oh. That feels good. I didn't know that could feel so good. Oh, Beth."

Flashing a grin, Beth cleaned her way up Alyssa's leg, repeating what she did on the right one. Alyssa quivered in anticipation. She put her hands on Beth's head. Beth pulled her head back. "Ah, Ah, Ah… Put those hands back where they belong," Beth almost sang to Alyssa.

"God, just stop teasing me. I'm right there. Make me come!" Alyssa reached back over her head to the headboard.

Beth flicked Alyssa's clit once, and Alyssa clamped her thighs around Beth's ears, preventing her from hearing her stream of obscenities as the powerful orgasm rippled through her. Beth continued to lick Alyssa's labia, avoiding her clit, until Alyssa relaxed her thighs. She moved her head across all Alyssa's swollen lips, then lowered her head to lick the nether hole. She spiraled out to the sensitive insides of Alyssa's cheeks, licking and nipping with her teeth, then spiraled back in. Alyssa writhed, and her pussy continued to drip, helping Beth devour Mike's cum.

When Beth wriggled her tongue over Alyssa's ass, Alyssa grabbed Beth's head and pressed it into her. The tip of Beth's nose dipped between Alyssa's open lips. Alyssa groaned. Beth finished her off by whipping across Alyssa's clit in a blur. Alyssa came again, then pulled Beth up for a slow kiss.

Beth felt Alyssa's muscles soften and her limbs sag onto the mattress as she snuggled beside her. Alyssa's eyes closed, and her breath slowed. Beth pressed up to get out of bed.

"Don't get up. You feel great," Alyssa said without moving or opening her eyes.

Beth lay back down. "I thought you were asleep."

"Just really happy and relaxed." She stroked Beth's thigh with the hand pinned between them. "I want to return the favor."

"As good as that sounds, I have to be at work soon."

"You have a three-minute commute."

Beth laughed. "True, but I only have thirty minutes. I still have to clean up and get ready." She traced her finger over Alyssa's closed eyes in a figure eight pattern, venturing as far as her eyebrows, then circling in. "I want to enjoy you for another few minutes. Lie still and let me feel you."

Alyssa luxuriated in Beth's gentle caresses. *Her touch is so light. It's exciting and soothing at once. Who knew my eyelids could be so sensitive?* Alyssa felt the warmth of Beth's body pull away but didn't open her eyes. "Don't stop. Keep me warm and relaxed all day."

Beth cackled. "Stay as long as you like. I have to be downstairs in fifteen minutes."

Alyssa sat up. "I owe you. How can I help you get ready?"

"Oh, stay there…" She looked at the bathroom door. "You know, could you brush my hair out and put it in a ponytail while I wipe up? I'm going easy today."

"Sure. I haven't done someone's hair since Susan was little."

She stood nude behind Beth in front of the mirror. Beth tried to stand still while she wiped her body with the baby wipes. Alyssa moved as quickly as she could, given the intimacy of brushing and holding Beth's hair. She took a few extra strokes before tying off the ponytail and fluffing her blonde curls. "There. You look put together, with a hint of wildness in the curls."

"That does look good. Thanks." She kissed Alyssa on the cheek on her way to the door. "I mean it, stay as long as you like, but get to Starbucks early if you want any food."

"Thanks. Understood." Alyssa patted Beth's rump as she kissed her on the cheek.

Alyssa took a few minutes to clean Beth's room. She hung up a couple of shirts that had been on the floor and put the trash in the hallway for housekeeping to retrieve during their rounds. *That should eliminate the leftover burger smell.* She hung up the couple of dirty towels in the bathroom, unsure when clean ones would be available. *Not great but better. She'll appreciate not having to do it herself.* She wiped herself off and made sure both room keys were in her robe before heading to the elevator. *Walking the halls in just a robe after sex and acting like a slutty girl was only for last night, remember.*

Back in her room, Alyssa let her robe fall open and called Robert. "Hey, Babe. Have I told you that I'm ready to come home? I miss you."

"I miss you, too, Baby. Tomorrow can't get here soon enough. Have you thought about where you want to eat after I pick you up?"

"Our kitchen. Cook some steaks. Yours are the best in town, and way better than the food at any restaurant I'll be allowed into. I haven't showered since Tuesday." *And I've been fucking non-stop. He'll smell it before I get within ten feet.* "I want good food, a hot shower, and good lovin' with my husband, in that order."

"That, my dear, sounds perfect. Being cooped up seems to make you horny. Yesterday you wanted phone sex, and today you are scheduling a booty call. I'm not complaining, but are you all right?"

If you only knew. "I'm lonely, bored, and trapped in a hotel. I got revved up hearing the couple next door Sunday night, and my husband is a thousand miles away from scratching that particular itch. The anticipation keeps me focused on getting home."

"You sure it isn't my steaks?"

"Oh no, Babe. I want you to make me feel like that woman on Valentine's. And I want to make you feel like the man who made her scream." She twirled her hair with her off hand.

"You want me to call you a whore and spank you? That's new. Could be fun?"

"It would be different, but I wasn't talking about that. I want you to make me feel like the center of your world, and I want to make you feel like the center of mine."

"I always feel that way. I hope you do too. Is there something on your mind?"

Except when you are at work, or have work to do, or something with the kids, or... Don't get into it on the phone, even as much as you want to tell him what you are feeling. "No, Babe. I just miss you. That's all. I want to celebrate being together when I get home." *Remember, you are the one outside your marriage, not him.* "This has been the toughest week."

"It ends tomorrow. I'll be the happiest face you see at the airport."

"I'll be the one with that 'I haven't showered all week' look."

"You will still be the most beautiful woman there."

"Oh, really? Even if there is a six-foot blonde with huge tits?"

"What did you just say? Who is this? My wife wouldn't talk like that."

"I notice you didn't answer the question."

"I see. Objection, Your Honor. The questioner is using a foreign language."

Alyssa laughed. "It's okay. We have always allowed each other to look at beautiful things…and people." *More than look now?* "In fact, do you remember that time at Fuddruckers?"

"How could I forget? You always bring it up. Besides, every man in line was watching that particular six-foot blonde with big tits, to use your crude term. It's the story that describes how great you are in that regard. Do you remember Juan, our neighbor?"

"Mm. Juan. I loved it when he and his girlfriend would sunbathe. You did, too, as I recall."

"Not as much as you. He was way past her on the hotness meter. I'm not gay, but if I were…"

Alyssa laughed. She hadn't felt this at ease with Robert all week. *I haven't felt this at ease with him in a long time. How long since we laughed and played like this? I love his sense of humor. Will I get to see it again?* Her eyes watered, and she sniffled.

"Did you laugh so hard you are crying? My sense of humor is why you married me."

"That's it, Babe. I can't stop laughing around you." She collected herself. "I love you more than anything in the world. I can't wait to see you."

"That goes double for me, Baby. Oh crap. I'm late for a meeting. I have to run. We can talk later. Love you."

"Love you," she said into the silent phone. *That was great and awful at once. I can't wait to get home, and I dread it more than anything.*

❦

By the time Alyssa dressed and made herself presentable, Starbucks was out of food. Alyssa got a cup of coffee and sat where she could people watch. A beautiful, tall, dark-haired woman was letting two kids chase each other around two of the large columns in the center of the open space. She smiled as they burned off the energy that only being cooped up inside can generate. She gave them hugs each time they circled the columns and returned to her yelling, "Mommy!"

When she noticed Alyssa, she walked over. "Do you mind if I sit here?" she asked, pointing to the chair beside Alyssa's.

Alyssa was taken aback at the woman's forwardness. Many seats were available in the lobby. "Please feel free." Alyssa let the children come get their hugs and run off again before asking, "How can I help you? You didn't sit here by accident."

The woman kept her eyes on her children. "You made my job very hard last night."

"Excuse me? I've never seen you before."

"My name is Sonia. Michael is my husband."

Shit. She's mad. Shit. That asshole lied to me. Alyssa looked around to ensure nobody was eavesdropping, and to let the venom out of her voice. "Wait. He told me you have an arrangement. He even said you suggested how to dress for me. Did he lie?"

"He told you the truth. We do have an arrangement, as you call it, and I did suggest he leave his underwear at home." She hugged the children as they completed another lap. She told them to run all the way to the other end of the lobby before coming back. "You made it hard to reclaim him last night."

Alyssa sat dumbfounded. "I don't understand."

"It was hard to reclaim him last night. You made quite an impression."

"He made more of an impression on me, I assure you. He is very good at what he does. He said you taught him. You have my compliments." Alyssa felt her face getting hot. "I'm surprised to hear you had trouble. He was adamant that he return to you and that you were waiting. Wait a second. How did you recognize me?"

"Michael pointed you out to me yesterday as a woman he would like to enjoy. I agreed. You are ravishing, yet you act as if you are unaware of that." A smile touched her mouth. "I waited up, and yes, we made the best love we have in months. But his mind stayed with you."

"What do you mean?"

"When Michael comes home to me, or I to him, we describe the entire experience in detail while we lie in bed and kiss and touch. When the story is over, we make love. It is always erotic and powerful, and we affirm our commitment to each other when we are done. Last night was the first time he continued to talk about a woman after we made love."

"Oh god, I'm sorry. I didn't intend to hurt anyone."

"You did not. In truth, you made it better. I had to reclaim him a second time. We had never had to do that, but it was better than the first. He was taken with you."

"I don't know why. I was the one who couldn't get off the bed afterward. All I did was come from his masterful work."

"That might have been what got him so excited. He said you responded better than any woman he ever had. The state of constant orgasm he described was, I am sure, complimentary to his ego."

"I can't apologize for responding. His cock and technique are unique and thrilling."

"They are unique. He studies the women he fucks, the same way I try to learn something from the men I fuck. The variety staves off ennui. You create an interesting challenge. I have to reclaim him, and I am no longer his most appreciative partner." "I mean it; I don't want to hurt your marriage. Last night was a one-time thing before I leave tomorrow. I won't see him again." Alyssa looked at Sonia. "Aren't you in love? Doesn't that make you a better partner than someone he just fucks?"

"Yes. Michael and I make love. Nobody else makes love with us. Everyone else is just a fuck partner, even the ones we care for, like Beth or Ramon."

"Wait, Ramon? Is Mike gay?"

"Oh no. No, no." Sonia laughed. "Ramon is our neighbor down the street. He is the partner I visit the most, just like Michael does with Beth. We like them, even care for them, but our feelings for them are nothing compared to our love for each other. That is why reclaiming is so important. Reclaiming tells us that even immediately after sex with someone outside our marriage, we love each other enough to make love and wash away the outsider with passion. I had to wash you away twice last night."

Alyssa raised her hands as if surrendering. "I won't compound it by engaging with him tonight. I really am sorry for making things hard for you. I probably should get myself ready to depart tomorrow, anyway. I have a lot to pack up after this trip." Alyssa sighed. "Can I ask you something personal?"

"Our conversation has been deeply personal so far. Please continue."

"How did you get started...sharing each other?"

Sonia's eyebrows twitched upward, then settled as the corners of her lips turned up. "That is more deeply personal. Are you asking for simple curiosity?"

"I said I had a lot to pack up. That didn't refer to clothes.

I have been, um, experimenting behind my husband's back. I want to stay married, yet I think I want to keep experiencing new things as well."

"I see. You have put yourself at the disadvantage by being secretive. I cannot help you with that, but I can tell you how Michael and I came to our understanding."

Alyssa spun her wedding rings as she thought. "I know I have to make amends before he and I are on even footing again. I need to figure that out for myself. Once Robert and I recover, maybe your story can help me. Thank you for sharing it with a stranger."

"You are no longer a stranger, Mrs. Alyssa Davis. You are my closest rival, and you have shown yourself to be a friend today." She hugged her children and had them run the length of the lobby again. "Michael and I married in Bogotá years ago after a brief and wonderful courtship. We were in our late twenties. Both of us had experienced many partners before we met, but when we made a vow to be faithful to each other, we meant it. Both of us spurned offers of extramarital dalliances during the first year, and we worked together to make our sex life as interesting as we could. It was then that we started honing his anal sex techniques."

Alyssa closed her eyes, remembering last night as a faint tingle rose from her ass through her belly. When she opened them, Sonia smiled, having waited in silence. "Sorry. Reminiscing. Please continue."

"Michael got an opportunity to return to the US. It was a chance for him to become the breadwinner far away from my family's plantations in Colombia. We came north. It was good for Michael. He worked hard and made more money. I was bored. I was not yet fluent in English and did not work. Lying at the pool while one's husband works may seem glamorous, but it lost its appeal quickly. The only benefit was the attractive second-shift workers who came to the pool in the late mornings."

Alyssa interrupted. "Did they cause trouble?"

"Yes and no. Cognizant of my vows, we looked at each other across the pool, but I never even allowed conversation. The looking led to fantasizing, which led to longing, and I attacked Michael every evening when he came home. We would have sex in the living room of the apartment before dinner, then make love at least once every night when we went to bed. That part was wonderful."

"Sounds like it. What was the problem with that?"

"I did not notice that he was attacking me every night with the same fervor. His lust matched mine. I noticed the evening he called me Tiffany when he ejaculated inside me. We had the kind of fight that only happens when a Colombian woman feels betrayed." She smiled. "I accused him of cheating, which he denied. He left in the car. I slipped my smallest bikini on and went to the pool. In retrospect, it was beneficial that the handsome men worked second shift, or I would have shattered my marriage by bringing one or two of them into my bed for Michael to find. Instead, I wept behind my sunglasses and returned to the apartment."

Alyssa shook her head and spun her rings but, as she opened her mouth, decided not to speak.

"Michael was waiting. He was drinking beer on the couch and handed me one. He had seen me at the pool but waited in the apartment. He denied cheating but admitted fantasizing about the beautiful and sexy women he saw every day, both guests and employees. Tiffany was one of the staff he fantasized about. He said something I did not expect. He told me that he had not spoken to her because he did not want to risk flirting and what that might cause."

Alyssa sat back. "He was running a hotel and not speaking to one of the employees? That doesn't sound good."

"It was not. As we talked, he named four other employees he avoided because he feared hurting our marriage. He had extensive sexual fantasies about them, however, along with some previous guests. He had been having sex with me while envisioning those fantasies. I admitted to having the same fantasies about the men at the pool and not speaking with them for the same reasons. I also admitted hunting for them after our fight. That they were at work, as I said, saved our marriage."

Alyssa swallowed, returning the knot that had risen in her throat to her stomach. "Wow, you were lucky. How do you follow revelations like that?

"We reaffirmed our love for each other, and we admitted that we wanted more excitement. We talked about why we had the fantasies, and what those fantasies made us feel. We talked about keeping our marriage vows. Hours later we realized that fantasizing about someone else while making love to each other was not making love. It was merely fucking, and worse, it was a substitute for fucking someone else. We decided that being disengaged from your partner was the worst form of infidelity. We decided to ensure our most intimate moments together would be exclusive of outside thoughts, that they would reconfirm our marriage and our love. We would look each other in the eyes when we coupled, and we would always tell each other we love each other using our names when we finished. The love we made that night was the best we had ever done. We still have not eclipsed its passion, though we try."

"That's beautiful." Alyssa paused. "How did you proceed from there?"

"We talked intermittently about what we had discovered, and we made love every night, focusing solely on each other. Consistent with our focus on each other, we stayed even farther away from our temptations. I avoided the pool. Michael

---

remained in his office most of the workday. I had more time to consider our problem, but Michael had more motivation. Not speaking to one's employees causes morale issues."

"I would imagine."

"By Saturday morning, Michael appeared distressed. I rented a small beach cottage for the weekend. It cost more than we should spend, but it was on a small inlet and had a covered front porch. I thought we could talk there and, if it was as secluded as the ads indicated, make love there too."

Sonia kissed her children and sent them on another lap before continuing. "Michael wanted to talk as we drove. He had agonized during those hours away from his staff. We had strengthened our marriage, but he could not reconcile succeeding at work. He recognized his opportunity and that he was being monitored for additional advancement. He also knew that interacting with beautiful women would trigger a mistake. He felt he had to choose between providing for his family and having a family."

Sonia shook her head. "I felt differently. I remained at the apartment, taking care of the house. I had fantasized about the men in part because I was lonely and bored. Left with idle time, my imagination would eventually overcome me also. I needed a distraction."

Alyssa looked down when her fingertips tingled. The skin showed white from the pressure where her fingers interlaced. She relaxed her hands and shook them to restore the circulation.

"As we talked, we reached decisions. We decided to remain married. We decided we wanted to be married because of our love rather than for appearances and that we wanted to keep that passion alive. We decided that we would both work and that we both needed to succeed. We decided that working required the risk of infidelity, both physical and mental. We weighed that risk for some time. We decided that envisioning another instead of a spouse was a greater infidelity than having sex with another before coming home to a spouse. If we had to choose, we would choose having sex with others."

Alyssa raised her hand. "Who said that first, you or Mike?"

"I did. Michael hurt me when he called me Tiffany, and that slip of the tongue confirmed that I had been just a place to orgasm while he fantasized about other women. We never wanted that to happen again. It still upsets me."

Sonia wiped a tear. "We reconfirmed that thought throughout the afternoon's discussion. We could not decide how to protect our mental and emotional connection if we did stray. We did not want to open our marriage to outsiders without protecting the relationship at its heart."

The knot returned to Alyssa's throat as she imagined her coming discussion with Robert. "It sounds impossible to me as well. I dread mine. How did you get past it?"

"It was late, so we walked down the beach in search of food. Fate led us to a small shack with one waitress and a cook. We were the only patrons. We ate, but talking was difficult. Michael watched the waitress, and I was intrigued by the cook. We lingered and drank as the pair cleaned. We watched them the whole time. Eventually, the waitress flipped the closed sign, locked the door, and came to our table. She told us we could stay but she and the cook were going to dance. We watched them dance for a minute before we danced, too, still eyeing the attractive couple."

Sonia smiled with her eyes closed. *She's remembering.*

"When a slow song started, Michael and I clinched together like lovers do. I whispered, 'Are you fantasizing about them?' He replied yes in my ear while squeezing my ass. I looked over his shoulder to see the couple moving toward us. The cook asked if they could cut in. Michael and I shared a deep gaze and both nodded. The cook took me in his arms, while Michael whisked the waitress away in a flourish. After only a few seconds of dancing, the cook leaned in for a kiss. By the time I looked up, Michael had his head buried in the waitress's neck and his hands groping her ass. Soon I was nude, on my back, with the cook slamming into me while I begged for more. Michael did the same to the waitress on the adjacent table. The cook filled me at the same time Michael filled the waitress. She then climbed on top of me and slurped the cum out of me. She lowered her pussy onto my face, and I reciprocated. The men watched."

"You swapped, right there beside each other?"

Sonia nodded. "After both of us orgasmed again, she lay on the floor. Not me. I made eye contact with Michael. I knew I must purge the cook and waitress from our minds. I leaped from the table and kissed him, full and hard, with the taste of his cum and the waitress still on my lips. I dropped my mouth to his cock, saying, 'Let me remove her from you, my darling.' I sucked him hard and licked him clean, then straddled him. I said, 'Make love to me, Michael. Reclaim me from the cook. Reclaim my love.' I dropped onto his cock, taking it to the hilt. I am unaware how long we made love, but when we finished, I looked into his eyes and he into mine, and I said, 'I am yours alone, Michael. I love you.' He told me the same. It was spontaneous, but it was the solution we needed. We learned that night how to enjoy others and how to strengthen our love. We have done so ever since."

Alyssa touched her chest. "My god, that's amazing. What did the other couple do?"

"I know not. A note on the table said thank you and that the door would lock behind us. We never saw them again, but they saved us. While it was not their intent, they taught us how to make our marriage work."

Sonia's children returned, gasping and giggling. "Play with

your toys over there." She directed them to a rug across the seating area.

"I know you don't always, um, play…together, or you would have been in my room last night." Alyssa turned her body more toward Sonia. "Mike said he would tell you the details. Is that the substitute for being there?"

"It is, and it is not. Following the events in the shack, we still had much to discuss. We needed to distinguish an open arrangement from a license to have affairs. We considered seeking permission before playing, to use your word, with others. That is often impractical, so we agreed that we would trust each other to make the right decision when living out our fantasies. The one rule is that we tell each other the details afterward."

"Does that ever cause jealousy? Like if he has several opportunities during a dry spell for you?" Alyssa was leaning forward, taking in every word.

"It has the opposite effect. It excites us to see our spouse still desired and sexy. Moreover, a sexy story with all the details is astonishing foreplay."

"Really? I never thought of oral sex as simply talking," Alyssa chuckled.

Sonia joined her laugh. "I had not either, but I find that the largest erogenous zone is the mind. Engage it, and the body will follow. Beneficially, you can stimulate the mind in a hotel lobby, rather unlike other foreplay techniques. For confirmation, feel your nipples. They have protruded behind your shirt since I started our story."

Alyssa cupped her breast. The hard nub shocked her as she flicked it with her thumb. "Oh my. I am a bit turned on."

Alyssa looked down at the two nubs interrupting the lines of Sonia's silk blouse. When she met Sonia's eyes again, the dark-haired beauty whispered, "Now feel mine."

Alyssa didn't bother looking around to see who might be watching. She palmed Sonia's breast. She thumbed the hard nipple before pulling both hands into her lap and sitting back. "Yours are harder than mine."

"Yes. I have the memory to accompany the story. Michael will receive its benefit later. Now you see how the story connects two people. Our connection was such that you felt my breast without regard for observers. Have you ever felt another woman's breast in such a public place?"

Alyssa paled, aware of what her lust had inspired. She swiveled her neck, scanning the lobby.

Sonia smiled. "Do not worry. No one watched us. Your lack of propriety will be our naughty secret." She leaned closer to Alyssa. "If you like what you just felt, perhaps I could tell you another story in private, later."

Alyssa leaned closer also. *Yes.* "I did like what I felt. You are so beautiful. The thought of another story, and what it might lead to, intrigues me." *Jesus. Again?* She leaned back and sighed. "I need to repair my marriage, and the first step is not taking any additional lovers. Please understand, I am both flattered and interested, but I can't."

Sonia sighed. "I expected your reply. I would very much like to experience you. You are ravishing, and you overwhelmed Michael. You could provide stories for Michael and me forever. If you change your mind, please let Michael know."

Alyssa blushed, then took Sonia's hand. "You are one of the many wonderful and difficult things I'll ponder today. If I change my mind, I will indeed call Mike."

"Thank you. I hope you reconsider."

"I have to ask, and I don't mean to offend. Given your arrangement, is Mike the father of your children?"

Laughing, Sonia replied, "He is. When we decided to have

children, neither of us ventured outside. Me for obvious reasons, and Michael to maintain full potency. Perhaps because of our commitment, fertilization occurred quickly. After ten weeks' gestation, we allowed each other to act on our fantasies again."

"Both of you?"

"Oh yes. I had more sex during my pregnancies than Michael did. You would be surprised how many men want a pregnant woman. Perhaps the novelty excites them, or the fantasy of taking another man's wife. Do you have children?"

"Two. Much older than your little ones."

"Do you remember the urges when you were pregnant? I wanted sex always."

Alyssa shook her head. "I wasn't so lucky. I had morning sickness the entire time, so I only wanted to feel better."

Sonia wrinkled her nose. "You missed a wonderful time. My body was never more sensitive than when I was pregnant. Every touch was bliss. You are not old. Perhaps you and your husband will have another."

"Oh no." Alyssa shook her head again. "If I get pregnant, my obstetrician will pay child support. She fixed that during the last C-section."

"I see. If our conversation helps you, perhaps your new experiences will rival those you missed during pregnancy. I hope it will. Everyone deserves to feel desired and to feel desire."

"I hope so. Thank you for sharing your story and being so forthcoming. You've given me a lot to think about."

"I am glad. If you will excuse me, I need to pull Michael into his office. He will enjoy the benefits of our conversation. It has been a pleasure, Alyssa."

"Yes it has, Sonia. Good luck finding Mike."

Alyssa bought a fresh coffee and sat by the immobile escalator across the lobby for a change of scenery. She was hungry but could make it to dinner.

≼

Frazier followed Alyssa when she moved across the lobby, as he had since she had emerged from the elevator. He sat where he could see her while smirking at the last four pictures he had taken of her—the ones with her hand on Sonia's breast.

7
THURSDAY AFTERNOON

ALYSSA SAT BESIDE the escalator long after the change of scenery had provided any break in the monotony. The soft couch cushions had put Alyssa's butt cheek to sleep, and the hot coffee had long ago become cold dregs. She shifted her weight and drank the last swallow, seeking relief, knowing it was a mistake. The cold bitterness of the coffee settled into her heart.

The gray light on the unplowed snow outside the window mocked her inability to leave town like the flimsy canvas shoes and dark buildings defied her to even leave the hotel itself. Her phone popped up the low battery warning.

Eighty percent of my battery went to confirming that I still can't get home. The airports are still closed. There are no rental cars available in Houston, and it doesn't matter because most of the roads remain unpassable. Even if I rented a car and got out of Houston, the roads between here and North Carolina are bad because of this cold bitch of a storm. Texas had the worst of it because they opted out of the power grid and their wind farms were inoperable in this weather. Alyssa closed her phone. Some deep breaths and counting to ten didn't provide the attitude adjustment she wanted. She sighed and sagged into the couch, conceding that she had neither the energy nor motivation to leave it.

Limited food, no running water, no snow removal. She spun her wedding rings while she thought. *Come on, do better. I have some food and a warm room to sleep in. As long as the power stays on and the elevator works, I'll be okay. Please, please.* She looked up at the ceiling as if praying for help, then motion on the escalator caught her eye.

She saw the man stumble before she heard the little girl scream, "Daddy!" He landed, crumpled, a few feet from Alyssa. He grabbed his leg before his daughter reached him.

Alyssa crouched beside him. "Are you all right?"

"My leg really hurts, and I feel it swelling."

Beth, Mike, and a couple of the hotel staff reached them and tended to the man.

Alyssa touched the little girl's shoulder. "Sweetie, are you okay?"

She looked at Alyssa and crushed into her, bawling. "My daddy is hurt. Are they going to help him?"

Alyssa hugged the little girl. "Yes, sweetie. They are taking good care of him. See? They already have him sitting up. The hotel people are so kind. They take care of all of us. Can you tell me your name, sweetie?"

"I'm Emma, and I'm five. We're here because our house is too cold."

"Well, Emma, I'm Alyssa, and we are going to keep you warm right here while they take care of your daddy. Is your mommy here in the hotel?"

"Mommy doesn't live with us now."

"I see." Alyssa made eye contact with Beth, who mouthed thank you. "While they take care of your daddy, would you like some hot chocolate?"

"Yes, thank you."

Alyssa took Emma to get hot chocolate at Starbucks. They sat and sipped their drinks. When they finished, Alyssa kept Emma chatting, singing, and playing I spy. The ambulance arrived, and they loaded up the injured man. Alyssa walked Emma over to him. Emma gave him a hug. "Daddy, I'm going to the hospital with you."

"Oh, baby girl, you don't want to go there. The doctors are going to fix my leg, and as soon as they do, I'll be back." He looked at Alyssa. "Ma'am, Beth here has told me about you, that you are a mom delivering her daughter to college. She told me not to worry about you sitting with Emma." He wiped a tear from his eye. "I don't have anyone to take care of her. Could I ask you a huge favor and let Emma stay in your care until I get back? Please? I've been watching, and you are good with her. She likes you. The paramedics don't think I'll need surgery. The hospital is no place for her. I can pay you."

"Sir—"

"Devon. Devon Hanes."

"I'm Alyssa Davis. Mr. Hanes, I can watch Emma if you will allow me to share that duty with Beth in a pinch or if we have to go to your room. I'll feed her dinner if you aren't back. Does she have any allergies or medicines, or anything else I should be aware of?"

"Only that she is everything that matters to me. Thank you. I can't repay you for helping us." He turned to his daughter. She eased closer to give a light hug. "It's fine, sweetie. You can give me a hug. My arms work great. You won't hurt me."

She buried herself in his arms. "Daddy, are you coming back?"

"Oh yes, baby girl. I'll be back as quick as they fix my leg." He kissed the top of her head. "You stay with Mrs. Davis. She'll take good care of you, and I'll come get you when I get back." He leaned his head back to look her in the eyes. "I will be back, I promise."

He looked at Alyssa. "Take care of her, please." The ambulance techs rolled him outside.

Alyssa looked down at Emma. "Let's have some fun while your dad gets better." Emma smiled.

I haven't entertained a little one in a long time. This will be exhausting but fun. Remember…what did Susan like to do at five? "Let's get what we need." They strolled over to Beth at the front desk.

"Beth, by any chance are there crayons and paper in the back? And maybe a deck of cards?"

Beth returned from the back room with a box of old crayons, some printer paper, and a deck of cards. "Here you go. There is a bouncy ball from lost and found too. The second-floor ballrooms are empty, and the concourse there is open for little kids to run, if they need to."

"Oh, thanks. We will be there if Mr. Hanes comes back. Do the bathrooms have water for flushing? Or will we need to come down here?"

"We put water buckets in them. You should be okay, but you'll want to check before committing."

"Understood. Nobody wants that surprise. We will be in for dinner later, if her dad isn't back."

❧

After Alyssa and Emma climbed the stairs to the second floor, Emma nudged Alyssa's leg, yelled, "Tag, you're it," and took off running. Alyssa ran after her, glad she had slept well the night before. They played most of the afternoon. When Alyssa needed a break, they sat in front of a low table and Emma made get-well cards. The elevator dinged, and a man came toward them.

"Mrs. Davis?"

"Yes?"

He flashed his badge. "My name is Lieutenant Frazier. Could I speak with you about the incident Tuesday night for a moment, please? We may want to step in here for privacy." He gestured toward the nearby ballroom before nodding at Emma.

"I see. Um, yes. I am happy to talk, though I gave my statement that night."

"Yes, ma'am, you did. I just have a few follow-up questions."

"Okay. Emma, I'm going right over here to talk with the policeman. You stay here."

"I will."

The pair reached the ballroom. Alyssa stood inside the door where she could see Emma's back. "What questions do you have, Lieutenant?"

"Mrs. Davis, I want to start by thanking you for providing a statement. In situations like this, witnesses are often reluctant to get involved. You see, Sherry Capps, the lady who attacked your friend, is dangerous. She has multiple arrests for assault and has put people in the hospital. You saw that it took three men to subdue her. I'm glad she stumbled before she could use the knife. She has stabbed people in the past."

"Oh my. I didn't know that, of course, but I'm glad she is in jail."

"Me too. I need to nail down a couple of items. Had you and your friends been drinking that night?"

"We had some wine with dinner."

"How many glasses, would you say?"

"I don't know. Including before dinner and after, maybe six?"

"Six? So you were drunk?"

"No. That was over a few hours. I was not drunk. Why are you asking this?"

"Yes, ma'am. I'm just nailing down some details. Did you antagonize Ms. Capps during the evening?"

"Of course not. I didn't even see her before she stood up shouting."

"You didn't bump her at the bar and spill her drink?"

"No."

"You didn't have an altercation in the restroom over a toilet?"

"No. Why are you asking all this?"

"Well, you see, Mrs. Davis, she alleges that you instigated the entire incident. It appears you could have been quite drunk and not remember antagonizing Ms. Capps. Make no mistake, I believe everything you said, but the DA is releasing everyone from holding who isn't a clear-cut case because of the tight staffing. With this information, she will probably be released later this afternoon. I'd hate to see her come after revenge, against you or your friend behind the desk. And it would be a real shame if the little girl over there got hurt by accident."

"Oh my. What can you do? Can we get protection? Can't someone that dangerous be held, even with the demands of the weather?"

"I'm sorry, Mrs. Davis. Given that you had been drinking, the DA is likely to decide to let her go and see what surfaces as we investigate further, which could be a few weeks. And no, we don't have any people to provide protection. Most of our people are working double shifts and can't watch over a simple assault witness. I'm sorry."

"Surely she can't get in the hotel."

"Ordinarily that is true, but an emergency proclamation prohibits the hotels from asking people to leave because they have no power in their homes. The hotel staff don't like it, but she will be back."

Alyssa's head drooped. "Shit." *She could come after me for another day, but she could come after Beth for a long time. God, could this trip get any worse?*

"Mrs. Davis, you know, if these answers didn't make their way to the station, Ms. Capps wouldn't get released."

"How would that happen? You have them written down already. You would have to lose them intentionally."

"Mrs. Davis, now you are asking me to sacrifice my principles."

"No. I asked a question."

"I see. To answer your question, the paper could get lost. You see, sometimes sheets get torn off before they should, particularly when I can help someone who is in a tough spot, like yourself. And sometimes I get sidetracked and don't make it to the office to report what I've learned. Can you sidetrack me so I don't have to turn this in?"

Alyssa gasped. "What do you mean?"

"Oh, I think you know what I mean," he growled. "I saw you mauling your cunt yesterday, and you felt up that other woman a little while ago, and I think you still need relief. Some major relief, like what I have here," he snarled as he grabbed his crotch. "You want to fuck me to keep her in jail."

Alyssa flushed. "Absolutely not! What do you think you are doing?"

"I'm offering a way to protect yourself, your friend, and that little girl. Capps can be processed out in ten minutes if I say so. Do you want to take that chance? And if she finds a box cutter that just happens to be in the street between the processing center and here?" He sneered and ogled Alyssa up and down. "I tell you what. This paper can be turned in at any time. I can hold it tonight, and you can decide to fuck me tomorrow. The price for tonight is a blow job."

"Are you nuts? No." Alyssa's voice cracked. *Oh shit. He knows he scared me.*

Frazier smirked at her. "Take it, or Capps is here, armed, in fifteen minutes."

God, oh god, oh god. What if he's not bluffing? Tears welled in Alyssa's eyes as she nodded.

"Thought so. Get those tits out. I want to see them when I come in your mouth."

"With a five-year-old over there? You can't be that stupid."

"Nobody's even using this floor. The water situation has canceled all the events. If you don't want her to get bored with her crayons, be quick. Get 'em out."

The anger on Frazier's face scared Alyssa more than the threat of a knife-wielding maniac. Her tears flowed as she began to unbutton her blouse. Frazier had dropped his pants and stroked his cock. Alyssa looked at it and stopped her hands. *Shit. That thing is thick. My jaw is going to hurt. At least it isn't long enough to gag me. Fuck, how do I get out of this?*

Frazier jerked her shirt open, then yanked her bra below her breasts.

"Nice tits, baby. Just like I like 'em, available."

The tears spilled down Alyssa's cheeks.

"Yeah, bitch. Cry. It reminds you who's in charge. You're gonna treat me right so I protect you from the crazy lady. I bet your friend at the front desk probably wants protection too. I'll see her later. You are stalling. Get to it."

Alyssa stood still.

"Kneel, dammit. Now."

Frazier pinched her nipples hard and pulled them downward. Alyssa whimpered.

"Quiet, Mrs. Davis. You don't want to bring the little girl into this." He dropped one hand between her legs.

She winced.

"You can give me this tomorrow. Now suck."

She knelt in front of Frazier. She got a whiff of his pungency and gagged. She wrapped her hand around his cock as far as she could. She covered the head with her thumb and forefinger. *I am protecting myself and Beth. This is the only way right now. Get through this and figure it out.* She started to lean in, then looked up. She controlled her sobbing enough to say, "If I do this, you leave Beth alone. I'm the one paying for your sleazy protection. Leave Capps in jail, and don't approach Beth."

Frazier gripped Alyssa's hair and glared at her. "You are doing this for you, for your protection. Who I visit next isn't your business. Now get to it, or I'll withdraw the offer. Seeing your tits makes me want to fuck you till you can't move. Now suck me."

Alyssa guided the short cock inside her mouth. He tasted like locker rooms smelled. Alyssa's tongue convulsed as she gagged again. Frazier pulled her head so pubic hair invaded her nose. Her jaw was wide open, but his cock had not hit the back of her throat. *Small victories.*

Both of them jerked at the sound of a small voice outside the room. "Alyssa, I finished my cards. Can we go eat? I'm hungry."

The flash of panic gave Alyssa an opening. "I'll be right there, sweetie. Clean up the crayons and paper, and we'll eat." She stood.

"Wait, bitch, you haven't finished yet."

"If she comes in here, I'll tell her to run for help, and this place will be crawling with people. Do you want to explain why

I'm exposed and crying and you have your pants around your ankles? Think quickly, five-year-olds aren't patient."

"This ain't my first rodeo. I'll just say you are a slut who likes it rough and you asked for this."

"But you will be watched, and you won't get another chance."

"Hmm. You're right. We'll pick this up after dinner but with a new offer. I'll meet you in the lobby outside the restaurant, and we will go to your room. Nobody will disturb us while I fuck you all night. Decide by then. And not a word to anyone, or I'll make sure the brat is around when Capps gets out." He pulled up his pants.

"Bastard. Don't threaten a little girl. I'll decide by then."

"I'll be watching you." He gripped her jaw and ran his thumb over her lips. "I'm a detective, so I read lips real well. Don't say anything to anyone," He pulled out his phone, open to a picture of her masturbating. "Or this hits the internet before Capps comes to cut you and your friend open."

"You fuck. Where did you get that?"

"You wanted me to have it, or you wouldn't have been by an open window with the light on. You asked me to take it while you put on a show for me. At least, that's what I'll say when I'm asked."

Nausea swept up through Alyssa's belly. The bile stopped in her throat but made her cough.

"Your devotion to me has you all choked up. Good." As she straightened, he gripped her arm. "And I'll have your phone."

"I need it to board my flight and talk with my family."

"You can have it back after we've had our fun, so you had better make up your mind. Now give it to me." He held up his phone showing her the photo and some kind of submission form. His thumb hovered over the button. "Give it to me, or I submit this to"—he looked at his phone—"forty-eight MILF porn websites and Capps goes free with a razor and a grudge."

Oh shit. Buy time and figure it out. She powered off her phone and handed it to him. "You have me. Just, please, leave it off and I'll talk with you tonight."

"Okay…for now. Remember I'm watching." Frazier pocketed the phones and left.

Alyssa wiped her face on a nearby tablecloth. *Thank god I didn't wear makeup. I have to find a way out of this.* She straightened her bra and buttoned the undamaged buttons on her blouse. *At least there are enough left to keep it closed.* Alyssa took a deep breath and walked to Emma, who was putting the last of the crayons in the box. "Your daddy will love those pretty cards. Are you ready to eat?"

8

THURSDAY NIGHT

Alyssa and Emma got a table on the side of the restaurant. Alyssa faced the door. She was not surprised to see Lieutenant Frazier sit at the bar where he could watch her. *He won't give me a chance to get help. How do I get out of this?*

"Let me get you two ladies something to drink." Beth walked up to take their order.

"You aren't taking orders at the bar?" *I wanted to get her alone to warn her. I can't wait though.*

"We are, but you are keeping Emma, so you get table service tonight."

"Um, special service got us in trouble Tuesday, remember?"

"Yes, but that nut is in jail, and more cops are in the dining room."

Alyssa looked around. She noticed several cops in uniform and some more with the right haircuts. Beth stood between her and Frazier. *Be quick and keep smiling.* "I see. One of them is at the bar. A Lieutenant Frazier. He got me alone and said the lady from last night might get out and come to the hotel tonight. Then he made some very troubling requests. Stay in public if he wants to talk, okay?"

Beth overtly glanced at Alyssa's torn shirt and raised her eyebrows. "I understand. I knew cops like that back in California. Don't worry." She nodded just enough for Alyssa to notice. "What drinks do you two want tonight? The menu is burgers and chips again. I assume you both want one?"

"May I please have chocolate milk?"

"Yes, you may, sweetie." Alyssa smiled. "You have been so good today. I'll have a gin and tonic, then just water."

"Coming right up, ladies." Beth resumed delivering food while Emma and Alyssa resumed talking, this time about favorite colors.

While they waited, the two arresting officers from the night before walked up. "Mrs. Davis? You may not remember us. We were here last night. We wanted to thank you for making a statement. Not everyone does."

Alyssa looked up but didn't speak for a second.

"Oh, my apologies. I'm Sergeant Taggart, and this is Officer Colson. We didn't get properly introduced last night. Are you feeling okay? That kind of incident is scary."

"Yes. I'm fine, though I'm surprised to hear that Ms. Capps could be released tonight and come back to the hotel."

"Who told you that?" Taggart's face wrinkled. "I'm not aware of that possibility. That would be most unusual."

"Lieutenant Frazier told me that a couple of hours ago. He seemed quite certain."

Alyssa noticed that Colson had blocked Frazier's line of sight. She made eye contact with Taggart, who said, "Please know that we are here to help, Mrs. Davis. Here is my card. My cell number is on the back. Please call or text if you need anything." He handed her his card.

Alyssa's eyes brimmed with tears, and she shook her head almost imperceptibly. "No phone," she whispered.

"Mrs. Davis, are you sure you are all right?"

She took a deep breath and opened her mouth to speak. She gasped as she saw Frazier walk into her field of view with his phone to his ear but boring into her with his eyes. He shook his head and turned the phone so only she could see. She couldn't make out the image, but the coloring matched what he'd shown her earlier, with his thumb over the bottom of the screen. Ice formed in her chest that suppressed the nausea in her belly. Her hope, so clear a second before, disappeared under the avalanche of fear gripping her. *Nothing on the internet ever goes away. If he lets Capps out, even later, she could come after Beth. These two could even be in on it. I don't know what to think. Buy time and figure it out.* "I'm fine. It has been a long week, but I'm fine."

The two officers stood another moment while Alyssa forced a smile. "Again, thank you, Mrs. Davis. If you think of anything else, please call. We will be nearby."

Alyssa and Emma returned to chatting while they waited. Emma pointed to Alyssa's hand. "Why do you do that?"

"Do what, sweetie?"

"Turn your ring. You do it a lot. Does it itch?"

Alyssa chuckled. "It doesn't itch. I twist my rings when I think really hard, but I don't usually realize I'm doing it."

"My daddy helps me think."

"I bet he does. We all need somebody to think with sometimes, don't we?" For a moment, thoughts of Robert settled Alyssa's stomach. *He could calm me, help me find the answer my frantic brain is hiding. If only I could call him.* Beth brought the food quicker than Alyssa would have liked. "Here is your food, ladies. I hope you enjoy it. I'll be back with more chocolate milk and water."

"Go ahead and bring the bill too."

Frazier took a two-top only a few feet from them when it opened up some minutes later. He sat facing them. Alyssa knew she would have no more chances to talk with anyone.

Maybe Beth can help me think. Instead of signing the bill, Alyssa wrote "bathroom, fifteen minutes" on the signature line.

Alyssa took Emma to the restroom a few minutes later. She saw Frazier rise when they did, and she heard him follow them down the hallway, pretending to take a call. Alyssa waited at the sink beside a woman fixing her makeup. After Emma finished washing her hands, Alyssa asked, "Emma, can you walk to our table and sit quietly by yourself for a few minutes like a big girl? I need to go myself."

Alyssa let Emma out of the door, went back in, and washed her hands, waiting for Beth. The woman doing her makeup was the only other person in the room. As another woman entered and rushed to a stall, the makeup woman turned to Alyssa, then turned back to examine her teeth. She checked her breath by breathing into a cupped palm. After another few seconds, she turned back to Alyssa and asked, "Do you have any toothpaste in your purse? You look like the kind of person who would."

Alyssa pulled her hands from under the water. "Excuse me?"

"I need toothpaste. I'm here with my husband's family, and they don't drink, but I sure need to when they are around, so I snuck to the bar and had two shots. They will be annoying as hell if I go back to the table smelling like bourbon."

Laughter and a flush came from the stall. "Amen, sister."

Makeup Woman continued as the woman left the stall and the restroom, "Do you have toothpaste I can use?"

Alyssa looked at the door as she dried her hands. *Where is Beth?* "Um, I think so."

Makeup Woman flashed a badge. "Mrs. Davis, I am Lieutenant Langhorne of Houston PD. Your friend Beth seems to think you are in some kind of trouble, perhaps with our Lieutenant Frazier. Care to tell me about it?"

Bless you, Beth. For the first time in hours, the constricting bands around Alyssa's chest loosened. After a deep breath, she relayed the events of the afternoon quickly, including the threats, the photos, and Frazier's plan for her tonight. Her fear returned as she remembered his face in the restaurant. Her shoulders slumped, and she looked away from Langhorne. "I have to hurry. He's waiting for me to come out. What do I do?" Alyssa looked up when Langhorne's hands gripped her shoulders, straightening her back with a soft lift.

"That depends on what you want, Mrs. Davis. If you want, we can detain him and you can file a complaint. Yours are serious allegations and could send him to prison for a long time. There is little proof that the interaction isn't consensual, just like he said, so he will likely go free."

Alyssa shuddered, shaking her head. Her chin quivered, but she fought back the tears. "No, no. He can't."

"The other option takes guts on your part. It's risky for you, but if it works, he will likely never get out of prison."

Alyssa's chin quivered some more, and this time, the tears fell. The nausea returned to her stomach. Then she felt the strong hands still holding her shoulders back and straight. "What do I do?"

"You said he wants to go to your room tonight? You're sure?"

"That's what he said. He kind of taunted me with it."

"Okay. You need to do three things. First, delay going to your room for at least two hours while we set up the surveillance.

Second, let him take you there after that time to do what he intends to do."

"What? No. Just arrest him now. You aren't any help at all."

"Nothing will happen. That is the third thing. Remember that you are safe. We will be watching and will not let him do anything to you. We will enter and arrest him as soon as we have evidence that he is extorting you for sex. Let me make that clear. We will not let him assault you. We just want to get his threats on tape. You will be safe, and you will put a piece of shit behind bars. Can you do those three things, Mrs. Davis?"

Alyssa stood straighter when Langhorne's hands squeezed tighter. She wiped her eyes. "Yes."

"I'll arrange it. With everyone already here, we can make this work right now. And Mrs. Davis, more than anything else, remember that we will be watching and you will be safe. Just get him to your room in two hours. You'd better go if he's waiting."

Alyssa nodded and moved toward the door.

Two steps down the hall, Frazier stepped from an alcove beside her. "Took you long enough. I almost posted the photos for making me wait."

Alyssa stopped to look him in the eye. "Some nasty shit I had in my mouth has made me nauseous all evening. I had to deal with it, or would you prefer I puke on your shoes?"

Frazier laughed. "Now that you feel better, go finish your supper. You will need your strength tonight."

Alyssa and Emma sat a while after settling the bill. Emma started to look sleepy. *Shit. She will need to go to bed soon. I can't take her to my room or hers because of Frazier.* Alyssa looked at the clock on the wall. *It hasn't been two hours yet.* Frazier looked nonchalant lingering at the bar, which frightened Alyssa. "Would you like to sit on a couch, sweetie? I could tell you a story."

Emma yawned. "Okay." She reached up when Alyssa stood.

Alyssa picked up the tot, carrying her to a lobby sitting area. Alyssa chose a couch against the wall.

Seeing a couple of cops sitting nearby let a spark of confidence ignite in Alyssa's chest before Frazier took up a seat only two chairs away. A chill shuddered Alyssa's spine, yet a drip of sweat rolled down her side. Her hope for a happy ending tonight flagged, and frantic heat spread through her as she glanced around the room. She felt sweat on her abdomen but let Emma snuggle close. She hadn't told a bedtime story in years, and hoped she remembered one. Having Frazier nearby wasn't helping her concentration.

Before the big bad wolf had arrived at Grandma's house, Emma's head slid into Alyssa's lap. Alyssa stroked the girl's hair as her eyes closed. Alyssa watched Emma sleep, remembering when her kids had done the same. Her mind wandered to dark places. *I wonder if I'll see them again. The cops may be ready for Frazier, but they all have guns. What if someone starts shooting? What if Frazier has a knife? How can I get out of this without going through with it?* She focused on Emma. She felt the warm head in her lap. *She will only protect me while I sit here. Her dad will be back soon. I need to be ready then.*

Alyssa sat as the lobby emptied. She was unsure how long; it could have been thirty minutes or two hours. Her stomach knotted ever tighter the longer she sat, but she could neither see a clock nor wanted to. *If I could talk to Robert, if I had my phone, it would all be better. I'll call him the minute this is over. If I can.*

Only two people remained in the lobby when one of the desk staff walked over, accompanied by Mr. Hanes in a cast and on crutches.

Alyssa shook Emma. "Emma, your daddy's here."

The little girl roused slowly until her eyes settled on the tall man on crutches. "Daddy!" She hugged his good leg.

"Told you I'd be back soon. Did you have a good time?"

"Yes. We played tag, and go fish, and I had chocolate milk with dinner!"

Alyssa fished the girl's cards out of her purse. "Do you want these, Emma?"

"Oh, I made you some get-well cards." She thrust the cards at her father.

"Those look great, sweetie. Can you carry them? My hands are full." He shifted his gaze to Alyssa. "Thank you for keeping her. You were a real lifesaver. I can't imagine someone being so kind as to babysit a stranger's little girl. I hope she wasn't a bother."

"She was just what I needed today, Mr. Hanes. I'm glad she and I became friends. How is your leg?"

"A clean break, according to the doctors. Most of the time was spent waiting. It hurts, but the painkillers help. Best of all, Emma is going to take good care of me."

"I know she will. Emma, can you get your daddy up to your room, and then get in bed yourself?"

"I will. Alyssa?"

"Yes, sweetie?"

"I liked staying with you. It was fun."

Alyssa knelt to hug the girl. "I thought so, too, Emma. Now get your daddy to your room and take good care of him."

⁂

Emma and her dad hobbled to the elevator. Alyssa leaned back and rubbed her temples. *They need to get on the elevator before this vermin and I walk over.* Frazier looked over his phone and coughed. The knot in Alyssa's stomach rose to her throat. Her breathing accelerated. *Here goes. Oh god, here goes.* She went to the elevator without a glance at Frazier. He followed five seconds later. Both got in the car when the doors opened.

"Are you going to make the smart choice, or do you begin to worry which one sneaks up on you first: Capps or those pictures you posed for me?"

Alyssa sighed and showed resignation on her face. "Let's go. I'll do it, you pig."

"Hit the button for your floor."

Alyssa swiped her room key and pressed eighteen.

"Now hit twenty."

The knot in her throat burst, sending chills through her entire body. Fear manifested as an ache over her heart. Sweat popped on her brow and trickled down from her armpits. If he took her to twenty, she would be alone. "What's on twenty?"

"Everything you ever dreamed of. You are in for a real treat when we get there. Now hit the button."

"I'd be more comfortable in my room. I could put on some lingerie for you."

"Hit twenty. We're going to my room, and you will be naked, not in lingerie."

"Come on. If I have to do this, don't you want to make it fun?"

He shoved her against the wall of the car and hit the twenty button himself. "Bitch, you are going to get fucked and do whatever else I say. You are gonna have fun because of my cock, and your sweet ass will make it fun for me."

Before the elevator reached eighteen, Frazier gripped Alyssa's upper arm behind her back. The doors opened and closed with no noise. They rode to twenty and walked to 20011 without Frazier releasing her. He threw her inside before locking the door and flipping the latch.

Alyssa swept the room with her eyes. Where she had an

adjoining-room door, this room had a bare wall. The curtains were closed. A backpack sat on the desk beside a small tripod. The king-size bed was disheveled. The smell of semen fouled the air. *Oh fuck. It's going to be a long night. Nobody knows I'm here, and nobody's coming to rescue me.*

Frazier remained between her and the door as he took out his iPhone and put it on the tripod. "I'll make a little reminder of our fun together. I'll jack off to it for years. And if you ever say anything, a perfectly edited copy will appear on the internet. I'll make sure it shows your face when you come." He aimed the phone at the bed. "If you unlock your phone, you can have a memento too."

Not a video! Alyssa swallowed. "No video. I'll fight you tooth and nail if you try to film this. It will look like the rape it is."

Frazier bounded to her and punched her breast hard. Alyssa's legs buckled from the pain. She fell onto the bed, and Frazier was on top of her, holding her chin in one hand. "No bruises on that pretty face of yours, but I have other ways to make you understand who is in control. Do what I say or there will be more pain. I'm making a video. Stop arguing, or I'll live stream it right now."

Alyssa nodded, then he rose and helped her stand.

"Take your clothes off. Let's get started." Frazier put his service weapon in the safe and locked it. He noticed Alyssa watching. "Hoping to get this? I'm not that stupid." He pulled the handcuffs from his belt. "These though. You'll get these. Get those clothes off."

Alyssa hesitated. He grabbed the front of her shirt and yanked, popping off the remaining buttons, leaving it gaping and torn. Alyssa stood, stunned and crying. Frazier gripped her bra and tugged, breaking the front clasp and leaving the cups dangling to the side of Alyssa's breasts. He grabbed both shoulders and turned her around, then jerked the remnants of the torn clothing down her arms. He cuffed her hands behind her back. The cold metal pinched her wrist bones, and she yelped.

"There. You know I'm in charge. You can't fight me. You know that if you don't do what I say, I'll let Capps out to hunt you both, and your friends and family will love the snapshots of your Houston vacation. Now we can fuck until you can't even walk."

He turned her around to paw her breasts. His rough touch sent shocks from the breast he had punched, and Alyssa moaned. "Told you you'd like it." He stepped back. "I guess you can't do this," he sneered as he removed his clothes. When he was naked, he pulled his already hard dick a couple of times. He pushed her shoulders down. "Let's start with that blow job you owe me."

Alyssa knelt beside the bed, crying. *He smells awful, and he's so hairy. At least I can't see him clearly. Fuck, I bet he shows me the video when we are done.* Alyssa's mind went to another place. She took a deep breath and clenched her teeth. Her spine stiffened, and the butterflies in her stomach became molten lead. Her eyes narrowed, and the tears stopped. *I won't do this. I'm going to bite off that dick, and we will see what happens. Somebody will come to see what the yelling is about. God. Get ready for this. I'll have to be quick before I vomit.*

With a crash and men's voices yelling, the door burst open. Alyssa saw flashlight beams before Frazier was tackled to the ground by three men. A lady in a bulletproof vest jumped across the bed, landing between Alyssa and the struggling men, and held Alyssa's face tight to her chest. Within a few seconds, the sounds of the struggle stopped, and the lady relaxed her grip on Alyssa, keeping her hands tight on her shoulders. "Are you hurt?" Langhorne asked as she pulled back and looked over Alyssa's exposed body.

"He hit me. He handcuffed me." Alyssa's voice was soft but

steady. Her preparation to fight back burned within her, and she remained steeled for violence.

"I need a handcuff key and a blanket here, now please," Langhorne yelled over her shoulder. Someone removed the handcuffs before rubbing her wrists gently where the cuffs had been. A blanket draped over her shoulders. Alyssa pulled the edges close around her chest.

"I'm Lieutenant Langhorne. Do you remember me from the bathroom?" Alyssa nodded. "I am with our Special Victims Division. I'm going to stay with you until everything is over and you are safe. Do you understand?"

Alyssa nodded. "Yes. Thank you."

"He can't hurt you. Neither can Ms. Capps; isn't that what he threatened you with? She's in jail. Nobody can hurt you. You can feel safe. I have to ask, did he rape you or touch you in any way other than hitting?" Langhorne kept her arm around Alyssa.

"He fondled my breasts, but you broke in before he could do more."

"Mrs. Davis, we have crisis counselors on staff. They are available twenty-four hours a day, seven days a week. One is waiting in the lobby. Would you like me to call her up to talk with you?"

Alyssa pondered it. "Not tonight. Can I reach her later if I need her?"

"Yes. Any time. I'll give you her number."

Noise in the corner made Alyssa raise her head for the first time. She saw Frazier being lifted, cuffed and naked. Blood colored his face, and he had tampons stuck in his nose. He glowered at Alyssa.

She straightened her back and glared back. "You're lucky they came. I was going to bite off your dick." She turned to Langhorne. "The dumb fucker recorded the attack. You should have everything you need"—she looked where the phone had been on the desk—"if you can find his phone. He was black-mailing me with pictures he took through my window, and he recorded a video of what he was doing here too. He took my phone. Can I have it back?"

Langhorne turned to the room. "Find his phone. We don't want it damaged or remotely accessed. Get it to the lab, get the evidence off it, and delete all photos and videos from his phone. And find Mrs. Davis's phone for her." She turned back to Alyssa. "You know, biting off his dick would have been tough. They bleed a lot. You would have gotten a mouthful."

"Better than a mouthful of what he intended." Alyssa sput-tered a laugh at her own joke. She was regaining her mental footing. "How did you find me? You said you would be at my room."

An officer handed Alyssa her phone. "The lobby officer radi-oed that you were in the elevator, but you didn't arrive. Your friend Beth pulled up the elevator cameras that showed you exited on twenty. We came as fast as we could. She has been on top of us tonight, making sure you weren't exposed. She's a good friend to you."

As if on cue, Alyssa heard, "Let me in! Is she all right?" She saw Beth jumping to look into the room over the officer's shoulder.

"We can't let her into the crime scene, but we can take you out. Do you feel up to walking?"

"Can I get dressed first?"

Langhorne turned to the officers. "Can we have the room please?"

The officers stood outside the broken door, facing outward.

Alyssa picked up the torn shirt and bra, then handed them to Langhorne. "These look more like evidence than clothes. Do you need them? They aren't wearable."

"I can take them if you don't want to see them any longer. That is pretty common." She held up a black bag. "Is this your purse?"

"I don't want any reminders." She pulled the blanket tighter around her. "Yes, that's my purse."

"I know you weren't in here long, but can you please see if anything is missing?" She held the bag open in front of Alyssa.

"Isn't all this evidence?" Alyssa stopped short of reaching into her purse.

Langhorne shook her head. "He took them from you, but we have all we need. If we want to ask about anything on your phone, we can reach you, but it's more important that you have it for now."

"It felt like I was here a long time." Alyssa reached into her bag.

"I bet it did. It's over now."

Alyssa pulled her hand out of her purse with a shake of her head. "Nothing appears to be missing."

"I'll carry this for you." They reached the door. "Coming through, gentlemen." The cops parted and stood back.

Beth leaped to Alyssa and enveloped her. She asked through flowing tears, "Are you all right? Did that fucker hurt you? I was so worried."

Alyssa snaked a hand out the blanket and hugged Beth back. "I'm okay. They got him." They embraced until Beth got out all her tears. None of the cops moved or said a word. The few hotel guests who opened their doors were discreetly hustled back inside.

When Beth raised her head, she looked at Langhorne. "Where does she go now?"

Langhorne turned to Alyssa. "Mrs. Davis, would you like to go to your room? You can get fresh clothes."

"Yes. I feel most on display."

Beth snugged Alyssa's waist. "I'm not leaving you for a moment."

As they approached the elevator, Taggart made eye contact with Langhorne, who nodded. "Mrs. Davis, are you all right?"

"I am, thank you. You guys really saved my day."

"Thank Beth. She spoke to us when she brought our food, and she stayed on top of us all night. That said, you were quite brave keeping that little girl in this kind of situation. And you helped us catch a sleazebag cop. You are a real hero. The public will never know—we don't release victims' names—but we will know, and we thank you."

"Thank you. I was just trying to find a way out. You all and Beth gave me that, and I won't forget."

Langhorne ended the pause in the conversation. "Let's get you to your room, Mrs. Davis. You will be more comfortable there."

In the elevator, Alyssa turned to Langhorne. "Do we need to go to the processing station?"

"No. I can take your statement in your room." She renewed eye contact with Alyssa. "The crisis counselor is still downstairs. Now that you have had time to settle down, would you like me to call her? She can witness the statement, or I can call another female officer to witness."

"That sounds good. The counselor can hear my story at the same time. I'd like to finish this and get to bed. It's been a shitty day."

↤

Alyssa went to the bathroom to dress. Langhorne waited by the bed while Beth opened a bottle of water. Alyssa emerged wearing a T-shirt and a pair of shorts with socks. Beth put her arm around Alyssa's waist and handed her the bottle of water.

Alyssa froze. "Would you please close the curtains? That bastard photographed me through the window."

Langhorne closed the curtains, then answered when the crisis counselor knocked. Beth and Alyssa sat on the bed, leaning against the headboard.

"Hello, Mrs. Davis." She stepped close enough to offer her hand to Alyssa. "I'm Janice Walker, one of the crisis counselors for the HPD Special Victims Division. I am so sorry that this has happened to you. I am here to help you address the feelings and repercussions of this attack, as much or as little as you would like. I understand you would like me to listen while you provide your statement?"

Alyssa took Walker's hand. "Yes. I'd like to only tell it once. I don't know if I'll need counseling after, but I'd like to tell the story, then go to bed."

"I understand. I'll be available to you for the foreseeable future, so call at any time. I'll put my card on the desk."

Walker sat in the armchair between the bed and the window. Langhorne sat at the desk. She opened a notepad and placed a small cassette recorder in front of her. "Mrs. Davis, is it all right to record your statement? It can be written if you prefer."

"Recorded is fine."

Langhorne stated some preliminary information for the record. "Mrs. Davis, please describe what occurred between you and Lieutenant Frazier today. Please be as thorough and complete as possible. If you need a break, just say so and we will take one."

"Yes. Well…" After her initial hesitation, Alyssa let the entire story flow. She spared no details about the blow job in the ballroom and the threats against Beth and Emma. She stopped only once for a drink. "I had decided the only way to get help was to bite off his dick, and I mentally prepared to do that. Then you guys burst in. I guess that's it." She sagged onto Beth and rested her head against the headboard.

"Thank you, Mrs. Davis." Langhorne turned off the recorder. "What Taggart said is true. You are a hero. You were unbelievably brave. The world will never know, but we know. Every cop on that arrest team was impressed. With your friend Beth too." She looked at the young blonde. "We will need a statement from you as well. We can get it in the morning. For now, stay with your friend."

"Mrs. Davis, I hear too many of these stories, often more horrible than yours. Nonetheless, I am quite impressed with you. You are a tough lady, and you handled a tough spot." Walker placed a hand on Alyssa's ankle and looked in her eyes. "You are tough, you have friends here, and you will go home to your family soon. That is all good for your recovery. Please know, sometimes toughness isn't enough. If you feel guilt, despair, or fear, remember that I am the backstop to your support network. There are others who feel the way you will feel, and I help them too. I can help you get on your feet if you stumble emotionally. Please call whenever you need my ear, any time day or night."

"Thank you. Thank you both. It's been a bad night, but it would have been so much worse without you. Mrs. Walker, I will indeed call soon just to check in. I feel relief tonight. I'll check in to make sure I don't miss anything you might see."

"That sounds fine." She looked at Langhorne, who was closing her notebook. "Let's let these two get some rest. We can show ourselves out."

Beth locked the door behind them, then checked the adjoining-room door as well. She returned to the bed and held Alyssa as she wept herself to sleep.

9
FRIDAY

ALYSSA WOKE IN a room lit only by the sliver of sunlight prying between the curtains. She was pressed against a warm body, her head on a bare breast. She was still dressed. A gentle hand caressed her hair.

"Good morning," she heard from above her head.

Alyssa realized she was with Beth and hugged her tightly but didn't look up. "Good morning. It is going to be a good morning, isn't it?"

"Yes, it is. How do you feel?"

"Like I slept in my clothes. How did I get this way?"

Beth smiled. "You cried yourself to sleep last night after the cops left. I took your socks off, but I didn't know how you would feel if you woke up naked, so I left you clothed. As you can see, I undressed. You are a hot snuggler."

"Oh, I'm sorry. I bet you didn't get any sleep…"

"Wait. You are a great bed partner, Alyssa, and I slept fine. I enjoyed having you hold me in the night once I undressed." She raised Alyssa's chin and gazed into her eyes. "I'm glad you are okay. I was so worried that he would hurt you, that we wouldn't get to you in time, that something would go wrong. I'm sorry it went as far as it did."

Alyssa maintained eye contact. "Don't be sorry, Beth. You recognized my distress and acted to help. I owe you my life. If you hadn't told the cops, he'd probably still be raping me. You said you knew cops like him in California. I'm sorry you did."

"Me too. There weren't many, but a few. Most of the cops I knew wanted me to get clean and stay out of trouble, but a few thought they could exploit my weaknesses. They were right most of the time. I've fucked or sucked in more than a few squad cars to stay out of jail. It gave me a feel for the good ones. That's how I picked out Taggart."

"I hate that you knew bad cops, Beth." Alyssa dropped her eyes, then returned to Beth's gaze. "Maybe the silver lining was that you were able to help me with this one. I hope that makes it hurt a little less."

"You know, I hadn't thought about it that way, but it does. It feels good to have helped you. Maybe I owe those bad cops a thank-you."

"Let's not go that far. Maybe an anniversary card for their sentencing dates?"

Beth's smile dimmed. "Maybe one day. We got this one."

Alyssa's head returned to Beth's chest, relaxing with the even rise and fall of her breathing. *We got this one. The cops call me a hero. Some hero, getting photographed by the dirtiest cop in the hotel because your libido ran rampant this week. Almost raped because of poor impulse control?* Alyssa had lived her whole life in control. This week, boredom, loneliness, despair, and libido had cast that aside. *You thought you were only risking your marriage as you decided to have your little experiment, but this could have been worse.*

But could it have been? Being raped by Frazier would have been terrible, disgusting, violating, but the people who love me would have gotten me through it. They would have been with her to make her feel safe and protected, they would have distracted her when she got depressed, and Robert would have never left her side.

Now... I don't know. Robert will protect and support me when he hears about Frazier. Then he'll feel angry, followed by guilty that he wasn't here to protect me. Telling him about the rest of the week's activities would focus all that energy on Alyssa. Frazier actually made it worse; he was the fire that her fucking around got thrown onto like gasoline. *Was it worth it?*

The sharp fingernails tracing through her hair shot chills down Alyssa's spine. She gasped, then smiled after the shudder passed. *It was. This young woman scratching my head is one of the reasons Frazier was unable to rape me. She helped me because we slept together. I am safe today because she felt something for me after we fucked. Paul saved me from that knife-wielding maniac. I would have been defenseless if I hadn't been with him and Kate.*

Beth's warmth crept into Alyssa's chest, growing with every memory she recalled. Alyssa took a deep breath, feeding the fire in her chest, and sat up. *But in the end, I'm safe because I was ready to fight him, die if it came to that, rather than be a victim. I threw aside that victimized feeling and became a new, stronger woman in that moment. I was strong enough to face Frazier alone and do what I had to do.* Alyssa thought about going home. *And I'm strong enough to face the demons I have created.*

Beth pressed her hand flat between Alyssa's breasts. "How do you feel?"

Alyssa placed her hand atop Beth's. "I feel lots of things.

I'm angry at Frazier. I'm grateful to you and the cops. I like the confident, resolute person I became when I decided to fight him. Most of all, I have hope that things will get better, because I am going home today."

"Well, then, tough lady, let's get you ready to go."

"Wait." Alyssa pulled Beth up for a soft, slow kiss. "I haven't thanked you for helping me. Can we spend a little more time together first? Please?" *I want to feel good one last time before...*

Alyssa pulled her T-shirt over her head. She got tangled in the covers while removing her shorts and kicked them to the foot of the bed. She kissed Beth, and Beth cupped Alyssa's breast. Alyssa slid her hand across Beth's stomach in ever-widening circles while they kissed. Their soft caresses became gropes as hands gripped tighter. Alyssa climbed on top of Beth and slid two fingers into her while thumbing her clit. Beth pinched both of Alyssa's nipples and stretched them out from Alyssa's body, the pain becoming pleasure as it traveled from her nipples to her pussy. Alyssa rose, moved both hands to Beth's nipples, and pulled them just as Beth had done to her, resulting in the hot blonde arching her back, rubbing her pussy against Alyssa's.

Shocks exploded from Alyssa's clit. She had never felt a burst of pleasure like that before, and she needed more. Alyssa ground against Beth, seeking the explosion again and again. Each woman had her left leg between the other's legs, grinding their pussies together harder and faster. Alyssa pulled Beth's right leg straight up beside her face and kissed and licked the inside of Beth's ankle while she humped her. Both sets of lips chafed against the stubble, the sensations colliding behind Alyssa's undulating belly. After some adjustments, they established a rhythm of bumping their clits together on every stroke, Alyssa moaning as the shocks and the scratching, the bumping, and the pressure built the tingle inside her.

Beth came first, slopping fluid out of her lips onto Alyssa's leg and her own ass. She yelled as her leg pushed Alyssa backward, only intensifying the contact between them.

Alyssa followed right behind, soaking their pelvises further. Her back arched, but when she released, she fell forward onto Beth's chest. They lay there sweating, gasping for breath, allowing their bodies to regain some strength. "Oh my. I've never done that before, but it was wonderful. That felt amazing," Alyssa said.

Beth opened her eyes. "Oh god, yes. I haven't done that before either, but I will again. Every time we pressed together, it was like a mini orgasm. I'm glad we played one last time." She held her blink closed a moment. "I know this trip has been rough for you, but I am so happy we met. You have been a fantastic lover, and a better friend. I am sad to see you go."

"I feel the same way, Beth. Maybe because this week has been rough, you and the other friends I've made are so important to me. You've helped me see who I want to become. You have no idea the impact you've had. The others, too, but you most of all. I can't thank you enough." She kissed Beth, then grinned. "I do know which hotel I'm staying at each time I come to Houston!"

"We will always have a room for you." They lay together another few minutes before getting ready. Alyssa's flight wasn't until late afternoon, but she wanted to leave early to allow for traffic. She was packing and had not dressed when Beth went downstairs. Just a few minutes later, Alyssa's phone dinged with a text notification. Alyssa collapsed on the bed, crying.

⁓

"Hey, Baby. Can't wait to see you today," Alyssa heard when her husband, Robert, answered her call. She had regained her composure enough to call, but she lost it again when she heard his voice.

She sobbed into the phone.

"Baby? Are you okay? Tell me what is wrong, Baby. I'm here."

She cried into the phone, "They canceled the fl…the fl…," and started bawling again.

"They canceled the flight? Oh, Baby, I'm sorry. Just let it out for a minute, and we will see what we can do." Robert waited for Alyssa to settle, breaking the silence with soft, comforting words and assurances that he would help her, underpinned by the clicks of his keyboard.

When Alyssa could breathe again, she said, "I was packing up, and I got this text. The airport still doesn't have water, so they can't get flights in or out. I'm bumped to Sunday. I don't think I can stay here that long."

"It's okay, Baby. Let me take care of you. Tell me about it while I find you a way out."

"Robert, you have to work and take care of Clay. I know how busy you are this week. We've barely had a chance to talk."

"Relax. When I heard you sob, I cleared my calendar for the rest of the day. Clay is eighteen. He doesn't need me to take care of him. Even if he did, he'd want me to get his mom home."

"But your work…"

"Relax. I told you. I cleared my calendar. I told people that something came up at home, and they were happy to reschedule. Look, I knew from the first sound I heard that my workday was over. You come first. You're emotionally drained and stuck. I'll take care of this. You sit back and relax."

"Oh, Babe." Alyssa sobbed again. "Thank you. I knew you could fix this."

"Why don't you tell me about being in the hotel while I look for a way home?"

Should I tell him about Frazier? He couldn't get to her any more than she could get to him. He would only worry, or worse, fester.

Later. When I'm home. Everything can come out then. "It isn't good, but it is better here than the other hotels in town, according to the news. We have power, we have bottled water to drink and buckets to flush with, and we have food. The staff has done everything they can to take care of us. But you bring Susan back to campus the next time there is any chance of bad weather. I'm so ready to be home."

"I know, Baby. I'm ready to have you here. I'm sorry you've had to endure this, but it will be over soon."

If you only knew what I've endured. She felt a smile tease the corners of her mouth even as a knot grew in her stomach. "I knew you could help me, Babe."

"I see some flights out of Houston. Let me call to make sure the website is accurate. I'll call you right back when I'm done."

﹏

Alyssa hugged her knees to her chest and lay on her side. She woke to her phone ringing. "Hello?"

"Hey, Mom. How are you holding up?"

"Susan? Honey, I'm fine. How are you? Does the school still have power?"

"Everything is good here, Mom. Dad told me they canceled your flight. I'm sorry. To think we drove fast across the country so I could go to class on Monday, and classes have been canceled all week. At least I've been around my friends. You have been alone."

"I've made a couple of friends, all stuck here together. It will be good to get home though."

"Do you want to get dinner together tonight? One of the guys on my floor said that driving is not bad, but there are still a lot of stoplights malfunctioning. Ruth's Chris has some reservations on Open Table. The website says their power was restored. I can come get you."

"Sweetie, do you think it's safe?"

"Mom, it's fine. Dad taught me to drive in winter weather, I know how to treat a nonfunctioning stoplight, and you need a boost. I'll come get you. Come on. It is the least I can do. Dad's paying, of course."

"I haven't had a shower in days…"

"That's half of Houston, Mom. You will be fine."

"Okay. It sounds great. It will be good to see you."

"The reservation is for six o'clock. I'll pick you up at five thirty."

"See you then. Be careful driving, sweetie. Love you."

"Love you, Mom."

It will be good to get away. Now if Robert can just get me out of here. I'm going to have to tell him everything, but I want him to make me feel at home first. I want him to come inside me and tell me he loves me. I need that to wash this week out of my mind. Then I can tell him everything that happened, and try to convince him to stay married.

∽

Alyssa had moved to the chair by the window by the time Robert called back. "What did you find out?"

"You are on a flight to Charlotte tomorrow at two thirty. You aren't flying all the way home, but Clay and I will come get you."

"Babe, you will have to drive too far. I'll just wait—"

"Stop." Robert paused a moment. "Alyssa, stop objecting. Charlotte isn't that far, and it's time you came home. Aren't you ready to be out of there?"

"Yes."

"Then get on that flight to Charlotte."

"Why would American be unable to fly me home but they can fly me to Charlotte?"

"They can't. Southwest can. Hobby Airport opened today with limited service. Southwest is the main airline there. I booked you on Southwest."

"We don't need to spend that money…"

"Baby, I don't have a superpower, but I do have enough money to buy a second airline ticket when the first one doesn't work. You are coming home tomorrow. I'll see you in the Charlotte airport. I'll be the one with the big hug waiting."

Relief washed through Alyssa from her head down. Her shoulders relaxed. She sighed, then wept a few tears. *I knew he could find a way. I love him so much.* Alyssa sat straighter and twirled a lock of her hair. "I'll be there. I hope you have something else big for me too. Doesn't the superhero always get the girl?"

"That's for after we get home. The airport may not be the best place to get too celebratory." He chuckled. "I'm glad at least some of your spirits are still up."

"My hero has come to the rescue. You sent me a dinner date and plane tickets. You always save me when I need it. I love you, Babe. More than I can say. I can't think of a better way to say thank you."

"I'll always be here to save you, Baby. And there is no need to say thank you. Susan got you to go to dinner? Good. You need it."

"I do. I didn't realize how much until she called. I can't wait."

Robert laughed. "I bet. Ruth's Chris after several days of only burgers would get me excited too. Sounds like their suppliers recovered faster than the hotel's."

"I can't wait to see Susan." Alyssa laughed right back at him. "Some steak will be nice too."

They talked a while longer as Robert kept Alyssa focused on home, memories, and enjoying time together. The topics ranged but stayed away from all things related to Houston and hotels. After they hung up, Alyssa sat smiling in her chair until getting ready for dinner.

↩

The two of them had an easy ride to Ruth's Chris. It was brightly lit, though the shops across the street were dark. The limited menu still had filet mignon, so they ordered and drank their bottles of water. Susan had had a fun week with no classes, but she could see the work piling up as they got behind schedule. The steaks were perfect, and the two women wolfed them down. Alyssa saw two cops sitting across the dining room. *I should tell her about Frazier. It may be in the news. Langhorne said they wouldn't release my name, but what if Frazier does through some sleazy attorney?* Reporters would not take long to find Susan once Alyssa's name was public. *She deserves better than some reporter sticking a mic in her face coming out of class. Susan just needs to keep it to herself until I can talk with Robert.*

The waiter came with more water. Alyssa had an idea. "Sir, could I please order two more filets to go? Medium rare? I would like to say thank you to a couple of important people."

After the waiter left, Susan asked, "Mom, who earned filet mignon? And how? Just how have you spent your week? We have talked about mine, but it sounds like yours was better than you let on."

"Honey, it has been a tough week, and I wouldn't have made it through without some good people. I need to tell you about some of it because it may become public, and I don't want some reporter to catch you by surprise. Waiting on those steaks will give us time to talk. The only thing I ask is that you not talk about it with anyone before I get home and discuss it with Dad."

"Okay." Susan looked her mother in the eyes. "I'm listening."
Alyssa told Susan about the incident with Frazier. She left out
some details but provided enough that Susan knew the extent to
which Frazier had assaulted her. Susan held her mother's hand
and silently wept but didn't interrupt. Alyssa focused on how Beth
and Langhorne had worked to save her. She thought a moment
before telling Susan how she had planned to end the encounter
in Frazier's room. "If any cops needed to contact you, I don't
know why, but if they did, I wanted you to know which ones I
trust, and that you might see this on the news. They promised to
withhold my name, but some attorneys use the press more than
the courtroom. I didn't want you to be surprised if it came out."

Susan lunged from her chair and crushed her mother in a
hug. She kept repeating, "Oh, Mom, I'm so sorry," in Alyssa's ear.

Alyssa held her daughter and whispered back, "It's going to
be okay, sweetie."

When Susan sat back in her chair, her eyes were red and
puffy, and she needed to wipe her nose. "Mom, how did you get
through that? You must have been terrified."

"It was hard, and I had some friends help me. As awful as
it was, it made me tougher. I mean, I was going to bite off that
smelly dick."

Susan burst into laughter, and Alyssa joined her. Susan
straightened. "Would you really have done it?"

"Yes. I thought I was going to be at his mercy all night. I
couldn't bear the thought of him, well, soiling me like that. I
decided that I would take my chances with him hurt and yelling.
It didn't come to that, but I had mentally readied myself for it."
She smiled. "I was visualizing rare steak."

"You hate rare steak."

"I do. I said bite it off, not eat it."

The two women again burst into laughter.

❧

As they pulled into the hotel's portico, Alyssa received a text. "It's from Beth. She is checking on me because I'm not at dinner."

"I want to meet her. Ask her to come out, please?"

In the lobby, Beth walked over to Alyssa. Before Alyssa could introduce Susan, Susan grabbed Beth in a powerful embrace. "Thank you. Thank you for helping my mom. Thank you."

"Oh, honey, your mom has helped me so much more than I helped her. She is a special person."

"I know. That's why you are so important to me now. You helped her in the worst situation ever. I can't repay you enough. Thank you." Susan held the hug for a moment while she shed a few tears.

When Susan was breathing normally, Beth pulled back from the hug, smiling. "You must be Susan. Your mom has told me a lot about you." She wiped tears from Susan's cheeks with her thumbs. "She never mentioned how pretty you are. I guess she didn't want to brag. I can see how much you resemble her, inside and out."

Alyssa blushed but remained silent as the other two continued to meet each other.

"Thank you. If I end up half as great as my mom, I'll be blessed. Look at her. Even after all she's been through, with no showers, wearing the same clothes, she still looks great. So do you, I might add. You are even back there waiting tables, and you look great."

Beth's mouth fell open. "Oh gosh. I'd better get back. We are full of people, and we are still short some runners. I'm sorry, but I need to go. It was great to meet you. Please know that if you ever need a friend or a place to stay, we are here for you. You are always welcome."

"I'll remember that. Thank you—for everything."

Alyssa chimed in, "Beth, I have something for you and Mike, but I don't want to bring it through the restaurant. You are going to want it in the kitchen. Is there a back way in?"

"Ooh. Thanks! Go to the front desk and have them let you go through the back room. Keep going back and right, you will get to the kitchen."

Susan turned to Alyssa as Beth hustled back into the restaurant. "Mom, are you sure you are okay here? I can get you into the dorm, and you can use Tara's bed until she comes back to campus."

"Sweetie, as long as you can get me to the airport tomorrow, I'll be fine. Besides, your floor is coed. I don't think the boys want to pass an old mom going down the hall to the bathroom."

"Mom, a beautiful stranger walking around the dorm? Every boy on the hall would find an excuse to stay in the hallway just to watch you come back to the room."

"Are you sure *you* are okay staying there?" *That sounds like college guys. Always horny. Maybe they would want to ogle me too. Or something more.* Alyssa's nipples hardened.

Susan laughed. "These guys know how to mind their manners, but they are eighteen- to twenty-two-year-olds. They like beautiful women. Based on what I hear coming out of their rooms sometimes, they know what to do with them too. Usually, though, they just look. Kind of like you and Dad."

Alyssa started. "What do you mean, 'like me and Dad'?"

"Come on, Mom. Do you think we don't notice that Dad looks at every hot woman around us when we are out? And that you do the same to every hot guy? You have always told us that you and Dad believe getting married was no reason to stop appreciating the beauty of life. We know that means looking at beautiful people in addition to sunsets, you know. But the sunsets don't make you two all touchy-feely like the people do."

Alyssa stood silent a moment. *Sometimes those beautiful people really put us in the mood.* Alyssa's belly fluttered.

"Mom, close your mouth. I can't have shocked you that much."

"You did. You noticed that?" Alyssa felt the heat in her face as she blushed. "Well, we didn't stop living, did we?"

"I noticed, and I knew what it meant."

"You knew what it meant?" Alyssa covered her face with her hands.

Susan pulled them away and held them. "Mom, I went to school. I had the internet, and you trusted me. Kids said things at school about sex, and I verified it on the internet. It's amazing what kids got right, and also very wrong. Clay did the same thing, but he asked me about it too."

Alyssa hung her head and shook it, then looked up, smiling. "Yes, your father and I have an agreement to admire beauty in all its forms, including beautiful people." *My turn.* Alyssa gave an exaggerated wink. "And yes, sometimes that makes nights in the bedroom better, like tomorrow night will be." *He's going to hit that spot he always hits. So good. God, I'm getting really horny.*

"Mom!"

"It's my turn to shock you, huh?"

"Not shock, so much. I just didn't expect you to talk about it."

"Why? We've always treated you two like adults in conversation at home."

"That's true, but we never talked about your sex life with Dad. That's a little out there, even for our family."

"You brought it up. I'm glad you did though. Sex is an important part of a relationship, and I'm glad you know that Dad and I still enjoy it. I hope you will, too, with someone special."

"Mom, I also remember you and Dad talking about the need to have a 'toy' relationship or two along the way. That isn't someone special."

Alyssa blushed again. "Well, yes, we both believe that relationship experience is a good thing. Having a number of relationships during your single life helps you learn how to live in one, and how to identify the good ones versus the bad ones. But that doesn't mean that a 'toy' relationship can't also be special. It's just special for what it is. It isn't special like a marriage or serious relationship. It's special for being an opportunity to enjoy and learn sex for just sex, even if both of you know it will never be anything more." *Like what I've been doing this week.*

"You have thought a lot about this."

"Not really, sweetie. I just lived my life, and your dad has lived his, and we have talked about our lives, the parts before we got together and the parts since, many times. We've talked about what we wanted to teach you and Clay. One of those topics is relationships, and that includes sex. Well, I guess we have thought a lot about it." *Not as much as we are going to when I get home.*

"I'm glad you did. You shared a lot with us that our friends didn't get at home. It made for some strange and entertaining dinner conversation, but I feel like there is nothing we can't talk about because of it."

"That's right. No topic is off-limits. That's why we have always tried to treat you two as adults. We want to be a part of your lives beyond your childhood, and that starts with openness and respect."

"Mom, you and Dad will always be a part of my life. I love you, and I love the unique dinner conversations too much to give that up," Susan said with a wink. "Now all this sex talk makes me want to head back to the dorm and see what I can hear through the walls."

"Susan!" *You can start a lot by listening through the walls.*

"Openness and respect, right, Mom? Who knows? I might even meet the right 'toy' on the way to the bathroom," she giggled.

Alyssa laughed. "Fair enough. Good luck on your hunt. I'll see you tomorrow to go to the airport?"

"I'll be here at eleven o'clock. Love you, Mom."

"Love you, too, sweetie."

❧

Alyssa watched Susan drive away, then took the Ruth's Chris takeout bag to the front desk. She was surprised to see who was working. "Sonia? I didn't know you were on staff. I thought you were just Mike's wife." Alyssa's hand flew to cover her mouth. "I'm sorry, that didn't sound right."

Sonia laughed. "I understood your intent. I am 'just Michael's wife' most of the time, but I provide assistance when he is short-staffed. I am covering the desk while they serve dinner. You seem to have upgraded tonight," she said, pointing to the bag.

"It's actually for Beth and Mike, for being so good to me this week. I don't want to go through the dining room with it. Beth said I could go through the back to the kitchen. Can you let me through, please?"

"Your generosity and consideration set you apart. It is why we admire you. This way." Sonia smiled and led Alyssa through the door to the back room, then through another door into a long hallway with narrow windows on the outside wall. She stopped in front of one. "You should admire the way you look tonight. You have endured much, yet you exude class and beauty. Look at your reflection in the window."

Alyssa turned. This was the second time in a few minutes she had been called beautiful. She had not thought of herself that way since Susan was born. She put the bag down and stared, struck with what she saw. She tousled her hair and smoothed her shirt, emphasizing her firm breasts. She could see the hard nubs of her nipples pushing through her bra. Her skirt clung to her hips and thighs, giving her a sexy hourglass appearance, before stopping midthigh and showing her shapely legs. *I do look good, and I'm horny.* Alyssa slid her hands up her sides to cup her breasts, then closed her eyes as she massaged them. She was not surprised when she felt two breasts press into her back and a hand slide across her belly.

Sonia moved Alyssa's hair back and kissed her neck and ear. She opened the buttons of Alyssa's shirt below her breasts, and she slipped a hand inside, titillating the soft skin. Sonia slipped a second hand inside, letting this one drift up to hold a breast while she dove the other under Alyssa's skirt and into the waistband of her panties. *Her hands are strong like a man, but she caresses like a woman does.* "Mm-hmm," Alyssa moaned and reached behind to palm Sonia's mound through her pants.

Sonia pulled her hands out of Alyssa's clothes and spun her hips, planting a deep kiss on her mouth. She worked feverishly to unbutton the rest of Alyssa's shirt and unzip her skirt, letting both fall to the floor.

Alyssa worked just as quickly to slide Sonia's blazer and shirt off her shoulders and unzip her slacks. Sonia wiggled her hips to help Alyssa slide her pants down and gasped when she saw that Sonia wore no panties beneath them. She knelt to pull the pants to the floor and help Sonia step out of them, leaving her in only a bra and high heels. She kissed Sonia's thighs before she moved to plant just one kiss directly on Sonia's clit, then kissed her way up Sonia's deliciously tan body, pausing to lick her navel and the small jewel pierced into it. Alyssa rose farther and kissed and sucked Sonia's breasts through the lacy bra as she reached around to unfasten it. Sonia shrugged it off, and it joined the rest of her clothes on the floor. Alyssa sucked and nibbled Sonia's breasts, causing Sonia to moan low in her throat.

Sonia remained focused on Alyssa, unfastening her bra while Alyssa bent to suck her tits. It hung a while before Alyssa moved her hands from Sonia's hips to let it fall. Alyssa stood to kiss Sonia and cupped her ass with both hands, kneading and tugging the cheeks apart. Sonia grasped Alyssa's vulva on the outside of her panties, squeezing and rubbing it. The silky material created a smooth friction, and the gusset soaked the fluid that ran from Alyssa's lips. Sonia pinched Alyssa's nipple hard, causing Alyssa to yelp into Sonia's mouth while shocks flew from her nipple to her clit. They kissed and fondled each other a few minutes before Sonia slid the crotch of Alyssa's panties aside and slipped two fingers inside.

Alyssa's pussy gripped at Sonia's fingers, and Alyssa was satisfied to feel the hard fingers resisting her muscles, in contrast to Sonia thumbing her clit still outside the panties. The mix of sensation buckled Alyssa's knees, and Sonia gripped her pussy to support her. Alyssa's hips writhed as she ground into Sonia's hand, forcing the bony knuckles against her G-spot and the silky thumb against her clit. Shocks converged deep in her belly, heating the building orgasm to near boiling.

Alyssa slid her right hand to Sonia's pussy, giving the same treatment she received, matching Sonia's hand stroke for exhilarating stroke. She continued to hold Sonia's ass cheek, but she stretched her finger to rub Sonia's puckered back door. Sonia jerked her hips at the first touch, then pressed back into Alyssa's finger with a moan. Alyssa slid her finger inside, pressing against the fingers inside Sonia's pussy much like Mike had done when he fucked her ass so well two nights prior. Sonia's orgasm was instantaneous, her body shuddering before her legs weakened. Alyssa helped Sonia, panting, sink to her knees. When she recovered, Sonia dove in to lick Alyssa's slit.

She again spun Alyssa's hips and snatched her panties down

to her ankles. She reached up to push between Alyssa's shoulder blades, forcing her ass to jut out and her breasts and face to press against the cold window. The cold flowed through her breasts, but rather than dampening the orgasm close to boiling in her belly, it enraged it. The heat spread up to her ribs and down through her thighs. Sonia latched onto Alyssa's inner lips, driving her tongue as deep as she could into her juicy opening. Using one hand to flick Alyssa's clit, she used the other to keep Alyssa pressed against the glass.

Alyssa's legs began to tremble, and her breath grew more ragged as she neared orgasm on Sonia's tongue. She opened her eyes, and what she saw enchanted her. With her face against the glass, the light inside was blocked, so the window no longer mirrored what was happening inside. Instead, Alyssa was staring at a homeless Black man watching and masturbating his huge dick only inches from her. She shuddered, and her orgasm boiled over, feeling like hot water splashing inside her from the top of her vagina. She wailed and pressed her breasts harder against the glass, reveling in the coldness.

She blinked when the first spurt of cum shot out of the homeless man's cock, sounding like hard rain as it splashed. He continued to come, with spurt after spurt hitting the window in front of her face, with the last couple landing where her tits were pressed. Alyssa licked her tongue out on the window as if licking some of the cum off from the other side. The man wiped the head of his dick on the window, smearing the last few drops of his load across her nipple. Alyssa's spasming pussy clamped down on Sonia's tongue again in a second, smaller orgasm, or perhaps an aftershock of the first. She pressed her hands against the wall and lowered herself to the floor beside Sonia.

She rolled to face her and asked, "Did you know we were being watched?"

"Watched? By whom?"

"A homeless guy with a huge dick. Look at the window. It made me come a second time when he splattered the window by my face." Alyssa thought she was only pointing out the cum on the outside.

Sonia pointed to the imprint of Alyssa's tits and face on the dirty glass. Cum streaked the glass from the imprint of Alyssa's forehead down below the lifelike impression of her nipples. "Oh god. That is so arousing. They should never clean that window."

"I won't, if you will let me finish," said a voice from up the hallway.

Both women's heads snapped in the direction of the kitchen to see an older man wearing the hotel uniform. His dick was hard in his hand as he stared at the nude pair.

"Come here, Richard," said Sonia. "You may finish on me." She lay back on the cold concrete floor, spreading her legs and resting on her elbows.

Alyssa leaned against the wall, driving two fingers into her sensitive cunt with one hand and jiggling her clit as fast as she could with the other. *I am so turned on by this.*

Richard came over to stand above Sonia, stroking his cock steadily. He clearly did not want to rush this opportunity. Sonia licked her lips and watched his eyes, even as his roved over her body. He turned so he could watch Alyssa as well, still aiming his cock at Sonia. Alyssa humped her hips into her hands, and her head pressed against the wall as her mind reveled in the depravity of her actions.

Richard closed his eyes. "It's been so long," Richard said under his breath, as if to himself.

Sonia showed surprise, then recognition. She nodded. "How long since your wife passed?" Sonia asked, throwing off his rhythm.

Richard opened his eyes and stopped stroking. "Four years."

Sonia sat up. Taking his hand in hers, she resumed his stroking. "You have had no woman since?"

Richard opened his mouth to speak, then shook his head instead.

Alyssa couldn't stop herself before saying, "Would you like one now?" *Oh god, what did I just say?* She looked closer at Richard. *I am so horny, and his cock looks fine, if nothing special. I'll do this.*

Sonia smiled and asked, "Would you like two now?"

Richard's cock grew visibly harder as he shook his head. "Are you serious?"

Both women looked at him and said yes in unison.

Sonia looked at Alyssa. "I will get on all fours. You lie on your back on top of me. Let him see those beautiful breasts when he comes. Richard, our cunts will be lined up for you. Use them as you want."

Alyssa looked at Richard. "Come on my belly, Richard. Paint me."

They got in position, Alyssa supporting some of her weight on her toes. Richard lined up and plunged his cock into Alyssa's waiting pussy. It was about average in every way, with a tuft of gray hair above it and more adorning his balls. He took his time with her, letting the stimulation build a response within her. She rolled her head while he fucked her for a few strokes. He shifted his cock to Sonia's pussy and fucked her while Alyssa fingered herself, her thin fingers an inadequate replacement for the stretching sensation she wanted in her lips. Richard switched a few times, each time bringing Alyssa closer to another orgasm. Sweat trickled down her sides onto Sonia, whose back quivered with the exertion of holding both of them off the floor.

Richard shoved into Alyssa and quickened his pace, breathing heavily. His face turned red while Alyssa rubbed her clit and squeezed her pussy muscles, gripping at him, wanting to come before he finished. She lifted her legs and spread them wide as she arched her back for her orgasm. Sonia groaned with the additional weight but held up. Richard pulled his cock out of Alyssa and stroked it furiously, finally yelling out and shooting ropes of cum across Alyssa's tits, belly, and pussy. Alyssa lay in place until he finished, then slid off Sonia, who collapsed to the floor. Sonia rolled onto her back, panting. Alyssa climbed onto her and rubbed her cum-covered body onto Sonia's, listening to the soft squishing of his cum and their sweat mashing between them. "Since you offered first, here is Richard's finishing, also on you."

Sonia kissed Alyssa, holding her head in both hands, then rolled Alyssa onto the floor beside her. "Observe your accomplishment, Richard. Notice our beautiful bodies smeared with your cum. Look well. Ingrain the image into your memory. Memorize the details so you can properly recall the night you defiled a guest and your superior's wife in the back hallway, right by this window. Never clean this window. Never. This image of Alyssa's body in ecstasy will be a monument for us and a conversation piece for the staff. I will get aroused every time I see it. Will you get hard when you see it?"

"Yes, ma'am, I believe I will."

The three of them smiled at one another for a minute before beginning to dress. Richard refastened his pants and turned to leave.

Alyssa called after him. "Richard, wait. I want you to have this." She handed him her bra. "That window will eventually lose the image. I want you to have a more permanent memento of when you covered my breasts with your cum. Thank you for a great memory." She kissed him on the cheek and resumed dressing.

"Thank you, ma'am. I'll never forget. I hope you enjoyed it as much as I did." The bra created a large bulge in his pocket as he walked up the hall toward the front desk.

Sonia turned her naked breasts to Alyssa, offering them with her hands. "Would you like to clean them before we go to the kitchen?" Alyssa leaned to lick Sonia's nipples, then stood back and growled. "I don't think so. You should walk with me. Show your husband your shirt soaked with sweat and cum. He might reclaim you right there on the counter."

Sonia looked aghast and stepped back.

"Oh god. I'm sorry. I didn't mean to overstep. It's just, you told me how you like to reclaim each other and share stories…"

"You misunderstand. You did not overstep. Your idea is excellent, and I will do it. You shock me, however. The spontaneous sex in this hallway was quite a step for you, even though it could be explained as a momentary indiscretion. Surrendering your bra to Richard and walking into the kitchen wearing a cum-soaked shirt are more deliberate, overt actions. You have evolved since we first talked."

"I suppose that's true. This has been a stressful week, and my new friends have taught me ways to deal with that stress. I've become comfortable with my sexual changes, though things may revert when I get home." Alyssa buttoned her shirt and pressed it against her damp body, making it stick and hinting at her pink areolae against her white breasts. "Tonight, though, let's take these steaks to your husband and Beth."

Sonia buttoned her shirt, and Alyssa pressed it onto her, particularly her breasts, revealing more because Sonia's nipples were darker than Alyssa's and her shirt white. Sonia hung her blazer on a nearby door handle. "I see what Michael saw in you. You are unique in your qualities. Tonight may be his opportunity to reclaim me twice." They walked to the kitchen.

❧

Mike stood before a large flattop griddle full of burger patties. He focused on them until Sonia said, "Michael, someone has brought something for you."

Mike stared at the two women with his mouth open until hot grease popped onto his hand. "Wow. Sonia, I did not expect to see you in the kitchen tonight. Mrs. Davis, what a pleasant surprise."

Alyssa handed him the red bag. "I brought you and Beth a small token of appreciation from Ruth's Chris. You two have taken such good care of the guests, and me particularly, that I wanted to thank you. You may need to warm them; Sonia and I got sidetracked delivering them through the back hallway."

"I see that you did. Thank you. You didn't need to though. I already told you. You are a special person, and it has been our pleasure to treat you well." He looked at the young man toasting buns and the older woman cutting tomatoes across the kitchen from where he stood and lowered his voice. "You appear to have provided a second gift, based on Sonia's appearance. I can't wait to unwrap it." He leered at his wife. "Sonia, I'll get someone else to cover the desk. You need to wait for me in my office. Think about what you have done, but do not touch yourself. Remember, and imagine what I must do to reclaim you. I will see you in a while."

Sonia nodded to Mike and kissed Alyssa on the cheek. "Thank you for being magnificent. I will remember this night for a long time, much longer than that window will remind me. Have a good trip home. I hope your conversations there go well. Please return to the hotel when you are in town again."

"I will be back. And thank you…for everything." Alyssa turned to Mike as Sonia left. "I hope you like what she and I did. And really, thank you for all you have done. This could have been a disaster, and you made it all work out."

"It's thinning out, Mike," came from the dining room door as Beth hustled in. "Oh, Alyssa, I thought you had already come and gone." She looked closer as she approached the pair. She hissed at Mike, "Did you do this while you were cooking?"

"Not me. Sonia. She showed her the back way in, and they got delayed."

Beth smiled at Alyssa. "I knew she would delay you sooner or later." She looked at Alyssa's shirt and murmured, "Sonia didn't put cum on you though."

Alyssa smiled and whispered back, "If you come see me tonight, I'll tell you the story."

"I'm counting on it." Beth looked back at Mike. "We just sat the last six people. That only leaves twenty-seven who haven't been fed. We should be clear in an hour."

"That should be covered by what's on the griddle. Then we can enjoy what Mrs. Davis brought us." He pointed to the bag.

"Ruth's Chris? I love their steaks. Thank you!" The young blonde hugged Alyssa. "You didn't need to do that."

Alyssa smiled. "I know, but you two have been so good to me that I wanted to give a little something back."

"Thank you. I need to get these guests fed so I can dig in to that steak. Will you be in my room when I am done?"

"Why don't you come to mine? I need to pack."

"I'll see you there." Beth put three plates on a tray and headed to the dining room.

Alyssa gave Mike a hug. "Thank you again, Mike. I hope to see you when I come back to town."

"It would be my pleasure. Travel safe."

⸎

Alyssa gathered her clothes from around the room. She laid the least smelly of them on the desk to wear home. The rest she folded into her carry-on. She sat in the chair wearing only her panties. The TV was on for noise. Alyssa looked through the small opening she had left in the drapes and spun her rings. Her tight chest resisted the deep breaths Alyssa took to calm herself. *I'll know what kind of marriage I have by this time tomorrow. I want to be home, to be with Robert again. I miss him.* She ran her finger over her belly, the faint tingle in her nipples fighting to loosen her chest.

I want him inside me, making me come the way he does. I want him to spurt inside me, reclaiming me. Alyssa's finger traced lower, running along the waistband of her panties, more tingles penetrating toward her heart. *He'll hold me and tell me everything is all right. He'll tell me he loves me.* Alyssa's chest relaxed. The tightness shattered, and she took another deep breath.

Alyssa's stomach reassembled the tightness just banished from her chest, multiplying it with nausea that rose to her throat. Her eyes watered, and she felt a tear drip down her cheek. *Then I'll tell him everything. I'll ask his forgiveness; no, I'll beg for it. Then we will see what happens. I'll have to make it up to him, if he will let me. I'll do anything he wants if we can stay together.* Knowing the odds, Alyssa retched into her mouth, then washed down the remnants with some water and a deep breath. She stared out the window through blurred vision, waiting for the burn in her throat and her tears to dissipate.

Alyssa wiped her cheeks. A final shuddered breath reset her guts without untying the knot still churning there. *Will I? Do I want to give up this adventurous part of me? Do I want to stop feeling the way I have this week? Do I want to forgo the excitement of new lovers?*

A soft knock at the door roused Alyssa from her thoughts.

She padded across the room to open the door for Beth. "I thought you had a master key?"

"I do, but the security system logs when it is used on a guest room. I didn't want this visit on the logs."

"Why not?"

"Because someone auditing the logs would use the security videos to see when I left, and I plan on being here all night." She grasped Alyssa's face and kissed her hard before settling into a hug. Beth put her blazer and a pack of wipes on the desk before kissing Alyssa again.

Alyssa unzipped Beth's skirt and pushed it over her hips to let it drop to the floor. She spun Beth around and unbuttoned Beth's shirt, dropping it to the floor as well. Beth started to turn around, but Alyssa held her in place, gripping, then stroking over the smooth shoulders. She nibbled and kissed Beth's neck and ears as she removed her bra and cupped Beth's breasts, enjoying their weight. She ground into Beth's backside, moving her mound onto each firm cheek in turn. She scraped her nipples up and down Beth's back, noting and not quite noting the tiny imperfections providing the texture shocking her. She dropped her hand from Beth's breast to her vagina, rubbing it through her panties. Beth moaned, raised one hand to hold the back of Alyssa's head, and held the other on Alyssa's breast.

Alyssa told Beth, "Open your eyes." Beth stared at the reflection of her own body being loved and caressed by Alyssa in the full-length mirror. Alyssa slid her hand inside the waistband of Beth's panties to touch her needy sex, feeling its heat with her fingertips.

Alyssa watched Beth's eyes follow the movements of her hand as she spread her legs wider to give the older woman better access. Beth's mouth hung slack-jawed as she moaned. When Alyssa slid a finger between Beth's wet lips, Beth's belly rippled. Alyssa whispered, "You like that?" into Beth's ear before inserting her tongue and adding a second finger to her pussy. Beth ground her hips forward, making better contact between her clit and Alyssa's palm. Alyssa let her hump the heel of her hand and pressed her fingers harder and faster into Beth. Alyssa squeezed harder on Beth's breast and flicked the nipple. She watched as Beth's body lurched with pleasure, and the bottom of her lime-green panties darkened from a sudden gush of juices.

Beth's white chest flushed a deep-pink color that spread up her neck and cheeks to her ears. Her breath quickened, and she humped her hips against Alyssa's hand faster than Alyssa was curling her fingers inside her. Beth shifted her eyes along her reflection from Alyssa fingering her inside her panties to Alyssa's eyes. They held each other's gaze while Beth's orgasm buckled her knees and made the veins in her neck stand out during a silent scream. Alyssa supported Beth, shifting her upper hand across Beth's ribs and keeping her fingers inside her, flexing and straining her back and legs to hold Beth upright.

Beth took her weight back onto her feet and stood up, her eyes heavy-lidded and the hint of a smile on her lips. Alyssa relaxed her grip and let Beth turn for a slow kiss. "You really man-handled me. God, your fingers are magical. That was so good."

"Good thing you aren't heavier, or we would have fallen."

"As long as you kept fingering me, that would have been just fine."

"No. Watching you in the mirror while I pleased you was one of the most erotic things I've ever seen. It was like porn, with touch. I wouldn't have given up that view if my back had broken."

"God, yes. I couldn't take my eyes off your hand, even though it was inside my panties. Then when I looked into your eyes, it got even better."

"Yes, it did." Alyssa nudged Beth backward. "Let's get in bed."

The two women lay down on their sides, facing each other, each perching her head on one hand while lazily tracing her partner's body with the other. Alyssa told Beth of her encounter with Sonia and Richard.

Beth fingered Alyssa to an orgasm at the point in the story where Richard came all over her body. Beth sucked the wet fingers and smiled. She then licked Alyssa's breasts and belly, cleaning the dried cum. "If I hadn't seen you in the kitchen and couldn't taste the cum, I wouldn't believe you, that story is so incredible. You know, I'm going to touch myself every time I pass that window. I may touch myself every time I see Richard," she laughed.

Alyssa slapped Beth lightly on the shoulder. "Be kind. He caught us at the right moment, and ensured we came before he did. Not bad for an old guy four years out of the saddle. I'm glad he didn't have a heart attack though."

Beth laughed and snuggled up to Alyssa, who shifted to her back and let Beth lay her head on her chest. "You are good for me. I'm going to miss you."

Alyssa kissed Beth on the head. "I'll miss you too." Before long, Beth was snoring, but Alyssa stared at the dark ceiling. *I love the closeness of her, but I really miss lying against Robert. I hope I can do that tomorrow night.* Alyssa shed a few tears as she nodded off.

10
SATURDAY

Alyssa woke and felt Beth's ass touching her own. *She doesn't always spoon all night.* She rolled over and spooned Beth, sliding her lower hand under the pillow and draping the upper one over Beth's waist. Her hair smelled of sweat and cooking grease, but Alyssa inhaled it deeply. *Every time we have burgers, I'll think of this.* Alyssa enjoyed the closeness a while. She felt Beth's muscles tighten as she woke, but neither woman spoke. When Beth moved her hand to Alyssa's, Alyssa intertwined their fingers and moved their hands between Beth's breasts, pressing against her sternum. "Good morning."

"Mmmm. Good morning. You are a good snuggler."

Alyssa barked a laugh. "Nope, we were butt to butt when I woke up. You had given up on snuggling me last night."

"I'm sure it was only for a minute."

"Probably so. This feels too good to be apart for long." She squeezed her hand against Beth's chest.

"I'll miss this tonight. I bet you will be glad to snuggle with Robert."

"I will. I hope I get to."

"You will. You are a great woman. He'd be a fool to not want you beside him."

"Well, I cheated on him a lot this week, including with you, several times. I don't know how he will take it."

"You don't have to tell him."

"Yes, I do. We don't keep secrets." Alyssa sighed. "And I like who I am becoming. If I want to continue to grow, I want to do it with him as a partner. If he doesn't want to forgive me, then I'll be in for even more change."

"That's why he will forgive you. You are honest when you don't have to be, and when your consequences are dire. You underestimate the feelings that inspires."

"And just what feelings are those?"

"Love, admiration, respect, everything positive and admirable you can think of a person."

"Maybe. He'll have to get through the feelings of betrayal, mistrust, anger, and all the negative things you can imagine first. We will see."

"There is one other feeling you kindle, Alyssa."

"What's that?"

"Lust." Beth rolled over and kissed Alyssa. Alyssa rolled onto her back as Beth pushed her shoulder to the mattress. Beth climbed on top of her, the weight holding her entire torso against the mattress, the pressure making her feel safe more than pinned. Alyssa kissed back and rubbed Beth's breasts and buttocks. Beth kissed down Alyssa's body, tingles amassing where Beth lingered, each kiss increasing Alyssa's desire for another, providing no satisfaction, only hunger. At the same time, Alyssa grabbed the inside of Beth's knee to pull her hips toward her face. Beth shifted, and Alyssa pulled Beth's opening to her mouth, pausing when Beth nipped her clit, arching her back with pleasure.

They lapped and sucked on each other's slits, lips, and clits. Alyssa's body crackled with energy everywhere it touched Beth's skin. The pleasure that began building in her pussy traveled higher. Each lick, nibble, or bite of Beth's lips or clit pulled the shocks starting in her pussy to her mouth as she pleased her young lover. Beth's fingers pulled Alyssa open. Momentary coolness from the air on her opening and her anus was replaced by warm, wet pressure across them, followed by two fingers sliding inside, resisting her clenching walls. Yet the pleasure of all that cool, warm pressure flowed to Alyssa's mouth, becoming a hot coal as she mimicked Beth's actions with her own.

They attacked each other's bodies, moaning and yelling as pleasure built up, unconcerned that other guests could hear them. Each clamped her thighs around the other's head when they neared release. Alyssa came in an orgasm that triggered from her mouth when she sucked Beth's clit and felt her orgasm start. They were more in a zero than a sixty-nine as Alyssa arched her back to press her pussy into Beth's mouth while stretching to keep her mouth and fingers on Beth's spasming pussy. When they finished, Beth spun to snuggle with Alyssa one last time.

"Fuck, that was good." Beth laid her head on Alyssa's shoulder. "It isn't my place, but remember how sexy you are when you talk with Robert. No man can say no to a sexy woman, especially one as amazing as you."

"It was amazing. I've never come that way before." Alyssa kissed Beth again, the softness of Beth's lips fanning the embers of her own orgasm, letting it glow in her own lips for a moment. "It isn't your place, but I appreciate that you said it nonetheless.

It tells me you care and that I can use strength like you do when I get home."

Beth craned her neck to look at the clock. "The first thing you have to do is get there. Isn't your daughter picking you up at eleven o'clock?"

"Yes."

"It's ten fifteen. You need to get ready."

The two women cleaned up with wipes and brushed Alyssa's hair. Alyssa put on some makeup and dressed while Beth put on her clothes. At 10:50, they walked to the door.

"Good luck. You have my number, so let me know how everything goes tonight. I'm here for you, no matter how it ends up."

"Thank you, Beth. I'll let you know. I'm going to miss you."

"I'll miss you too." Beth hugged Alyssa, and they shared a last kiss before walking to the elevator.

Alyssa strode across the lobby toward Susan, who sat in a chair near the door. "Hey, honey. I'm so glad to see you." She bent for a hug.

"Hey, Mom."

"Sweetie, what is wrong?"

"Mom, can we talk a while?"

"Want to talk while we drive? We need to get to the airport."

"The roads are pretty good this morning. They didn't refreeze overnight. Your flight is at two thirty, and we built in travel time that we don't need now. Can we talk somewhere private before we go?"

"Yes, honey. We can talk in one of the empty lounges. Come on." She took her daughter's hand and walked deep into one of the open-air lounges. They sat at a dark table. "What has you upset, sweetie?"

Susan didn't speak immediately. Alyssa waited while the girl gathered herself. "Mom... All that talk. When you and Dad talked about 'toy' relationships and having sex for pleasure only... Do you have 'sex toy' relationships now?"

Alyssa felt her legs weaken, relieved that she was sitting. She braced her arms on the table and looked at her hands.

"Mom?"

"Sorry, honey. Your question surprised me." *I won't lie to her, but how do I answer?* "What makes you ask that?"

"Mom, please answer the question." Susan's big brown eyes pleaded with Alyssa.

"No, honey. We don't have 'toy' relationships or any outside relationships. All that was before we were married. Why do you ask?"

Tears spilled from Susan's eyes. "Mom, I got here about nine thirty. I wanted to help you pack. I still had the key from Saturday night and was going to surprise you. I heard familiar noises as I came down the hall, but I wasn't sure until I was at your door. You were having sex with someone." She swallowed and breathed. "Are you getting divorced?"

Alyssa slumped in her chair yet maintained eye contact with her daughter. "Sweetie, I had hoped to talk with Dad about this first, so he and I could sort it out, but I'll talk with you now. I don't yet have all the answers you want." She reached for her daughter's hands, but Susan pulled hers into her lap. Alyssa's stomach roiled as she pulled back her hands and steeled herself. "This week, being stuck here, has been tough. I have met different people, and I have learned things, both about them and about myself. I have done things that I would never have considered even a week ago, including having sex with other people. Your dad and I will talk about them tonight, face-to-face. I owe him that." Tears ran down Alyssa's cheeks, and she sniffled before continuing. "I love your father dearly, and I want to be with him the rest of my life. If he can forgive me, then I will be the happiest woman in the world. I don't know if he will, so I can't answer your question about a divorce."

"So it's my fault our family is broken? Because you brought me back to school and got stuck here? Oh god." Susan hung her head.

Alyssa lifted Susan's chin. "No! No, no, no, no, no. None of this is your fault. Not one minute of it. You are the best daughter in the whole world, and I love traveling with you and wouldn't miss bringing you back to school, even if I got stuck in an ice storm every time. What I have done, I have done on my own, consciously. Any mistakes made or damage done are my fault. If you never hear anything I tell you, please, please hear that."

"Is this because of what that cop did to you?"

"No, but because of what I did, the people I connected with, what he did was not any worse than it was."

"Hold on. You mean you and Beth?"

Alyssa felt a flush of heat beneath the tears on her cheeks and nodded. "You heard me with Beth this morning. She has helped me so much. She is a good friend."

Susan's face hardened, and her tears stopped. "You said 'people.' More than just her?"

"Yes. There have been others. The week has been a bit emotional, and my emotions have led me to experiment a bit."

"Men too? Or just women?"

"Both."

Susan stood and slapped her mother's face, then did it again. "That's for Dad, because he would never hit you. You took vows. You bore his children. Then you had a weeklong orgy just because you couldn't handle the weather? Some wife you turned out to be."

Alyssa sobbed once but stared Susan in the face. Blood flowed to the searing handprint forming on her cheek. She waited, counting to ten, then fifty.

"Say something, Mother."

Alyssa took a deep breath. "Susan, I am ready to talk when you are. Would you please sit down? I don't want to be slapped again."

Susan sat. "I shouldn't have done that, but I won't apologize. What you did was reprehensible. How do you explain it? And did that cop pursue you because he didn't get his turn?"

Shame gripped Alyssa's lungs, forcing the air out of them. Anger at the accusation lit a fire in her belly. Shame prevented her breathing in an attempt to suffocate the anger before the unfairness of Susan's statement exploded through the shame with a gasp. "That isn't fair, Susan. He extorted me and would have raped me. What I did with anyone else had nothing to do with it. I told you all about that, and I told you the full, unadulterated truth. Don't intermingle my mistakes with what he did."

"Okay. So he wasn't involved. How do you explain the rest?"

Alyssa told the story of the entire week. She explained how things had started and how they had progressed. She talked about the emotional conflicts, the guilt and excitement competing within her. She stopped to cry twice. Susan neither interrupted nor consoled her. She finished by reminding Susan that if Robert divorced her, she would still be her mother, and she loved her more than anything. Alyssa slumped, exhausted from the tale, her stomach knotted tighter after hearing herself lay out everything without interruption as more tears fell. *It sounds even worse when I tell it.*

Alyssa wiped her eyes and held her folded hands toward her daughter. "Susan, I had wanted to talk to your father in person about this first, but you asked, so I told you everything out of respect. Will you please keep this to yourself until I have a chance to talk with your dad?"

Susan wiped tears from her eyes. "I'll wait until tomorrow night. That will give you time to get home and have some privacy, even if you get delayed. After that, Dad needs to know. He's been in the dark long enough."

"Thank you, sweetie. That is more than I could expect. I'm so sorry you found out this way, and I'm sorry for whatever consequences come from it. Please remember that I love you, and Dad, and Clay. Nothing can change that."

"I know that, and I even believe that you still love Dad. Understand that I am furious at you, and how it turns out will probably not change that. I guess I understand how you used to tell me that you were very angry with me but you still loved me." Susan leaned across the table, her lips set in a thin line and her eyebrows leaving no question as to her intent. "I still love you, but your cheating makes me livid. I'm going to think before we talk again. It feels like you threw away our family because you were drunk and horny. If I came home pregnant for the same reasons, how would you react? I'm really fucking angry, Mom."

Alyssa fought the urge to look away. "You have every right to be. I hope we can get past it. I'll talk with you whenever you are ready. I want to remain a part of your life, a good part that we both enjoy. Maybe after I talk with Dad, you and I can talk again?"

"I don't know right now. I'll call when I'm ready."

"Okay." Alyssa looked at her watch. Her stomach turned at what she needed to ask. "It's time for me to go. Would you like me to try an Uber?"

Susan took a deep breath. "No, Mom. I'll take you to the airport. You are still my mom, and I promised I would. Come on. The car's out front."

Alyssa relaxed. *A small victory.*

They drove most of the way in silence, but as they exited the highway, Susan asked, "What about Clay?"

"What do you mean?"

"When will you tell Clay?"

Alyssa's heart dropped low in her chest. "Your dad and I will figure that out. He's still in the house, so he will know something is going on. Will you let us tell him?"

"Yes. He deserves to hear this from Dad, or you, or both of you face-to-face. I won't say anything until you have talked with him."

"Thank you, sweetie."

The car stopped in front of the Southwest terminal.

"I'm sorry our time together ended this way, Susan. I hope we can talk soon."

"We will, Mom. I'm just really pissed right now."

"Can I have a hug?"

Susan leaned forward and gripped her mother tightly. Alyssa returned the hug and let Susan cry on her shoulder.

She kissed Susan's head behind her ear and stroked her hair. "I love you, sweetie."

"Love you, too, Mom. Now go. Don't miss this flight."

Alyssa was glad to have a window seat. She couldn't believe the snow covering the ground from Houston all the way to the Appalachians. *Driving home would have been impossible. I really was stuck.* She typically slept on long flights. Today she thought of Robert. She thought how he may react to her tale, but mainly she dreamed of him fucking her. *How different would I be today if he had come with me? What would he have done if he had been there and I had stayed home? How would I feel if he had experienced Beth and Sonia and Kate without telling me? Ooh. I would like to see that. What I really want to feel is him plunging into me and hitting that spot just right, the way he does. I want that. A lot.*

When the plane touched down, Alyssa shifted in her seat just to put some different pressure on her tingling clit. As she slid forward, her pants gripped the seat, tightening on her mound. She pressed her hips forward and smiled. She texted Robert. "On the ground. See you soon!"

"At the arrivals exit. Can't wait to see you."

Alyssa looked through the security gate and smiled at Robert. She ran through the crowd and jumped into his arms, sobbing into his shoulder. He held her while she let the emotions of the week escape, his arms clenching her into his chest. When she stopped crying, she squeezed him tighter. Alyssa inhaled the scent of their laundry detergent as if the feel of him needed confirmation.

Eventually, she looked up. "I really missed you. Thank you for getting me home. I couldn't do it myself. The week was so hard. It's good to be back with you."

"Baby, it's good to have you home. I missed you too."

Alyssa looked around. "Where is Clay? I thought he was coming."

"He had a chemistry test he couldn't miss. He's at home and can't wait to see you."

"Okay. I missed him, too, but tests come first. I'll give him a hug when we get home."

"Sounds good. Let's get you home." Robert wrapped his arm around Alyssa's waist and took her carry-on with his other hand. She leaned against him for the entire walk to the car.

"The deck is never this empty," she noted.

"Yeah. I noticed when I came in. I got to park on two, and we usually end up on level four or five. Must be light because of the weekend."

They put her bag in the back of the big Suburban and got in. Alyssa turned to Robert. "Let's see how empty this deck is. Go up to level four."

"Why do we care? We are just leaving."

"Trust me, and go up to four, will you, please?"

"Okay, Babe. You are the one who has been traveling all day, so if you want to look around, I'll oblige."

Alyssa pointed to an empty corner of the fourth level. "Go over there and park. I want to show you something."

Robert laughed. "Okay. Here we are."

"Turn off the car."

He did, and Alyssa kissed him more passionately than she had in years. She dove her tongue into his mouth and pressed the back of his head toward hers. He responded by wrestling her tongue with his. His hand slid into her hair, while his other rubbed her back. He pulled his head back. "No bra?"

"I took it off in the restroom. Let's get in the back. I need you now."

"Deal."

They opened the back and climbed in, using the button to close the tailgate behind them. "The seats are missing. Did you have this in mind?"

"Nope. And it was you who started this, Baby."

"Let's finish it." She climbed onto him, kissing him before pulling his shirt off over his head. He unbuttoned her shirt and cupped her breasts, the warm palms cradling her just the way she'd anticipated. Just the way they always did. She moaned as he rolled her nipples between his finger and thumb, lighting them on fire as he had thousands of times before, satisfying her and making her want more. He trailed one hand and then the other down and back up her sides just the way she liked, sending electricity pulsing from his fingertips to her nipples, making her pussy throb.

She reached between them and grasped his hard cock through his pants before unbuckling his belt and unzipping him. He raised his hips to let her pull the pants down, then unbuttoned the front of her jeans. He slid his hands inside them and cupped her ass.

"Panties? You didn't take them off too?"

"I was too wet. I didn't want to drip through the airport. Why don't you feel."

He slipped one hand in farther and touched her pussy through the material. "They are wet. You should probably take them off before you catch cold."

Alyssa laughed and replied, "God, yes. Take them off, then make me warm."

He hooked the waistband of her jeans with his thumbs and tugged, catching the panties as he lowered them. She shimmied her hips to help him strip her and sloughed off her shirt. Once they were naked, Alyssa rolled onto her back and opened her legs. "Come on. I'm ready for you. I've been ready for you since Sunday."

Robert positioned the head of his prick at her dripping opening. He shoved inside a couple of inches while Alyssa growled.

"Oh god, that's good. Keep going. Give it to me, Baby. Come on. Fuck me right, the way you do."

He pulled back, then shoved all the way in. Alyssa locked her heels behind his ass and pulled him inside her. She raised her hips to meet him, pulling his cock across her G-spot. The slight curve of his cock back toward his belly and his large head rubbed her there every time they coupled, going in and pulling out. His cock wasn't huge, just a bit bigger than average, but its shape made Alyssa groan deep in her chest because her walls savored squeezing as he parted them on every single plunge. "Oh, that's right. Come on. Hit that spot. Fuck me, baby. Fuck me."

Robert did. He slammed his dick into Alyssa on each stroke, and she bucked upward to meet him.

Alyssa's body flushed and her belly churned as her orgasm rushed to overtake her. She wailed and gripped Robert with her arms and legs, holding the head of his cock right beside her cervix as her pussy convulsed around his swelling shaft. *He's going to come.*

Robert's cock shrank ever so slightly during the stillness. *Not yet, he won't. Give me more.* Alyssa relaxed her grip, and Robert started fucking her again, hitting that same spot over and over, exactly like he usually did, and exactly what Alyssa had dreamed of the entire flight home. Her pussy boiled at its top, another exploding release driving Alyssa to writhe and babble broken syllables. She came again, dripping juice across his balls as he kept his cock buried in her.

Her arms lost their strength, and her legs fell to the side, opening her fully for him to finish. He leaned back until his head brushed the roof of the truck. That angle always increased the pressure of his cock on the front wall of her vagina, making her groan like she always did after a big orgasm. She lay still to feel him pump her for a few more strokes, feeling her breasts bounce and her head loll around as she surrendered to him.

She felt his cock harden and grow as his orgasm approached. She found strength to grasp him again and pull him deeper. "Come in me, Baby. Fill me full. Reclaim me." She looked into his eyes, unblinking as she held on tight.

Robert's cock nudged beside her cervix and stayed there. Alyssa's pussy kept spasming against him, and her cervix fluttered across the head of his cock. He groaned and skewered harder against Alyssa, the warm splatters reviving her orgasm every time they hit her cervix.

Robert fell forward onto Alyssa. She wrapped her arms around him, feeling happier under his body than she had in a week. His warm lips on her eyes, her cheeks, and her mouth built the usual glow in her chest she had never appreciated until she had missed it this week. *This is what I needed.*

He stroked her hair. "I love you, Baby. I'm so glad you're home. You should come home like this more often."

"Oh, Babe. I've missed you so much. This was a great way to celebrate getting home. I love you. More than I can ever say." She pulled him tighter to her with both arms, feeling the sweat on his back and smelling the faint cologne over the smell of their love-making. "You put on cologne? You haven't done that in years."

"I wanted to make you feel special. You've had a rough week, and you needed to know how happy I am that you're home." He rubbed her cheek. "I would have driven to get you, but even on Wednesday, the roads were a mess through Louisiana and Texas."

"Babe, I know. I looked at renting a car and driving home, but there were no cars and no clear roads. This week was just something fate wanted me to go through, it seems."

"Well, we missed you. I missed you. I'm glad your tough week is over."

Robert shifted sideways to roll off his wife, but Alyssa stopped him. "Not yet. I love feeling you on me and in me. Stay."

"Okay, Babe." He brushed her hair off her forehead and kissed her there. "We have to get home eventually though."

Alyssa closed her eyes. "I know. I just want to enjoy feeling you a little longer before we leave." *If this is the last time, I am going to savor it.*

A few minutes later, Robert's cock softened and slid out of Alyssa. A dollop of their combined orgasm followed, which ran down the crack of Alyssa's ass. She shuddered beneath her husband. "God, I love that feeling."

"I'm glad you do, baby." He rolled off and lay on his side, looking at her. "You've been getting that feeling for twenty-three years. What has you worked up about it today?"

"I guess I just missed it. Maybe it's that we are in the back of your truck in a parking deck like a couple of teenagers. Maybe it's that my Valentine's night was spent listening to the neighbors in the hotel instead of being with you. I'm not sure, but I really loved it today."

"I'm glad. It is fun to be here doing this. I don't remember the last time we made love outside of the house or a hotel."

"Maybe in that first house you owned, when we sunbathed nude on the deck?"

"Or maybe when we went camping with Carol and Chris, out on that island in Lake Philpott when we stopped the boat to explore?"

"Those were good times," Alyssa said. "We should do that more often. We could use a little more adventure."

Robert bowed his head, then returned her gaze. "Yes, we could." He grinned. "Want to drive home naked?"

Alyssa cackled. "Oh! You are so bad! Maybe we wait on that, since we have to pay the parking attendant?"

"He gets one look at your boobs, and I bet we don't pay."

"If it's a woman, though, I'm going to have to get you hard to get a freebie."

"Getting hard has never been a challenge around you."

"Mm. No. And I love that you are always ready." She stroked his slick cock.

Flashes of yellow light on the ceiling caught Robert's attention. "Be still. Security is coming."

Alyssa kept stroking Robert's cock as they lay in the back of the Suburban. "In case it's a woman…"

They listened as the security car drove through the deck in front of the Suburban and made its way away from them. Robert kissed his wife and said, "We have probably tempted fate enough today. Why don't we get dressed and get you home. You need a shower, and I am happy to provide washing services."

✂

During the two-hour ride home, Alyssa moved the conversation away from the events of her week, focusing on Robert and Clay's week as bachelors and Susan's move back to school. Clay had eaten dinner by the time they arrived, so she visited with him while Robert made a small supper. They ate and cleaned up before heading to the shower.

She and Robert made love again after toweling each other off, slower this time, lovingly and long. Alyssa rode Robert in their bed, patiently coaxing an orgasm from him, both of them aware he was slow to come when she was on top. They came with a final frantic rush, releasing with the muffled cries of two parents whose child is at home. Alyssa leaned forward onto him, his body warming hers, his arms wrapped across her back with his hands holding her sides.

Alyssa raised her head to look at Robert beneath her. *It's time. Suck it up. Tell the truth.* She pulled off of his cock and sat sideways, resting her shoulder against the headboard. "Robert, you probably noticed that I didn't talk about this week yet."

"I figured you would when you were ready."

"I don't know that I'm ready, but I won't delay any longer."

"Okay. I'll listen as long as you want to talk. You know there is nothing we can't discuss."

"I know. I love that about us." She took a deep breath and let it out. "This week was a lot worse than I told you. I didn't want you to worry, and I wanted our talks to be escapes from what was happening. Most important, I wanted to talk with you about it here, face-to-face."

"Okay, Baby. Whatever it is, I'm here to support you. I love you. You talk; I'll listen."

"I'll start with the worst thing. There was a fight on Tuesday night. A crazy lady attacked one of the workers. She got arrested. That part was bad, but it got much worse on Thursday. A dirty cop named Frazier used the situation. He tried to extort sex from, well, he tried to rape me." She told the story, including every detail, from the first encounter with Frazier until Langhorne left her room that night. Robert remained silent, holding Alyssa's hand. As she told about Frazier, his head flushed bright red. It always did when he was angry. "I may have to testify, but I don't know. Langhorne said they would not release my name, but I told Susan last night in case it makes the news. I was scared, but in the end, I was mad and ready to fight. I'm stronger because of it. It made me look at who I am and how I want to live life. It reminded me how important you and the kids are."

"Baby, I'm sorry you had to go through that. You're home now. You're safe. Is that how you got that bruise on your breast?" Robert asked, caressing it with his fingertips.

Alyssa put her head on Robert's chest and squeezed his ribs. "Yes. He hit me there, hard. I didn't know how much that could hurt. But I feel safe now. I feel at home."

"I can see how that's the worst. Is there more?"

"Yes." Alyssa clasped her shaking hands together. She swallowed, but the nervous lump in her throat remained. "It takes longer to tell, and it isn't as scary, but I believe it will hurt you more. It hurts me, but it also makes my life better, if that makes sense. Please, listen while I tell the story, and we can talk after, okay?" Alyssa held her breath, wondering if Robert could hear her pounding heart.

"Okay. I'm nervous about what you have to say."

"I am too." She kissed him and sat back against the headboard, glad she didn't need to support her own body while she talked. "Remember what I told you about the people in the room next door having loud sex on Valentine's? I never met them, but their noise, the dirty way they had sex, it had me horny that whole night and the next day. I masturbated a few times, and I came so hard, but I stayed excited and turned on. It didn't help that there was nothing to do. So they fucked and I listened. I went to the lobby that afternoon just to clear my head and cool my body."

Alyssa saw the flush begin in Robert's neck. "Too much detail?"

"Not yet. I don't like where I think this is headed." His glare tightened her chest again.

Alyssa imagined Kate saying, "Have the conversation, whatever it takes." She pursed her lips and looked him in the eye. "No, I don't think you will, but I need to tell you."

The flush filled in Robert's face. He nodded.

"I ended up meeting a couple and having dinner with them. Remember, the hotel was packed, and people were sharing tables. Paul and Kate and I drank wine while the food cooked, and we got a bit drunk. I asked Kate how tall Paul was when he went to the bar for a refill, and she told me that it is true that men with big feet have big dicks. She also told me that they have an open marriage and they would like to have me join them, both of them, for sex."

Robert's jaw clenched.

Alyssa bit her lower lip. "Babe, I'll tell this with as much or as little detail as you want. Either way it hurts. How much do you want me to describe?"

After a couple of false starts, Robert responded. "And to think I was glad when you got home. Stupid me." He sighed. "Do this. Tell me every single sickening, salacious detail. Tell me everything he did to you so I don't have any questions when you are finished except maybe why you bothered to come home at all. If this is going to be the worst night of my entire life, rip off the damn Band-Aid like a big girl, and don't stop until I know everything I need to know, might want to know, or might ever ask about, just in case it's the last civil conversation we ever have."

Alyssa sobbed a breath and put her head in her hands. "I'm sorry. I don't want to make it worse."

"Then don't leave me in suspense. Talk."

Alyssa took a couple of deep breaths and wiped her tears, then nodded. "So Kate called me beautiful and desirable, and told me they didn't think I was old. I told her I couldn't hurt my marriage. Kate licked my neck when she whispered to me. She rekindled the arousal that had been smoldering inside me all day. We kept eating, and nothing more was said about it. Kate got drunk, so when we finished, I helped Paul take her and the extra food we ordered, like you recommended, up to their room. Kate made sexy comments about me to her husband between the restaurant and their door."

Robert grunted and rolled his eyes.

"Are you sure you want the detail, Babe?"

"Talk."

"I made my first mistake. He was holding her, and I had to get the room key out of his pocket. I grabbed his dick before I pulled out the key. It was big, and I was turned on. He had me help her out of her dress, and I got hornier. She was beautiful. He kissed me and told me that I was the hottest woman in the hotel, but I told him I needed to leave. He understood, and I went to my room and called you. I had stripped and was rubbing myself. I wanted to have phone sex with you, but you were playing video games with Clay."

Robert, head flushed red, interrupted. "So this is my fault?"

Alyssa's hands went up in surprise. "No! Not in any way.

Robert, what I did, I did. Nobody is to blame but me. Please understand, I'm not rationalizing or blaming. I'm confessing. I'm only confessing. I'll ask your forgiveness when I am done. I hope you can find it in your heart to give it."

Robert sat back. "Go ahead."

"I didn't know how to say how much I needed you that night without sounding like a horny slut, or an idiot, or both, so I got off the phone and left you two to play. That was my second mistake. The loud neighbors had left, and masturbating alone wasn't satisfying me, so I got dressed and went back to Paul and Kate's room. That was my worst mistake. I fucked Paul. Well, he fucked me."

Robert's neck strained under the skin. His chest muscles rippled, and his fists clenched.

Alyssa leaned away from him. "Maybe less detail?"

Robert leaned toward her, not speaking until he was inches from her face. "Don't like the way I'm reacting? You should have thought of that before you fucked somebody else because I was taking care of our son. Keep going. Every fucking detail."

Alyssa nodded, then talked through her tears. "Maybe because I was so horny, or maybe because his huge dick stretched me like I've never been stretched, or maybe because what I was doing was wrong, I don't know, but it was the hottest pure fuck of my life. I came so many times I lost my reason. I felt so naughty, no, dirty. I had him come on my tits because it felt so dirty. When Kate licked his cum off my body and ate my pussy, I felt myself slipping into depravity. Paul ended up fucking her while she ate me, and it was the hottest, most perverted thing I've ever done or felt. My body was on fire. I just kept coming."

"At least you enjoyed it. What next?"

"I woke up later and went to my room. I just stared out the window and thought about what I had done. I cried, and I considered calling to tell you but decided to talk in person on Wednesday. It was a once-in-a-lifetime experience, and it was enjoyable and fun and spontaneous, and I didn't feel guilty."

Robert sagged. The tension in his chest and neck abated. For the first time since Alyssa had started talking, his eyes shifted down. He turned away from facing her, shifting instead to lean against the headboard beside her. "You didn't feel guilty."

Alyssa reached for his hand.

He jerked his away.

"I was sad. I knew I would tell you, and it would hurt our marriage. I weighed how good I had felt: being desired by beautiful people, feeling the unique physical sensations and excitement of being with new lovers, enjoying the orgasms, feeling the naughtiness and debauchery of cheating and being with a woman, against how bad I felt: hurting, maybe ending, our marriage, hurting you, hurting the children, hurting myself by not having the strength to forgo the temptation."

"Well, at least you made a conscious decision to trade our family for, what did you call it? Oh yes, the best pure fuck of your life. It isn't as bad as being swapped for just a run-of-the-mill fuck." Robert turned his head toward the wall away from Alyssa. She knew without following his gaze what he was staring at: their wedding picture. "Finish."

"In the end, I accepted what I had done. I had enjoyed the experience, so while I wouldn't seek anything out, I would be open to more if the opportunity arose. I knew there would be consequences when I got back, potentially terrible consequences, but I couldn't undo what I had done."

Alyssa took a breath and wiped a tear from her eye. She then proceeded to tell Robert about the rest of her sexual escapades during the week. She trimmed the detail but covered the new experiences and sensations. She described the adventure and new pleasures of exploring anal and lesbian sex. She talked of the differences between the women and the men. She described the thrill of being watched by the homeless man while pressed against the window by Sonia. She described the tenderness that had developed between her and Beth.

She told Robert that Susan had caught her with Beth and given an ultimatum for talking with him.

Robert's head spun to her for the first time in fifteen minutes. "She knows? God, Alyssa. The more you talk, the fucking better this gets." He turned back toward the wall.

"I'm not proud of it. I wasn't going to hide from what she knew, and I wasn't going to talk with her about it over the phone." Alyssa sighed, then turned back up on her hip to face him before continuing. "The best part, though, was making love with you in the back of the Suburban at the airport. It was naughty, and spontaneous, and dirty, but also loving and tender and healing, all at once."

Robert's head reddened again, but he neither spoke nor turned.

Alyssa continued. "I needed to feel your cock please me the way only your cock pleases me. I learned that yours is special and my favorite. You may think I'm saying this to soften what I have told you, but I'm not. It was absolutely, certainly, the best lovemaking I've had in a long time."

Robert's red head turned. "So that's what that 'reclaim me' shit was?"

"Yes. I needed you to take me back and make me yours again. And you did. I am yours."

"I didn't know that you had become someone else's, did I?"

"No. I needed to feel your love again, and if it was to be the last time, I wanted it to be happy. It was one final deception."

Robert frowned. "Anything else?"

"I have one last confession. I want to talk about having an open marriage. As much as I love what we have, I think it can be better with some variety in the bedroom. I don't know what that looks like, and we can decide together what we want. That said, if you're against it, I'll give up that desire and never mention it again, if you can forgive me and we can rebuild the loving marriage we had before I broke it."

Alyssa scooted back on the bed, supplicating herself before Robert and holding his hand with both of hers. Tears ran down her nose onto the sheet inches below. "I beg your forgiveness, Robert. Please forgive what I did. Please let me repair the damage and let me heal the hurt I caused. Please think about what I have offered. You have always been a fair man. You would be right to throw me out naked and penniless. Please don't. Please know I will do anything to make this up to you." Her face fell to the mattress. She sobbed while holding his hand.

Robert let her cry a few moments before pulling back his hand. He got up, got dressed, took his keys and wallet, and left. Alyssa wailed as the bedroom door closed.

11
SUNDAY

THE ALARM CLOCK read 4:26 a.m. when Alyssa looked at it before letting exhaustion and sadness take her. A firm hand shook Alyssa's shoulder. "Alyssa, wake up. We need to talk." She roused slowly, reaching to put her hand over his on her shoulder but keeping her eyes closed. Robert shook her again. "Come on. Get up. Let's talk." She saw the clock—7:49 a.m.

Alyssa registered what was happening. She looked at her husband and gave a wan smile.

His stern look didn't change. "Meet me on the back porch." He stood and left the room.

Alyssa pulled on some sweatpants and a sweatshirt and grabbed a pair of fuzzy socks. She walked to the back porch barefoot. Robert was sitting on the small sofa, watching the dew sparkle in the early light.

"May I sit here?" Alyssa asked, looking at the empty spot beside Robert.

"Sure. We are just talking, and the neighbors don't need to hear."

Alyssa sat and slipped her socks on. She hugged her knees to her chest, hiding her heart from what she feared Robert would say. The protection didn't slow the hole growing in her chest. As she watched him, her eyes brimmed with tears.

He watched the grass for another few minutes, then began to speak, not looking at Alyssa. "I've been driving around. Almost everywhere I went, we have memories, mainly good ones. I don't want to lose those good memories or become bitter about them. I think that's what would happen if I threw you out. It is tempting, you know. Divorce was my leading option until I turned into the neighborhood by the little playground. We were so happy there with the kids, and when we passed it on our walks, we always reminisced. I don't want to be angry at you every time I pass that park."

Alyssa loved that park. She started to agree with Robert, then stopped as her throat tightened, threatening a sob if she tried to speak. She imagined being angry every time she went past it, feeling the hole in her chest continue to expand until nothing remained inside her ribs. She waited, wringing her hands.

"So, for now, I don't want a divorce."

Alyssa exhaled and hugged her knees to her chest. *We have a shot.* She felt like her heart resumed beating. A smile fought into her throat, but she swallowed it down. *Not the time.*

"We have some work to do. You hurt me badly, and I am both angry and sad. You have broken my trust and faith in you. I don't like you very much right now, and I am struggling to find the love we shared for all these years. If I can't recover the good feelings, we will divorce. To do anything else would be worse."

The smile stopped fighting its way up, and her heart retreated to the empty ache in her chest. Alyssa's hands lost the strength to hold her knees, and her feet slipped from the cushion to the floor. Her head drooped. *Divorce still looms, so fight.* She raised her head. "I'll do anything you say. What can I do to help us heal?" "I thought about that after I decided to try to reconcile. I took a long time."

"Since you pulled back into the neighborhood?"

"I've been back since about six o'clock, thinking. To be honest, I thought about how to punish you, how to take my anger out on you, how to make you hurt the way I did when you said you didn't feel guilty about it."

"I didn't mean for that to hurt you." She turned to reach for him.

"You didn't intend a lot of things, but you did them." He held up his hand to stop her. "I thought about how to get even. I'm relieved to say that those thoughts gave way to thoughts of fairness. Maybe that is the first step to forgiving you, I'm not sure."

"I hope it is. What do I do?"

"Here's what I think is fair. You had sex with six people, three men and three women. It seems fair that I have sex with six people too. I don't want that, though, certainly no men. So here is what's fair. I have sex with one woman, one night, all night, any way and every way I want to. That is almost what you did on your first foray outside our marriage."

Alyssa felt her stomach settle. *That is okay, and maybe a step toward an open marriage.* She nodded and leaned toward him.

"Two things will make this fair. First, you have to set it up. You have to find an attractive…no, didn't you describe your lovers as beautiful? A beautiful woman willing to do this, who is not married, and is, of course, on contraception, and arrange it with her. And don't think of calling in a favor from one of your women from last week. This needs to be hard for you. Second, you have to watch. Wherever we go, whatever we do, I'll have the, what was it, yes, the hottest pure fuck of my life. We will be depraved, and dirty, and mind-blowing. While you watch."

I have to do the dirty work. Alyssa's stomach roiled again, the butterflies only a fraction of what she expected when she asked someone to fuck her husband. *While you watch.* Alyssa had fantasized about watching Robert and Beth or one of her other lovers, but she'd planned on being involved. This was different. *You have to watch, not participate. Then maybe he'll tell you he doesn't feel guilty for having an epic fuck, just so you can see how it feels. What if he likes her better?* Alyssa looked at Robert and pulled her knees up to hide her chest again. He was hard. *No, no, no. Does hurting me turn him on?* "That sounds like a punishment."

"No, a punishment would be telling you to set it up with your sister, Carolyn, who would hold it over you forever in her own nasty way. I decided that would be too much, but it did cross my mind."

"Wow." Alyssa choked back a sob, imagining her sister whispering in Robert's ear and laughing at every family gathering just to make Alyssa uneasy, or signing her Christmas card, "Your Replacement." "You think as little of her as I do. Thank you for not making me do that."

"I want us to be married on the far side of this," Robert sighed. "Hurting you, hurting us, didn't seem like the best way to accomplish that. I did think about making you tell your mother what you did. She has always liked me and might punish you more than I would."

At least hurting me didn't make him hard. That's what he said. Maybe he just wants to fuck somebody else. "I am sure I will tell her sometime if we get through this. If we don't, then she'll know anyway. Is there anything else?"

"You are going to sleep in the guest room. That may change, but right now, I don't want you in our bed. We need to reestablish closeness, but not yet."

Even though she had expected it, being banished from their room tightened her throat in a sob. She nodded, then rested her face on her knees. When she raised her head, she sighed. "We need to talk with Clay."

"Yes. It would have been better to keep this from the kids"— Robert scowled at her—"but since Susan knows, it isn't fair to make her keep a secret from Clay. You know how close they are, anyway. He doesn't need the details, but he deserves to know. We should talk with him together so he understands that this is a problem between us and not with anything he has done."

Another thing you messed up. "How long do I have?"

"To set something up? Let's not set a deadline. Instead, simply know that until that night happens, it will be impossible to reconcile, and the longer we wait, the harder it is. Will you do this?"

"I want to think about it. Can I talk with you later, maybe after you sleep?"

"Fair enough. I'm going to get a few hours' sleep. When I wake up, I'll expect an answer." He went inside.

Alyssa sat, watching the sun burn the dew off the grass. *I've never seen him this mad at anyone over anything. Should have thought about that before I went to Paul and Kate's room. Is this fair, and am I willing to do it?* This was what an open marriage might be like. Either of them could find a replacement every time they tried a new partner. *Except I have to find the woman, then watch. I could have called Beth and flown her here, or Kate, but he thought of that.*

Alyssa sat and cried, blaming herself. After a while, the strength she'd found in Houston returned. She put aside her self-pity. *I am willing to do this. I have to. It is the price for his effort, and I will pay it. And I'll be damned if the new bitch will replace me, no matter how hard she fucks him.* She sat on the porch, spinning her rings.

~

"Mom?" Clay stuck his head out the door. "Are we going to have breakfast?"

"Sure, honey. I was waiting for you to get up. Let's cook."

The two of them made a big breakfast, talking and laughing the entire time. They cooked and ate and caught up on what he had done while she was gone. *This feels good. I'll never give this up, whatever Robert demands.*

A few hours later, Robert woke Alyssa, who was napping on the couch. "What have you decided?"

Alyssa sat up and looked around to make sure Clay was out of earshot. "I'll do it. I'll do whatever you ask to keep this family together. I'll sleep in the guest room. I'll find you someone to fuck all night. I'll watch you do it. I'll help you do it if you want me to. And then I'll make you fall in love with me all over again, whatever that takes."

Robert hung his head. "Okay. I'll let you try to repair our marriage. To be honest, I didn't think you would."

"I meant what I said. You, our marriage, our family, mean everything to me. I'll do whatever I have to do to save them. Whatever you require."

"Very well. I'll leave you to figure it out." Robert went to play basketball in the driveway with Clay. Alyssa went to the kitchen and poured some grape juice.

"He doesn't realize how my heart beats when he's a good dad," Alyssa said to the empty room, watching her boys through the kitchen window. Robert spent time with the kids whenever he could, and never was too tired or not interested to join them. Every time he did, Alyssa reconfirmed she had married the best man she knew. *He's still so strong and handsome.* A delicious ache grew in her chest. Her hand on her chest warmed the ache, just as it had so many times in the last twenty-three years.

Tears fell. *If you don't fix this, you don't get to see this anymore.* Juice splashed on her shirt when her cup fell from her hand into the sink, but the cold she felt came from the inside, not the juice. Fear gripped the warm ache, freezing her body despite the sweatshirt. Tears became sobs while the love she felt faded into despair. She sagged forward, resting her chest on the counter while she cried on her crossed arms.

The sound of the kitchen door opening behind her shook her from her stupor. "Alyssa?" called Robert.

She looked over her shoulder before easing her chest off the counter. "Hey. I just got emotional watching you play with Clay."

He frowned, pointing to the stain on her shirt and the flush on her face. "I see that. Why don't you get a shower before Clay comes in? He doesn't need to see you looking like you drowned your tears in merlot."

"Grape juice." She wiped her eyes while the tiniest flicker of warmth danced through her chest. *Do I ask this? Might as well.* She looked at him with pleading eyes. "Would you like to join me? You are all sweaty."

Robert's face showed a flash of red that immediately vanished. "I appreciate the offer, and what you are trying to do. I don't think so. You go ahead."

The avalanche of ice in his stare snuffed the flicker, making Alyssa gasp. Alyssa nodded, then forced a smile as a tear fell. "I will. If you change your mind, the offer stands. It always stands, if it helps me earn your love back. I'm willing to start anywhere."

Robert shook his head. "I understand. You go ahead."

✥

Alyssa nodded and shuffled to the guest bathroom after gathering some fresh clothes. The warm water thawed the cold rejection lingering from the kitchen. Her hands moved across her body, yet her mind focused on Robert's demands. *Who can I talk into this, and how? Nancy at his office has always flirted with him, and even got a little handsy at last year's Christmas party. She is gorgeous, and divorced. I bet she would jump at the chance.* She pictured Robert pulling up her skirt and bending her over the back of their couch to fuck her from behind so hard he slid the couch across the floor. She pulled her nipples. *He wouldn't want that with a coworker.*

My friend Carol would. She cheats on Chris a lot. She's a slut. Robert likes her body. He can't take his eyes off her when she wears bikinis on their boat. He said not married, but maybe I can talk him into fucking her? Images of Carol, her tits bouncing out of her black bikini top as Robert pounded her on the back seat of Carol and Chris's boat, while she and Chris watched, made Alyssa's pussy ache to be filled. She worked her hand across her slick labia, spreading them open and running her fingertip in the moist slit. *He likes Chris though. He knows she has slept around, but he wouldn't be a part of it.*

Amelia at work…she is young, and hot, and talks about her sexy weekends. Wait. That kills that. Alyssa's fingers were inside her, driving toward an orgasm as she envisioned Robert fucking these women. She shifted the shower to massage and moved her body. Her pussy throbbed slower than the pulsing water, but every delicious impact of the shower stream pounded her clit, making her pussy pulse harder, chasing release. *I heard her tell someone she fucked a guy on his desk during the day. That's so hot.* As her mind placed Robert in the story, nailing Amelia on his desk, her legs tensed and her back arched. She moaned deep in her chest. Her vagina clenched her fingers as she pinched her nipple with her other hand. Her orgasm drove her head back against the wall of the shower as she let it wash over her like the water.

Alyssa dried off and dressed. She heard the shower in the master bedroom running. She yelled back to Clay's room, "I'm going to take a walk. I won't be too long, if Dad is looking for me." He grunted his acknowledgment. Despair crept into Alyssa's thoughts. Robert had given her a chance, but she had no idea how to make it happen. How ironic. In a Houston hotel, where she'd known no one, she had fucked six people in five days. At home, where she knew hundreds of people, she couldn't think of one person to fuck Robert. Alyssa wandered the usual path she and Robert walked together, focused on women they knew. The more women she thought of, the more she crossed off the list, and the more she realized she might not win Robert back. She sat on a bench in the empty playground. Her head fell into her hands as she wept.

"Alyssa, do you need help?"

Alyssa turned toward the woman a few feet away.

"Hey, Jessica." Alyssa recognized her neighbor from down the street. They knew each other sufficiently to chitchat at the neighborhood parties but were not friends. "No, I'm okay."

"No offense, but you don't look it. Can I sit with you?"

Alyssa nodded. "Was it the tears or the runny nose that gave me away?"

"Holding your head made me wonder, but the puffy eyes confirmed it." Jessica chuckled as she put her arm around Alyssa's shoulders.

Alyssa fell into Jessica's shoulder and cried some more. Jessica held her, stroking her hair occasionally. Alyssa finished crying and sat up straighter. "Thank you. I thought I was the only one out here."

"You were. I saw you as I walked by and thought I'd check on you."

"I'm glad you did. Sometimes I need a shoulder to cry on. I'm sorry if I ruined your walk."

"Nonsense. This is a good place to have a cry, and I am glad I could help you. Would you like to talk about it?"

Alyssa hesitated.

Jessica nodded. "It's all right; I would be uneasy sharing something personal with someone I barely knew also. If you change your mind, I'm just down the street. So you know, I never break confidences."

Alyssa remembered noticing that Jessica stayed away from the neighborhood gossips and that when they did talk about her, it was speculation, never facts. "Actually, it might help to get this off my chest, and I can't turn to many people about it. It may take a while. Could I impose on you some more?"

"It's not an imposition. When I got divorced, two of my friends were always available for me, even when they didn't have time. I remember that when I can listen for someone else. Take all the time you need."

"Thank you." Alyssa took a deep breath. "You see, I destroyed my marriage." Alyssa unloaded everything that had happened. She kept the details to a minimum but didn't gloss over what she'd done or how she'd felt about it during and after. She talked about coming home and talking with Robert. She told Jessica of her desire to make everything right, and how she couldn't meet Robert's demands. "I have been sitting here thinking that I will need to pick up some woman in a bar or hire a prostitute. I don't know what to do, and I think he wants me to fail so he can say he gave me a chance."

"That is some tale, and some spot you're in. I'm not judging, but I know how he feels, at least a little. My husband cheated on me for two years before I found out. I had a threesome with two of his single friends the day the divorce was final, just so the story would get back to him. I understand why Robert asked for what he did. You hurt him, and you did it behind his back."

"He wants to get even, and to humiliate me. I can't argue with him about it."

"You are right, and no, you can't argue. You can't even negotiate at this point. I wish I could help you."

Alyssa shrank back. "Oh my, no. I wouldn't consider asking you."

"Why not? Am I not pretty enough? You don't think Robert would like me?"

Alyssa's face got hot. "No, it isn't that. You're gorgeous, and he has always had a thing for tall, leggy blondes like you. I mean, you have been so kind to talk, I wouldn't dream of asking you to sleep with him to help me."

"You think I wouldn't like it?"

"No." Alyssa flushed again. "Robert is good in bed, at least based on my experience. He's just, well, I think he's looking to use someone in every degrading way to hurt me. I wouldn't know how to even ask someone to do that, much less a friend."

"I'm glad to hear you call me a friend, though we are just getting to know each other. Being pretty and divorced tends to keep me out of the couples' parties around here. I don't have a lot of friends in the neighborhood."

"Only a friend would have stopped to help me today. I wish I had realized it sooner."

"A friend might learn that, sometimes, I like being used in degrading ways. I just don't like that known around the neighborhood."

"What?"

Jessica shivered. "The chilly air is getting to me. Why don't we walk to my house and have a cup of coffee? We can get to know each other better."

Alyssa nodded. "That sounds great."

～

The two women strolled the few blocks to Jessica's. Alyssa ran two cups of coffee through the Keurig in the kitchen while Jessica turned on the gas logs in the keeping room. They sat on the love seat in front of the fireplace.

"Put your feet up and get warm," Jessica said, putting her bare feet on the hearth and setting her coffee cup on the end table.

Alyssa mimicked her, enjoying the warmth on her bare skin. She noticed the bright pink toenails on Jessica's long, slender feet, and the dainty gold chain around her ankle. "You have lovely feet, if you don't mind me saying so."

"Thank you. My ex used to call them skis."

"He must have been a real jerk. You have long legs, and you are so tall. Your feet fit you. The pedicure and the anklet are the perfect touches."

"Oh, he called them skis, but it didn't keep him from fucking them."

"What? He did your feet? How?" *Paul could fuck my feet and come all the way to my belly, I bet.* She felt that familiar warmth in her crotch and moved her legs to get some relief. *Easy, Alyssa.*

"Oh, he fucked every part of me he could think of: pussy, mouth, and ass, of course, but also feet, tits, thighs, underarms, butt cheeks, whatever. He even brought other people to bed with us on a vacation. I think he wanted to do anything someone else might have ever done with me. He ensured I knew he owned me. Don't get me wrong, it was really good, right up until he decided that owning me meant he could do those same things with other women." A thin smile crossed her lips, then faded.

Perfect teeth too. "So you liked what he did in the bedroom, all the different ways? Even with other people there?" Alyssa remembered Mike fucking her ass and how hard she had come. She moved her thighs together again. *I wonder if some other ways would make me come as hard?*

"Oh yes. We only had bedmates that one vacation, but it was exhilarating and hedonistic. He was a great lover. And not just in the bedroom. It was wherever, whenever, however, and I loved it." Jessica placed her hand on her chest. As it drifted over her left breast, her nipple hardened, poking noticeably from inside her thin shirt. When her hand slid onto her belly, she resumed talking. "It worked for us until he cheated."

Alyssa shifted her eyes from Jessica's breast to the fire. "That must have hurt a lot. I did the same thing to Robert." Her gut tightened as she pondered what she had done to her marriage. She looked back at Jessica. "Why are you being kind to me? I must remind you of your ex."

"First, I'm being kind to you because you are my friend and you need someone to be kind to you today. Second, you don't remind me of him. What he did, he did because he felt he could, because he was in control. Funny that he hid it from me." Jessica placed her hand on Alyssa's thigh. "It sounds like you wanted to explore, and you have been honest about it. You still love your husband."

The warmth of Jessica's hand spread up Alyssa's thigh, and she let her leg sag outward as a signal for Jessica to keep it there. "I do love him. I also have these desires to explore other things and people." Alyssa sat back to look at the fire and enjoy Jessica's touch. "Robert hasn't said if this deal means he is willing to explore those desires with me or not. I will abide by his decision, either way."

"But what do you really want?"

Alyssa stared into the fire a long moment, then whispered, "I want it all."

"All what?"

Alyssa turned to Jessica, warming from the sudden surge of energy in her chest. "All—everything. I want variety and excitement, and I want to be with other people." Alyssa put both hands in front of her, palms up. The excitement in her chest flowing down her arms made them tremble. "Men and women. I want Robert to experience all that with me, if he wants that. Most of all, I want my husband to love me for who I am becoming."

Jessica kissed Alyssa while rubbing her thigh. Her off hand cupped Alyssa's breast, causing her to moan into Jessica's open mouth. Alyssa grasped Jessica's breast, returning the affection and flicking the hard nipple with her finger.

Jessica broke the kiss but kept her hands engaged. "Are you sure? You really want all that?"

"Absolutely. And I want to start with you." Alyssa leaned toward Jessica, then pulled back, shaking her head. "I can't. Not right now. I'm on thin ice as it is. Another lover right now and Robert would divorce me for sure." The thought of Robert's reaction if she walked in smelling like sex doused Alyssa's libido. A chill shuddered up and down her spine. "I couldn't control my urges in Houston. I have to do better here at home."

"I understand. You need to work on your marriage." Jessica smiled. "Now that we are friends, know I'm always here to listen and help you stay strong." She gripped Alyssa's shoulder. "I'll help you remember what you want."

"Marriage first, then everything else." She was no closer to a solution than when she had left the playground with Jessica. "Now to figure out how."

Jessica stood. "Most human thought actually occurs at the subconscious level. Let's talk a while, and maybe an idea will strike us. More coffee?"

✧

Two cups and an hour later, they both stared into the fire, warm from its heat and enjoying a pause in the conversation. Jessica broke the silence. "I will help you."

Alyssa looked up. "You will? How?"

"I'll help you plan it, and I'll fuck your husband."

Alyssa sat forward when for the first time all afternoon, she felt some hope inside her body. "Are you sure?" Confusion overcame the hope as she realized what Jessica had said. "And what do we need to plan?"

"I'm sure. We need to plan so he not only wants to save your marriage but wants to open your marriage. It will take some work on your part. You talked about not keeping secrets from him, so treat this like a birthday surprise. You have to keep the plan quiet for now."

Alyssa smiled and nodded. "I can do that."

"Also, I have one condition."

Oh shit, the conditions I've had to live with today. Alyssa swallowed the lump in her throat. "What's that?"

"When this is done, I get a night with you."

Shit. What if Robert doesn't want to open our marriage? He would never tolerate Alyssa stepping out on their marriage again. Alyssa wrung her hands. *If he does, he won't mind. He might even like it.* Alyssa's competing hope and dread flipped again, dread racing through her chest, constricting her throat on its way to her brain. *If he doesn't, we likely end up divorced, and I won't need to worry.* Accepting her lack of options settled her dread, letting hope grow in her chest. Alyssa smiled at the only option she had to save her marriage, who sat beside her, watching. "That's a deal."

They planned over a glass of wine before Alyssa returned home to make dinner. A phone call later that night finalized everything. Alyssa prepared for a long, orchestrated week ahead. She smiled.

∽

After they ate, Alyssa and Robert spoke with Clay about their sleeping arrangements. He revealed that he had heard Robert leave and Alyssa cry the previous night, so he expected something. They told him they needed to work through some things that had happened in Houston, leaving out the details. They emphasized that they were working things out, and that their issues were not caused by him or Susan, and they both still loved him every bit as much as ever. Outside of Alyssa sleeping in the guest room, the family would function normally. Clay held his emotions as teenage boys will, and when they finished, he went to his room.

Alyssa and Robert watched TV after cleaning the kitchen. They discussed how the conversation went with Clay, and how they would spend extra time with him the next few days. Outside of family issues, they didn't speak. Robert said good night and walked to the bedroom. Alyssa didn't look up. *Wait, Alyssa. This has to look natural.* She fidgeted on the couch, watching the clock tick off four minutes before she got up. *Step one.*

Alyssa entered without knocking, heading to their large walk-in closet where she knew Robert would be undressing. She stood gazing at his muscular naked body, shifting from foot to foot. She held her breath to calm her fluttering stomach, knowing things could go badly when he turned and saw her.

"What are you doing in here?"

Act natural. She swallowed her smile behind a small cough. *He didn't throw me out.* "Getting ready for bed, same as you." Alyssa removed her shirt and bra as she had done countless times since they'd married, but she continued to face Robert, watching him watch her.

"You're sleeping in the guest room."

"Yes, but my clothes are in here." She turned her back to

Robert and bent over to wriggle out of her jeans and panties, giving him a good look at her naked backside and the cleft beneath it. She looked over her shoulder without straightening. "Would you prefer that I move them? I want this arrangement to work for you. I want to make you happy." *Look at me and remember how happy I can make you.*

She watched Robert's cock thicken as she retrieved a thin nightgown from her drawer and slid it over her head. She had placed this one on the top of the stack, knowing her nipples showed through it and that it barely fell below her ass. "May I dress in here for now?"

Robert broke his stare and shook his head, his cock continuing to harden. "Yes. You can leave your stuff in here. Let's not make this harder than it is." He looked her up and down. "You don't wear that one often."

She shrugged. "Huh? Yeah. I just grabbed the one on top." Alyssa looked into Robert's eyes with a soft smile. Her heart pounded in her chest, and she fought throwing her arms around his neck, knowing he still wanted her. "Well, good night." She headed to the guest room. "Love you."

12
MONDAY

Alyssa waited until she heard the shower running to head to the master bathroom Monday morning. She dropped the thin nightgown in the clothes hamper before going in to brush her teeth, knowing her sink was directly across from the glass shower enclosure. Following Jessica's advice, she kept her normal ready routine but thrust her hips to the side a little more than usual and arched her back a little more. She emphasized her assets without posing for him. She smiled that Robert's dick jutted in front of him after he noticed her presence. She waited until he turned off the water and toweled off before speaking. "I figured I would get ready in here, if you don't mind. Just like keeping my clothes in the closet?"

Robert wrapped the towel around his waist, which did nothing to hide his sizable erection. "Uh, yeah. It's fine. We don't need to make this hard. But you don't normally get ready naked."

219

"Yeah. It was hot in the guest room. The nightgown was sweaty, so I took it off. You used to like seeing me this way." She turned the shower on, reaching to get the temperature right.

Robert grunted, "It's fine," and shook his head, then started getting ready at his sink. Alyssa took her shower, making sure to caress herself when she caught Robert watching in the mirror. *I have his attention. That's a good sign.*

She finished her shower and got ready, staying in the bathroom with Robert, and staying nude. Alyssa engaged in conversation about Clay and his reaction to their conversation last night, turning and facing Robert when she spoke so he got good looks at her body. She made sure that she joined Robert in the closet to get dressed, and that she had his attention while she put on her clothes. *He's having trouble getting that hard dick in his pants.*

Ready to go to work, Alyssa said goodbye and walked to Clay's empty room. He had left for school early. She knew her son would want to talk, and she would be ready when he brought it up. While she thought about it, she texted Susan. "Your Dad knows everything. We are working through it. Clay knows we are having an issue, but not any details. I'm ready to talk with you when you are ready to talk with me. Love you. Mom."

Dinner that night consisted of all Robert's favorites, with Clay's favorite dessert. Alyssa celebrated being home and made sure that they felt loved. She worked through her lunch to leave work early and buy the groceries. She bought a good bottle of wine as well and let Robert drink most of it. Dinner conversation was strained, but it improved as they talked about their days. After dinner, Clay again retreated to his room and Robert watched

TV. Alyssa changed into loose shorts and a V neck T-shirt, then joined Robert. Alyssa sat with her feet on the couch, one knee up, making sure that her panties flashed at Robert when she spoke to him. She also gave Robert a good view down her shirt when she filled his glass with the last of the wine.

Alyssa noticed the bulge in Robert's pants when he headed to bed. Excited, she again waited four minutes before going back herself. Encountering Robert in the closet, she took her time stripping off her clothes, giving him a good show. She again opted for a thin, short nightgown that revealed more than it hid. Robert's erection achieved, she again said good night and turned to go.

"If you're hot, you can turn down the heat," Robert said before she left the room.

Alyssa faced him, appearing to ponder his offer as she gave him another veiled view of her body. "No, you and Clay shouldn't be cold just so I can be comfortable. I can sleep in these thin nightgowns and not use covers. Thank you though. Love you, Babe. Good night." She left, swaying her ass as she did.

Tuesday morning repeated Monday's ready routine. Alyssa waited until Robert was in the shower, then got ready naked, showering seductively while he watched. She wanted him to feel aroused and excited by her body, hoping that lust would cascade into more tender feelings. She knew that although he had seen her naked countless times, her body still aroused him, unlike what some of her friends had revealed about their husbands. She wanted Robert to remember the sexual part of their relationship, how good it had been, and what he was forgoing by sleeping apart from her.

Alyssa again worked through her lunch to get home and make more of her family's favorite foods for dinner. Dinner conversation flowed a little freer. Robert enjoyed most of the wine. They even laughed a little. After dinner, Clay again retreated to his room, Alyssa again dressed in revealing, comfortable clothes, and Robert again sat in front of the TV. Alyssa tried to engage him in more conversation, but she held his eye more than his ear. She propped her foot on the cushion to look natural spreading her legs for him. "Robert, can we talk a minute?"

Robert tore his eyes away from her crotch. "Sure. What's on your mind?"

"How are you feeling? About me, and us? Have you softened any?"

"Alyssa, why are you asking?"

"I want to know how your feelings are progressing. You've had a few days to absorb all this. I want to know if we have a chance."

"Have you done what I asked? You know the price of reconciliation. I think it is best if we let you show just how remorseful you are. I'm not trying to be an asshole; I'm trying to be fair. You need to feel some of what I feel so we can talk on an even plane."

Alyssa dropped her gaze to the floor. "I haven't set anything up yet. I'm being careful in who I pick."

"I see," Robert growled. "Were you careful last week?"

Alyssa ignored the question. "I'm thinking of your reputation. I'm sure you wouldn't want Nancy from your office, though she would, right?"

"Hmm. She's an interesting option. A hot slut always available, perhaps making you jealous. But you are right, I don't need to be featured in her rumors."

"And I know you like Carol's body. You always have. And you know she sleeps around. But you don't want to hurt Chris, right?"

"Right on all counts."

"That's what I am up against. I'm trying, but I haven't found the right option."

"You'll figure it out, Alyssa. You always do. It's one of the things I love about you."

Alyssa sat stunned. "You still love me?"

Robert pursed his lips as he looked over her body. "I do still love you. I always have, and I always will. A marriage takes more than love though. It takes trust and respect, too, and those are hard to come by right now. You have to earn those back, and the clock is ticking."

"I thought there was no deadline."

"There isn't, but the longer we wait before trying to revive our marriage, the harder it will be."

"You mean sleeping together? We are almost normal in all other regards."

"Sleeping together, yes, but also regular life. I see what you have been doing. You are home early to cook special meals." Robert smiled. "I get text alerts from the house alarm, too, you know. You are paying extra attention to Clay and me every night, even though we aren't responding. You are trying, but I remain skeptical. You need to do whatever you're going to do, and then we will see what happens."

"I understand. Please know I'm trying." *Trying to get you in the mood for what's coming.*

"I see that. Make it happen."

Alyssa waited, looking at the ceiling to show Robert her concentration. She shrugged. "Would you accept an escort?"

"What? No! Prostitution is illegal. Not an option."

Alyssa sighed and looked at the floor. "Okay. I'll figure something out." Alyssa lay on her belly, then slid, moving the legs of her loose shorts enough to show a hint of her ass. She watched the news before Robert headed back to the bedroom. Alyssa followed four minutes later to dress for bed in what had become a bit of a routine: She got nude, he got hard, then she sauntered out to sleep in a flimsy nightgown.

Tonight was different. Robert was naked as he had been the previous two nights, but tonight he was hard before she entered the large closet. Alyssa subconsciously licked her lips and smiled at Robert, who unabashedly watched her. She stuck to her routine, sexily stripping her clothes, giving Robert long, slow looks at all of her. She pulled yet another diaphanous nightie from her drawer, slipped it over her head, and turned to leave. Alyssa turned back and gave Robert a kiss on the cheek. "I know you are trying too. I love you. Good night."

✍

Wednesday proceeded as the previous days had: Alyssa enticed Robert when they were together, and they conversed more like the married couple they wanted to become again. Wednesday night had Alyssa show her body, eventually stripping for an excited Robert before heading to the guest room. Thursday started the same way.

✍

Thursday night, Alyssa upped the ante. She opened a second bottle of wine and made sure Robert drank more than he had the previous nights. When Clay retreated to his room, Alyssa changed into a thin, tight T-shirt and pulled thin, gray yoga shorts into the cleft of her pussy, leaving nothing to the imagination. She tweaked her nipples into hard points, and she stroked her clit until the shorts darkened from her wetness. Alyssa took her usual position where Robert could see her, and she selected a sexy movie on TV. They didn't talk, but Alyssa made a show of fondling her breasts during the sexier scenes, keeping her nipples hard. Robert just as openly watched his wife stimulate herself.

When the movie ended, Robert headed to the bedroom, his erection tenting his pants. Alyssa smiled and waited four minutes before heading back herself. She met Robert, naked and erect, in their walk-in closet. Alyssa began to strip again, moving slower than she had during previous nights. She made the hem of her shirt catch under her breasts, raising them before slipping the shirt past her nipples and letting her full orbs fall and jiggle. She pulled the soaked yoga shorts down, rolling them inside out to show Robert the moisture on the gusset and on her spread lips. Alyssa looked through her legs to watch Robert slowly stroking his cock as he stared at his wife.

Alyssa moved to her lingerie drawer, selecting the sheerest and most revealing nightgown she owned.

Robert broke the routine, speaking for the first time. "Would you like to stay tonight?"

Alyssa stepped closer, grasping his cock and kissing his neck. "It will be best if I show how remorseful I am. We want to be on an even plane, don't we?" She stepped back. "Love you. I'll see you in the morning." Robert's loud laugh put an extra swing in her hips as she left the room.

13
FRIDAY

ALYSSA GOT READY early Friday morning, still nude and teasing Robert, but more efficiently, with an eye on the clock. She worked through her lunch again to arrive home before 4:00 and make a pot of soup. She put ham and cheese sandwiches for grilling in the refrigerator. Jessica arrived just before 5:00.

Alyssa answered the door. "Are you sure about this?"

Jessica smiled. "Alyssa, I'm sure I want to help you. I'm also sure that I need a good fucking. This will be good for both of us."

"Okay. I don't know how to thank you."

"Yes, you do. One night with you, remember?"

"I remember, and I look forward to it." She gave her sexy neighbor a long, passionate kiss. "Let's put your bag in the bedroom."

"We need to change also."

Robert stopped dead when he walked through the kitchen

door about thirty minutes later. Alyssa made eye contact with him over the three glasses of wine sitting on the table in front of her. Robert looked to her right, then up and down the blonde sitting there in a black cupless push-up bra, clearly ignoring his wife's similarly bare tits.

When Robert's face flushed, Alyssa swallowed the lump that Robert's indifference had lodged in her throat and spoke. "Welcome home, Baby."

"What the hell, Alyssa? Did you decide to explore your sexuality some more?"

"No, Robert. This is Jessica. She lives down the street, though you probably didn't recognize her dressed, well, undressed, so differently. This isn't exploring. This is reconciliation. Jessica is yours for the night."

"Where is Clay?"

"He's staying with Mom. I told him we were going to have a long talk and he should stay there." She watched the blood begin to drain from his face. *Now it begins.* Her stomach tightened, but she forced a deep breath. "Robert, do you want to welcome our guest?"

"Ah, yes," Robert stammered. "Jessica, welcome to our home. You look stunning."

"Thank you, Robert. I hope I can help you and Alyssa get back on track. She loves you very much, and she agonized persuading me to do this for her." She stood, giving Robert a good look.

Alyssa gritted her teeth and plastered a smile on her mouth to hold in her fear of being replaced. She fought her fear back to fight for her marriage. *Play the part you must.* "I tried hard, Babe. I know what you like. Long, blonde, wavy hair. Big blue eyes. Beautiful face. Long body with big, full tits. I bet you can't wait to suck on those little pink nipples and kiss those toned"—her voice cracked, and she inhaled—"those toned abs. Long legs, ready for you to slide that tiny little thong all the way down to her high heels. All for you."

"I take it from the bulge in your pants that Alyssa chose well."

"Yes, she has. I never doubted her." He turned to his wife. The lips that had been parted pressed together. His fingers clenched but not quite into fists. His eyes narrowed a tiny little bit, the way they did when he was scolding someone. "Alyssa, Jessica is beautiful; you checked every box of what I like, even the faint tan lines. If she is willing, I'm going to fuck her as many times as I can get hard, and I expect you to watch every one. This will hurt you the way you hurt me. I hope tomorrow morning, we can begin to heal together. Are you sure you want this?"

Alyssa's breath caught as she tried to respond. The hot tear rolling down her cheek seemed to settle her. "I'll watch. You do whatever you and Jessica want to do. I want to begin to heal tomorrow too." She turned to Jessica. "Are you sure you want to do this, now that you are both here?"

Jessica strode to Robert and grabbed his hard cock through his pants. "Oh yes." She turned to Alyssa. "Are you sure?"

She is everything he likes. Alyssa nodded, spilling more tears down her cheeks. "Go ahead. Bring my husband back to me." *Please don't take him from me.*

Jessica turned to Robert. "I'm yours for the night, starting now. How do you want to start?"

In her heels, Jessica was nearly Robert's height. He kissed her without bending his neck. His hands moved to her ass, and he ground her pelvis against his straining cock. He rubbed and pulled her firm, smooth cheeks. She pinched his nipple through his shirt while kissing him back. He cupped his hands underneath her butt and sat her on the kitchen table beside his wife. "Lie back. Let's get you ready," he said, pushing between her breasts. Alyssa stifled a gasp. They hadn't had sex on the kitchen table since before the kids were born.

When Jessica lay on the table with her legs pointed upward, goose bumps arose on her body. Alyssa touched the table. *The wood is cold.* Robert used both hands to pull the thong over her hips and up her legs, handing it to Alyssa without looking at her. *So was that.*

Robert sat in a chair between Jessica's legs. Hooking her knees over his shoulders, he kissed and bit the insides of her thighs, alternating one leg, then the other, growing ever nearer to her pussy. Alyssa stretched taller to see. *I know how well he does this. I don't want to see, but I do.* Robert used his lips to part Jessica's, pulling the puffy outer lips to the side one at a time, then gripping the inner lips and pulling.

When Jessica moaned, Robert licked between her folds, long and slow, reaching her clit with an aggressive flick of his tongue. Jessica's hands gripped the edge of the table, and she pressed her hips into his face. Robert backed away before licking from midthigh upward, skirting his tongue across her perineum and down the other thigh, then returning. When he reached her pussy this time, he dove his tongue into her like a little cock. He scraped his teeth on her clit and pulled her labia apart with his fingers, filling the gap with his tongue.

Alyssa wept silently as she watched Robert make Jessica writhe and moan with his tongue. The empty feeling in her chest fed on her insecurity even while growing it. She still watched, leaning toward the two even though her back weakened with fear. *That should be me. This has to happen, but I don't have to like it. Stay quiet. I won't let him hear me sob.* Her nose ran, and she tasted the salt on her lips. Alyssa watched Robert perform on Jessica. He was holding nothing back, using the techniques Alyssa loved best.

Jessica's thigh muscles and tendons flexed and rippled as she pulled Robert to her with her calves. Her belly rose and fell faster with each breath. Her moans confirmed that Robert was devastating her. *I love when he does that, and so does she.* Even through her tears, Alyssa grew horny watching the live porn show on her kitchen table. Subconsciously, she stroked her bare nipples.

Jessica moved her hands from the table edge, pinching and pulling her nipples, distending her breasts. Her head rolled from side to side. Alyssa pinched her nipple, anticipating Robert's next move and Jessica's reaction. He shifted his mouth over her clit, sucking and flicking it with his tongue. He replaced his tongue with two fingers in her cunt, hooking them forward to stimulate her front wall. Jessica's first orgasm exploded out of her. Her thighs clamped on Robert's ears. She cried out and arched her back, slamming her hands on the table and pushing.

The sound and smell of Jessica's orgasm shook Alyssa. The long wail resonated in the quiet house, and at this distance, the smell of her sex obscured the aroma of the soup on the stove. Alyssa continued to cry, pained that her Robert was doing to another woman what he should be doing to her, but rubbing her nipple inflamed her pussy, and her lips warmed as the blood flowed to them, preparing them to meet a need she knew would not be met. *I did this to myself.* She dipped her head briefly before returning her stare to the two lovers in front of her. Her heart ached, but her body crackled. The contrast met inside her like a thunderstorm. She slid her panties aside, flicking her clit and massaging her lips, making them wet and slick before inserting a finger. She inserted another finger and twisted her nipple, tears still flowing as she did so.

Jessica's legs relaxed. Her fingers stretched away from the table's edge. Her breathing slowed. Alyssa smirked. She was ready for what was coming.

Jessica was not.

Her body arched and her legs contracted when Robert growled and pumped his hand furiously between her legs. Alyssa smiled and pulled her nipple, letting the pressure in her breast and the pinch in her nipple fire bolts of white electricity deep into her body. *When he sucks and flicks your clit at the same time he punishes your G-spot, it's almost unbearable, isn't it?* She spread her fingers, pushing back at her walls squeezing them, feeling pleasure in her lips and up to the G-spot she stroked, but feeling empty farther inside.

Alyssa came just after Jessica did. *That's my husband making you come so hard. You love it, but he's mine when you are done.* Her pride stifled the jealous ache in her chest and freed her explosion. The orgasm that followed racked her body, making her fall over in the chair. When she recovered, she sat, still agog at the sexy scene before her, still crying quietly.

Robert stood to remove his clothes while Jessica lay limply on the table. He looked at Alyssa, who met his eyes. The three fingers inside her own cunt and the small puddle on the chair indicated she'd had at least one orgasm herself. Cool tears dripped onto her tits, but she knew she had to acknowledge what Robert was doing. He needed her to feel this way, and to tell him to continue. She nodded at him and whispered, "Give it to her."

He smiled as he hefted his thick, curved cock in front of her before lining it up with Jessica's gaping entrance. He tapped the tip on her clit, making her belly jerk, before slipping just the head inside. Robert leaned back as his hips inched forward. Alyssa watched Jessica's belly rise above it as he advanced. She groaned but lay limp, obviously still recovering. Robert held still, then withdrew just as slowly as he had entered. When he rammed into her, Jessica's legs rose and her shoulders curled forward as she silently screamed. Robert pulled her legs over his shoulders, and she gripped his arms as he hammered her pussy and strummed her clit with his thumb. Alyssa watched, pride and jealousy still battling in her chest, absent-mindedly tweaking her nipple.

"Ooh fuck. God, keep doing that. Oh, fuck me." Jessica wailed as Robert hammered her. He squeezed her breast with his free hand, holding it in place while the other danced on her chest. He maintained the pace. Jessica's breasts resonated in time with his thrusts. Rapt, Alyssa watched them circle, wondering if hers looked the same, while she reinserted three fingers, letting the sting of stretching her lips electrify the top of her vagina. With a grunt, Robert buried himself in Jessica, who tensed yet again.

Jessica's legs slipped from his shoulders, hanging limp off the table. Robert bent forward, resting his head on her sweaty chest as they both caught their breath. Alyssa ground her hips on her fingers and stroked her clit, trying to have another orgasm. His face turned to her for the first time since he'd put Jessica on the table. Alyssa locked her watery eyes with Robert's narrowed ones. His disdain chilled her spine, but his attention warmed her heart, and her throat tensed while she came, moaning deep in her chest. For a glorious instant, connection replaced sadness. As the glow in her pussy dissipated, unease returned, tightening her gut.

"Fuck. You get that all the time?" Jessica asked Alyssa.

Alyssa closed her eyes as if her inability to see Jessica and Robert allowed her an escape while she wrestled with her emotions.

"Answer the question, Alyssa," Robert said after a pause.

She smiled, eager to brag on her husband. "I get it a lot. I told you he was good in bed."

"You used to get it a lot. We will see what happens now, won't we?" Robert corrected her.

"Yes," Alyssa said, his reprimand loosening her stomach like dropping through the floor.

Jessica stroked Robert's head. "I hope you are rested. I promised all night, and I want that all night."

Robert chuckled. "As I recall, you were promised to me all night, and I intend to see what you can do. All night."

"Challenge accepted. You will remember tonight, young man."

Robert looked at Alyssa. "Would you like to participate? Perhaps improve my attitude?"

Tingles linked between her breasts and her pussy. She leaned forward but swallowed the smile coming up her neck. *Don't appear too happy about it.* "I will do anything you want if it gives us a chance."

"Good." Robert slid his prick out of Jessica. A glob of semen flowed down her ass to the table. "Come clean my cock with your mouth, then clean Jessica. We don't want to get too messy too early."

Alyssa knelt before Robert, the cold floor easier on her knees than Robert's tone was on her heart. She took as much of his cock as she could in her mouth, trying to dispense with the humiliation of cleaning another woman off him. Jessica's scent mingled with his familiar sweat. She bobbed her head over the end, savoring the taste and his returning hardness before lowering her body to lick the base of his cock clean. "Don't forget to clean my balls," Robert reminded her with a gentle push on top of her head. She sucked one ball, then the other, feeling his semihard, wet cock smear her cheek as she moved.

The smells and tastes of sex took root in Alyssa's mind. When her tears stopped, she cupped her pussy, and Robert grabbed a handful of her brown hair and pulled her head back, turning her face upward. "That's good enough. Now clean Jessica." He pulled her head, placing her mouth on the puddle of cum at Jessica's ass. "Start with that, then suck the rest out of her. I want to fuck a clean pussy tonight."

Chills radiated from her chest when it touched the cold table edge, making Alyssa flinch. She hissed when she pressed forward to make a show of slurping the cum off the table, making it sound like she was getting the last drops of a milkshake from a straw. Each swallow warmed her chest like coffee on a cold morning, but disproportionate to the few drops she managed at a time. Her pussy echoed her heartbeat, amplifying it in a plea for attention. Alyssa answered by stroking her satiny panties across her lips.

She didn't hesitate moving her tongue to Jessica's ass, lingering to clean every drop of leaking cum and making Jessica purr. *Like Kate and Beth but with cum. My husband's glorious cum.*

When she moved her tongue to Jessica's slit, she licked it, keeping the lips apart. She mimicked her tongue with her hand on her own pussy, the satin teasing her own lips apart before she drove her tongue inside Jessica. She latched her mouth onto Jessica's opening and sucked. Jessica wove her fingers into Alyssa's hair, the slight tug gripping Alyssa's pussy a hundred times stronger than it felt in her scalp. The slick friction no longer sufficient, Alyssa answered her pussy by sliding her hand inside her panties. Her legs quivered at the feel of warm skin on warm skin.

Robert broke the mood, tamping Alyssa's rising pleasure with an icy tone. "Show me what you have cleaned, Alyssa. Open your mouth and show me."

Alyssa pulled her head back, turned to Robert, and showed him the cum she hadn't already swallowed. Jessica protested at the interruption, and Robert smiled. "Alyssa, Jessica wants an orgasm. Let's start by giving her mine. Kiss her and let the cum in your mouth flow into hers."

That's new. Did he make a list of things we've never done? It's like he's mapping my limits. Alyssa straightened. *No limit yet.* She stepped to the other side of the table to reach Jessica's head. As she bent to plant the kiss, Jessica winked at her, easing her discomfort about the perverted act. Their lips met, and the salty cum flowed over her tongue, lingering on her lips before falling out. After only a second, Jessica dipped her tongue into Alyssa's mouth, as if hunting for the remainder. Their tongues twisted across each other, tasting and sharing the juices before Jessica pulled her tongue back and swallowed. Alyssa rose and opened her mouth for Robert's inspection.

He chuckled. "Very good. Do that with the rest. Make her come while you retrieve it, Alyssa."

Alyssa stripped off her red thong before she returned to Jessica's pussy, kneeling on the hard floor and sucking cum while stroking Jessica's clit with her thumb and rewarding her own with her fingers. When she had a full mouth, she broke contact, again making Jessica moan her complaint. Alyssa walked around the table, and the two repeated their lusty sharing for Robert's amusement. Returning to Jessica's crotch, Alyssa focused on making Jessica come, letting her own pussy simmer. She sucked what little of Robert's spend remained and held it in her mouth while working Jessica's clit. Jessica pulled Alyssa's head to her pussy and groaned. Her lips compressed between her teeth and Jessica's pubic bone until Alyssa thought they would pop from the pressure. Alyssa caught Jessica's little splash of fluid in her mouth, showing it to Robert before strutting around the table. She dipped her head to kiss Jessica, but when Jessica opened her mouth, she rose about six inches and let the combined cum flow over her lips, into Jessica's mouth, before again dipping to complete their kiss.

"Most impressive." Robert leered at the two women across the table. "Alyssa, what is for dinner? It smells good, and we should keep up our strength."

Alyssa rose from Jessica's lips. "Chicken soup and grilled ham and cheese."

"Sounds good. You get those ready. Jessica, why don't you join us?"

Alyssa bent to get her apron out of a drawer. *Cooking in lingerie works better in stories than real life.* She and Jessica had purchased matching outfits for tonight. Alyssa didn't expect to participate at all, certainly not in the way she just had, but the red lingerie made her feel included. Her sadness at seeing Robert with Jessica had abated as her arousal grew, and her body tingled from the orgasm she'd abandoned moments ago. She focused on preparing dinner, hoping to bond with the other two while they ate, not yet daring to hope that Robert would make love to her. Alyssa got out the sandwiches and poured a little olive oil on the griddle.

Robert stood at the far end of the kitchen island from Alyssa. "Jessica, would you come over here, and bring the olive oil with you, please?"

Jessica picked up the olive oil with a quizzical look and walked to Robert.

"I want you to do what my wife has never done for me but that she recently did for someone else." Robert looked out the corner of his eye to Alyssa. "Would you bend over the island here? I want to fuck your ass." For the first time, Alyssa's ass didn't tingle when she remembered Mike fucking her there.

"Ooh. I like that," Jessica said with a smile, resting her elbows on the counter and jutting her ass toward Robert.

Robert poured his palm full of olive oil and rubbed it on his cock, then stuffed two oily fingers in Jessica's back door, lubricating her. Jessica tensed, then relaxed. He withdrew his hand, and he pressed the head of his dick against her opening, applying enough pressure to slip inside. Jessica gripped the edge of the countertop. Robert used a dish towel to wipe his oily hands, then reached under to cup Jessica's breasts. He pinched the nipples between his middle and ring fingers as he held her. Using them for leverage, he pushed farther inside her oily ass, making her groan. He stopped about halfway in and let her get used to the thickness inside her. When she nodded, he pushed forward more, not stopping until he nudged her cheeks with his abs. They were still. Jessica's face softened from red and strained to normal, then she licked her lips and nodded. When Robert started moving inside her, Jessica bit her lower lip and muttered, "Mm-hmm."

Robert looked at Alyssa. "I never knew an ass could feel this good, baby. And fucking it while you cook for me? Man, what a great way to spend an evening."

Alyssa looked in their direction, but she didn't look at Robert. The sheer ecstasy on Jessica's face captivated her. Jessica's eyes had rolled back in her head, and her mouth hung open. Her long hair just brushed the countertop, obscuring Alyssa's view of her breasts, but she could see Robert's arms straining to keep his grip on them as he rocked his hips. Alyssa boiled at Jessica's pleasure. *That should be me. I want his cock in my ass, goddamn it.* A pop of hot grease interrupted Alyssa's jealousy, and she flipped the sandwiches before they burned. As she turned her focus back to the rutting couple, arousal overpowered the jealousy.

Robert picked up speed, bouncing Jessica into the countertop. He pulled his hands back to her hips, then pressed her chest onto the cold granite. He spanked her cheeks on some strokes, making them pink as he reamed her.

Jessica emitted a long, low moan, inhaled, and did it again. With her head on the counter, Alyssa couldn't see her face, but when her fingers scrabbled against the granite, unable to grab, Alyssa knew Robert had made her come again.

Robert grabbed a handful of Jessica's long hair and pulled, making her look like a horse being ridden. He pulled her hair just enough to raise her face, but he kept her tits rubbing against the counter. He announced his orgasm, pressed deep into her, and stilled. He reached for some nearby paper towels, squirted some soap on them, and wet them in the sink to his left. He washed his cock and Jessica's ass with them, removing all the oil and other fluids, drying them both with more towels. *He even cleaned her up. He's full service. I want mine.*

∽

"Good timing. Dinner is ready." Alyssa had managed to avoid burning the sandwiches while she watched her husband bugger her beautiful neighbor. She had not been able to give herself any release while she watched, and her pussy had loosed a small trail of juice down her right thigh, almost to the knee. She caught it with her finger, swiping up, then licked her finger clean. She served dinner without touching herself, but she was so aroused that she couldn't sit still, instead choosing to rub her wet lips across and around the seat of her chair.

The three of them sat at the kitchen table, eating and having as normal a conversation as possible given their plans for the night. Robert and Jessica learned each other, having never talked at neighborhood events. Alyssa played hostess, using what she knew of them to keep the conversation moving. They realized how hungry they were when they started eating, and dug in. They finished the bottle of wine, then switched to water to remain hydrated. Alyssa took the dishes to the sink, but before she could sit back down, Robert stood.

"Jessica, let's take this to the bedroom. My wife hasn't been sleeping there, and I want to fuck in our bed." Painful cramps gripped Alyssa's sides at the comment. She winced, then led the way to the bedroom. Robert pulled one of the wingback chairs from the corner of the room beside the bed. "Sit here and watch, Alyssa. We've done depraved and dirty. If this is mind-blowing, we might match what you said made yours the hottest pure fuck of your life. Is that right?"

Alyssa gasped, then nodded and sat. Tears welling in her eyes couldn't relieve the pain his comment buried in her chest. The tingle in her nipples, the grasping of her pussy, the hot churn in her belly that raged while she watched her own live porn performance retreated, replaced by the pain Robert drove into her chest in the last three minutes. Alyssa pulled her knees to her chest, protecting her heart from further injury. *This is how I made him feel. We do have some healing to do.* She gritted her teeth and let out a long breath. *So do your part.* Then she wiped her eyes and watched.

Jessica dropped her bra on the floor and crawled naked onto the bed, turning on all fours to face Robert. "Why don't you bring that marvelous cock over here?" She smiled. "I'll get it hard so you can fuck me again."

Robert stood at the edge of the bed as Jessica sucked his full length into her mouth. Alyssa watched his cock harden and swell every time it emerged from between Jessica's lips, imagining the feeling in her own mouth every time Jessica's nose touched his abs. Imagined pressure flowed from her throat to ease the pain still sitting in her chest.

Jessica swallowed his fully hard cock a few times, then pulling back, grinning. "You're ready. How do you want me?"

Robert climbed onto the bed and lay on his back in his usual spot. His cock stood straight up. "I want to watch your beautiful body ride me. I want Alyssa to watch that too."

Jessica kissed Robert and slid her knee across his hips as he held her hair. She rose, reached between them, and lowered herself with a hiss. She rolled her hips around before lifting and dropping down, hissing again. She repeated her pattern two more times before settling all the way down on his abs. There she stayed, grinding her hips. Alyssa leaned over the side of the chair for a glimpse of her husband's cock buried in her neighbor's cunt, and her heel pressed against her lower lips, the hard bone reawakening them. She imagined his cock pressing there, shifting, teasing while seeking entry.

Jessica ground on Robert a while, then rose and plunged down. Her ass rippled with each impact as she rode with long strokes. Alyssa righted herself in the chair but kept her heel grinding her entrance, the big tendon firing her clit as it made contact. Every time Jessica plunged down onto Robert, Alyssa's pussy gripped at the emptiness inside, wanting more and building the pleasure in her belly that rose to meet the pain abating in her chest.

Robert dropped his hands to Jessica's hips, allowing her tits to flop and bounce in time with her plunges. Alyssa watched their movement and slid a hand behind her thigh to pull her own breast, pretending the stretch came from her riding in Jessica's place. Jessica accelerated and crashed down, her body tensing with a low whine.

Alyssa watched, rapt, as Jessica continued to spasm, her entire torso flushed pink, her buttocks clinching, hollowing out on the sides. *God, he really is good. He never comes in that position. She's in for more, if he lets her have it.* Jessica mewled unintelligible sounds while impaling herself violently on his cock. Jessica's hair stuck to her face with sweat, and the muscles on her side rippled as she moved.

Alyssa imagined her own hair stuck to her face, and her muscles clenched while her mind put her in Jessica's place. Her heel insufficient for her need, Alyssa spread her feet on the floor and rubbed her clit. Pain and pleasure combined as her fingers pressed harder and moved faster over her sensitive nub. She moved the hand on her breast from the underside to pinch her nipple hard for the shock, then pulled until it hurt. Jealousy and pain forgotten, Alyssa chased her own orgasm.

When Jessica collapsed onto him, Robert grabbed her ribs and rolled her onto her back. He pounded into her. The sound of their bodies thudding together filled the room. He rode her hard. She lay there as he worked her, his hair becoming wet and his muscles flexing as hers had done, and Alyssa felt what she did.

It's good when you give out and he takes over. Alyssa's legs sagged out as if she were the one exhausted beneath her husband, but her hands held firm to their work, pulling, pressing, flicking, and plunging with all the vigor Robert gave to Jessica. Alyssa watched from the side, but she felt what Jessica did. She remembered and let her mind give her body the feelings her husband would not. She came, pussy clenching her fingers, legs curling up until she became a ball, every muscle in her body tensing to hold and release the cataclysmic orgasm that came more from her mind than her fingers.

Alyssa relaxed just in time to see Robert pull out, rise above Jessica, and point his cock at her body as he jacked it. His first spurt landed across one eye. The spurts after that fell across her tits and belly, with the final few drops falling onto her gaping pussy. She rose from the chair to clean Robert's cum from Jessica's body.

"Stay seated, Alyssa," Robert said before she reached the bed. "I have painted Jessica with my cum. It's a good look. It says, 'She's mine,' don't you think?"

Alyssa sat, glancing from Robert to Jessica and back again. "It does indeed. She is so lovely covered in your cum too." Her body ached to be touched despite the trick her mind had just played on her. She had been jealous of Robert's affections toward Jessica earlier, and now she was jealous of the powerful fucking she received at every turn. Masturbating took the edge off, but Alyssa's fingers didn't do what she needed Robert's cock to do. She looked at the bedside clock: 12:27. *Maybe we will sleep and the time will pass until I get my turn. He'd better be ready.*

"Jessica, please sleep in my wife's spot, since my wife isn't using it. And please get my cum everywhere so she knows it was well used in her absence." Jessica rolled onto her side, facing Alyssa. She scooped the cum out of her eye and wiped it on the pillow. Robert snuggled behind her. He draped a hand to hold her breast. "Alyssa, you sleep in the chair. We'll wake you to watch us fuck in a little while."

While Jessica and Robert snored softly, Alyssa struggled to get comfortable. She took off the lingerie because it pulled and bound her as she tried to sleep. She retrieved a small blanket from the chest at the foot of the bed to keep her warm, but it slid to her waist unless she kept it tucked against her neck. The chair lacked the depth she needed to slump into it, and it wasn't wide enough to lie across. The back was so straight that when her head nodded, she woke up rather than fell forward out of the chair. She ended up wedging her head between the back of the chair and the side wing about 2:15, exhaustion finally taking her.

14
SATURDAY

"Oh, right there" woke Alyssa. She saw Jessica facing her on her side, her right leg extended upward at the hip. The covers were flipped back, and the bedside lamp was on. Robert's cock sawed in and out of her from behind. His hand pulled her breast. Jessica bit her lower lip, and her fingers traced tiny circles around her clit. Her hips humped backward every time Robert thrust forward. "Keep going. I'm close." Jessica's stomach tightened, and her chest flushed pink. Jessica gripped the sheet with her free hand. Her eyes squeezed shut.

Robert sped up after Jessica came. His breathing grew louder, competing with the slats squeaking as the bed wobbled sideways. He gave two rapid strokes, then pulled lout, shooting cum all over the inside of Jessica's thigh, on her pussy, and on the sheets. After the number of orgasms he'd had already, it was an impressive load. He peeked over Jessica's shoulder and made eye contact with Alyssa, then pulled the covers over him and Jessica, turned off the lamp, and snored.

Alyssa had indeed noticed the cum on her side of the bed. If Robert intended that she would feel betrayed by his cum while another woman lay there, he'd miscalculated. Alyssa wasn't hurt. She was horny. She loved sleeping in puddles of their cum. She had for years, and it gave her a little dirty excitement. Jessica sleeping there enhanced that feeling. Alyssa wanted to rub her leg along Jessica's, getting some of the warm, sticky fluid on her. Then she wanted to slide her dirty body onto Robert's and get a load for herself. Instead, she remained in the chair. She rubbed her clit, but when she didn't get close to orgasm, she stopped and tried to sleep.

⁓

Alyssa started awake. The lips on her forehead jerked back. Alyssa recognized Jessica's face in the dim light.

"I'm going. It's morning. I had a great night. I hope you did, too, or at least that this works. Call me later this afternoon. Good luck, Alyssa."

Alyssa cupped Jessica's cheek, pulling the beautiful face down for a kiss. "Thank you. This may not work, but you sure did your part. Get some sleep. You've earned it." Alyssa listened to Jessica walk to the kitchen and out the door. Alyssa left the chair, stealing into the bed. The lump in the covers revealed Robert's erection.

Should I? If he wants to keep punishing me, he may be mad. Maybe I can let his body help me ease his mind. Alyssa slid her head under the covers and inhaled as much of him as she could. She bobbed her head and let the saliva drip down his shaft onto his balls and belly. When his thighs tightened, she knew he was awake, and she sped up.

The covers flew off her, and she looked up at Robert's surprised face. "I thought you were Jessica," he said. "I figured you went to the guest room to sleep."

Alyssa smiled around his cock, shaking her head without breaking her rhythm. She pulled off. "I hope you aren't disappointed. Jessica just left. It's morning, and you're hard. I can help you with it, if you don't mind."

Robert smiled. "If you must. I won't stop you."

She crawled up his body until her breasts dangled in his face. As he lifted his head to kiss one, she lined up his cock and plunged down, taking all of it inside. She moaned with the fullness, feeling his girth stretch her and the tip of his cock press against her cervix. *I've wanted this all week.*

She looked into Robert's eyes as she rose and plunged down again. She knew he could last in this position, and she was going to enjoy him for a while. After one hard plunge, she stayed down, grinding her hips forward and back like riding a horse, his cock pulsing against her pussy while it clutched at him, and she squeezed so he could feel all of her. He gripped her hips, so Alyssa stayed in place and massaged his cock that way until he groaned.

She leaned forward to kiss Robert and slide her clit across his belly and her nipples through his chest hair, changing her angle yet again. Her tongue scoured the inside of Robert's mouth. Her forearms bore her weight on either side of his ribs while she rubbed all her erogenous zones on Robert's body. Her orgasm neared. She studied Robert's face, desperate to read his feelings. The softness around his eyes had returned for the first time in a week. The corners of his mouth hinted at a smile. *Maybe we will be okay.*

Her pussy replaced her heart as she studied him, noting that he was not showing any signs of exertion. *Good. I want to come a lot before he does.* She ground onto him, pressing his cock beside her cervix and her clit against his pubic bone. She flexed against him harder than she could ever remember, grinding in little circles as the orgasm overflowed from behind her belly. Her ass clenched. She muffled her scream on Robert's collarbone and humped his cock.

Robert grasped both her breasts when she straightened up again. They compressed as he held her up and pounded into her. Shocks from the pressure snaked to her pussy, reassembling the pieces of her orgasm into the next one. His balls flipped up to smack her ass on every stroke, and his head pushed on her cervix, both adding strands to the knot of pleasure building faster than Alyssa could imagine. She flicked her clit. Her thighs strained to tighten around Robert, but he was strong and continued driving into her. Robert slipped her hand aside to thump her sparking clit with his fingernail. The shock launched Alyssa into a third climax. She collapsed onto Robert's body when it abated.

Not willing to stop, Alyssa lifted just her hips for a while, fucking Robert's cock through her exhaustion. She nibbled his neck and kissed his jaw. She pinched his nipples while she struggled to writhe atop him. Her skin glistened with sweat; she smeared it on him as she worked. After this brief rest, Alyssa sat up again and rose until only his head remained inside her before dropping full force onto him.

Over and over she rose and fell, knowing she had to work to coax out his seed. She felt sweat drip from her chin onto her tits, and she watched it drip from her tits to his chest. *I won't quit until he comes, even if it kills me.* Her grunts mixed with the liquid sounds of her pussy every time she dropped her body, and she rejoiced with every collision.

Robert swelled inside her. She quickened her pace yet again, urging him to come while compelling every ounce of energy from her quivering thighs. She squeezed her pussy muscles, tightening her grip on his cock. She stared into his eyes as she dropped two more times onto him. She talked dirty with her last bit of energy. "Come on, Babe. Fuck me. Come for me. You can do it. Fuck me and flood your cum in this pussy of yours. It's your pussy. Use it and fill it, Babe. Come for me. Come in me."

His mouth firmed, and he held his breath. She slammed one last time as he erupted inside her. She ground her hips, keeping his cum as deep inside her as she could, never breaking eye contact. When his spasms stopped, she fell forward and kissed Robert. "I love you, Babe. Have I reclaimed your love?" The last of her energy knotted inside her belly. She held her breath.

"I love you too. You never lost it. You just buried it."

Alyssa's heart swelled to force her breath out. She sagged further onto him. His embrace felt like coming home after a long trip. Maybe it was. He swept her wet hair from her face. They lay there until his softened cock slipped out. Alyssa rolled on her side beside Robert, facing him with her head on his arm.

"So is there a chance to save our marriage?"

"You earned that chance, Baby. I didn't think you would be able to arrange it, and I really didn't think you would be able to watch. I underestimated you."

"It was hard. Jessica and I had fun planning it and surprising you, but I hated when you started fucking her. I was jealous, and I wanted to yank her out and replace her."

"Why didn't you?"

"I meant what I said. If watching you fuck her was the price for our marriage, then I would pay it. I wasn't going to get this close and wimp out." She took a ragged breath to fight a sob. "The hardest part…was the way you invited her into our bed using my own words to describe how good it was. Saying that I had not been there for the best fuck of your life almost broke me."

Robert stroked her arm. "I wanted to give you a chance to stop things there, before anyone from outside could intrude upon our bed. An emotional response at that point would have been understandable, and a way to keep you from being too hurt."

"It felt like you were trying to hurt me."

Robert grimaced. "Just the opposite. I wanted to give you the chance to call a halt if you needed to. Yes, I wanted you to feel what you made me feel, but not to the breaking point."

Her body began to recover some strength. She stretched her leg across his and hooked her heel on his calf. She let her smile rise, spurred by the happiness building behind her ribs. "Is that why you turned on the light in the middle of the night? You usually just fuck in the dark when you wake up horny."

"Yes, and I wanted to check on you. Staying in the chair all night, thinking about what was occurring, I wanted to see your face." He grinned. "And I did want to fuck Jessica again. She's good."

Alyssa play-slapped his belly and smiled. "You dog, you." Her belly clenched. *Say it. Be honest with him.* "I want to see how good she is, too, Robert."

"You just watched how good she— Oh. You want to sleep with her?"

Alyssa nodded. "I have to."

"You have to?"

"How do you think I persuaded her to do this? She and I talked beyond meaningless chitchat for the first time on Sunday. I told her everything, including that I asked you to consider other people. I promised her a night with me as a trade for helping me"—she swallowed hard—"and I want to pay my debt." She lay frozen, every heartbeat echoing in her ears. Robert's lips pursed the way they did when he pondered a problem. Alyssa waited.

"You need to honor your agreement, then."

Robert's face revealed nothing. Had he just given up on her? Alyssa's throat tightened. She cleared her throat and swallowed. "What does that mean, Robert? Are we going to stay married?"

"I very much want to be married to you. Do you want that?"

The tension in her entire body released a warm wave from her chest. Elation followed in its wake. Her voice caught in a sob, her first happy one in a long time. "I do. Being married to you means the world to me." She hugged him, then pulled back, looked at his smile, and hugged him again, weeping with joy. When her tears stopped, she released to look him in the eye. "What do you mean by honoring my agreement with Jessica?"

"First, never break a deal that personal. Second, she worked hard and deserves her reward." He sighed and grazed her side with his fingers, making her shiver. He smiled. "Third, if you still want to, we can discuss some kind of open marriage."

Alyssa didn't believe what she had just heard. As hard as the night had been, as punished as she had felt as Robert used Jessica for his own pleasure, as guilty as she'd felt on the flight home a week ago, that one sentence was too good to be true. "Really? Robert, do you mean that?"

"I do. I was dead set against it, even a couple of days ago, even though the thought of sex with other women titillated me. Last night with Jessica, I felt the new-lover excitement you described feeling in Houston. I liked it, and you saw how it kept me horny. There are some downsides, and we can deal with them. Your friends have agreements in their marriages. We can make an agreement too."

Robert tightened his arm behind Alyssa's neck, pulling her close. She squeezed him back. Though she'd been exhausted only moments before, the adrenaline rush of this outcome made her entire body tingle with energy. "We'll do it together."

Robert kissed her head. "We both know how much we love each other now, but we both enjoy exciting new lovers. Besides, I can't get over how you reclaimed me. You haven't worked that hard in bed in years, Baby."

"You haven't seen anything yet, Babe. I love you so much. I'm so happy we worked this out." She snuggled against him, absorbing the heat of his skin from her head to her feet. "Let's talk more about it after a nap and some breakfast." Alyssa smiled and kissed her husband. She laid her head on his shoulder and draped her leg over his. *Maybe you really can have it all.*

Alyssa's adventures continue at
www.sagemallory.com/books. Go there now.

ACKNOWLEDGMENTS

I must thank Beth, who pointed me in the right direction, shared her secrets, and told me writing would be a lot of work and worth every second of it. I must also thank Lyss, who made the story better, got me in the correct head, and taught me that alright is not okay. If there are errors or shortcomings, they are mine, not hers.

ABOUT THE AUTHOR

Sage Mallory lives near the water, working by day and creating adventures for sexy, determined, evolving women by night. Sage enjoys cooking, hiking the mountains, discussing the meaning of life, and escaping the hectic pace of life inside a great story.

Printed in Great Britain
by Amazon

60380922R00150